Kingdom of Machines
Sister Worlds Book 2

TIFFANY NICOLE TERRY

DEDICATION

This book is for all the friends who have believed in me, especially when I struggled to believe in myself.

This is for my old-school heifers, my Charlie's angels, my rocky mountain women writers, and my Jiu Jitsu mamas.

No matter how far apart we are, I am forever your friend.

CONTENTS

ACKNOWLEDGMENTS

Thanks to my mother, Mandra, for keeping us fed while I spent my evenings writing and editing after completing long days at the office. She is the reason I have been able to achieve my dreams.

GLOSSARY AND MAPS

Places	Pronunciation	Description
Naldash	Nahl-dash	The planet where Kingdom of Men takes place.
Denlerack	Den-err-ahk	The sister planet, where Kingdom of Machines takes place.

Dragons	Pronunciation	Description
Klackire	Klak-ire	Mythical dragon.
Anissa La Alani	An-ih-sah Lah Ah-lah-an-ee	Mythical dragon's real name.
Nala	Nah-lah	Race of flying dragons, extinct. Lived on Naldash.
Dynack	Dy-nak	Race of land dragons, extinct. Lived on Denlerack.

People	Pronunciation	Description
KaLeah Trapper	Kuh-lee-uh	Brown-haired girl from Erion village.
Clegg Trapper	Kleg	Man who raised KaLeah as his daughter.
Princess Amirra	Ah-meer-rah	Princess, daughter of

		King Erazus.
Prince Nikolat	Nik-o-lot	Son of King Erazus
Elektra Dean	Ee-lek-trə	Black-haired rebel from Sarda
Colt	Kolt	Rebel leader
Keldon	Dayn Kel-don	Dictator of Denlerack and KaLeah's biological father
Ash	Ash	Brown-haired orphan child
Huntra	Hun-trə	KaLeah's mother
Lina	Lee-nə	Rebel twin
Lainie	Lay-nee	Rebel twin
Rustin	Rus-tin	Rebel
Alister	Al-is-tewr	Rebel
Von	Von	Rebel
Zuri	Zewr-ee	Rebel
Felisha	Fə-lee-shə	Rebel

Animals	**Pronunciation**	**Description**
Draggot	Dra-guht	Horse-like, covered in scales and fur, main, talons and hooves.
Doquer	Doh-kər	Wolf-like.

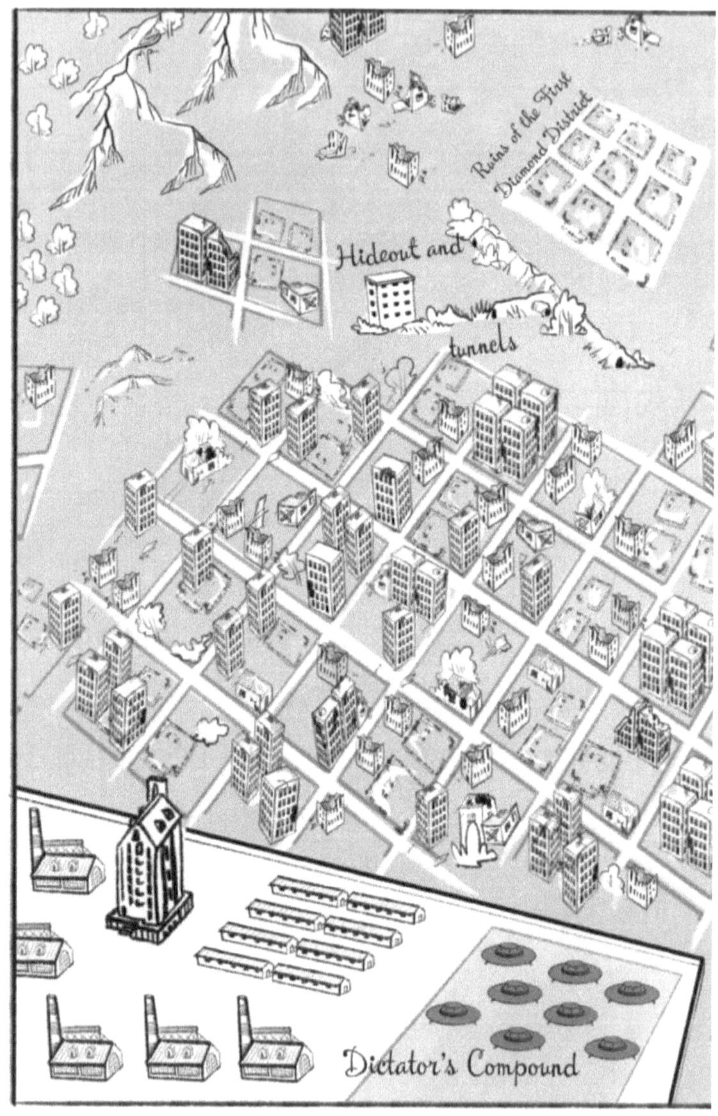
Ruins of the First Diamond District
Hideout and
tunnels
Dictator's Compound

Morbel Diamond District
Prof. Wheelwright
Sarda
The Mud Lands

1 FLAMES

Elektra sat on the couch and stared at the small fetus floating in a goo-filled glass chamber across from her. The blue light underneath it cast an eerie glow around the living room and up into the tank, illuminating the creature's tiny arms and legs.

The hum of the artificial womb machine, keeping the fetus warm, was the only sound in the room.

She and her mother lived with her new stepfather in his pristine apartment in the princess section of the Morbel diamond district. It was hard to believe that a little over a year ago they had been fighting for food and tech scraps in the Sarda slums.

A lot had changed in a year.

Inside the district they had found a better life, but Elektra was growing restless and suspicious with the simplicity and ease within their new community. She also had an overwhelming feeling that she didn't belong there.

Elektra had been conceived and born naturally, although she had been an accident. Growing up without a father had been difficult, but Elektra had learned to be strong and clever.

From a young age, she'd taught herself how to piece

together scraps of discarded tech they would sell or trade for money or food. When they visited her mother's friend, a professor and inventor who lived on the outskirts of the slums, he would show her new ways to repair the technology, pulling from various broken pieces and welding them together.

Her dark brown hands were covered in scars from burns and cuts from the years she had spent developing the skills.

Her mother, though lovely and kind, had not been prepared to raise a child on her own. As soon as Elektra had been capable enough, her goal, even though she was still just a child, had been to make sure the two of them stayed fed and protected. She had become her mother's protector.

Kids stopped trying to rob Elektra once she got the reputation for throwing punches strong enough to break noses. Her secret was the metal knuckles she'd made herself and built into a pair of gloves she wore that hid her scars.

When she found a discarded gun among the heaps of technology trash one day, she snuck it back to their garage workshop where she and her mother lived. She repaired it and taught herself how to load, unload, clean, and of course, shoot it.

The slums were dangerous, and they had to be careful. They had to protect themselves.

They would admire the clothing and technology the diamond district residences would casually toss away. To Elektra and her mother, it was treasure. It was a window into another world that they so desperately wanted to be a part of.

That world was salvation from the slums. There was a perception that safety and abundance existed within the district walls.

That's why Elektra had built a device to intercept the airwave calls between legal secretaries in Morbel, who were laxer in their security standards than other professionals.

They discovered a position was just about to open, and

Elektra's mother, Zatia, dressed the part from discarded clothing they had washed and patched.

Zatia used a reengineered access card to get into the district and into the law firm in time to ensure an accidental bump into one of the firm's partners mere moments after he'd heard about the opening himself.

Zatia was beautiful but with a soft smile and gentle charm that kept her from seeming too intimidating or suspicious. Elektra manipulated the technology, but it was her mom that convinced everyone that she already belonged in Morbel. She hid her street smarts behind flirtatious giggles, tossed her hair, and batted her long-lashed eyes.

Elektra knew her mom had grown up strong and savvy. She had experienced heartache, loss, starvation, and devastation, but she never showed her scars. She was firm with Elektra, but never mean or harsh. Aside from their dark head of curls, they didn't have much else in common.

Elektra was proud to have a woman like Zatia as her mother, but she had always felt she needed to protect the woman. She saw her mother as a tired, worn-out soul, who had lost the drive to be more than who she was.

It was Elektra's desire to get her mother into a better life that propelled them into sneaking into Morbel.

Zatia claimed to be a widow, struggling to make an honest living while bringing up her daughter alone.

Elektra didn't mind the lie since it sounded so close to the truth. In fact, if she hadn't found, mended, and washed the professional clothing, and if she hadn't forged the new worker access card, Zatia never would have been able to pass as a diamond district resident.

Zatia charmed her way into the position, and then Elektra used another forged card to join her on the other side.

The slums outside the city were dry, and everything was coated in a thick layer of orange dirt. The air smelled of smoke and chemicals.

Walking into the diamond district that first day had felt

like a dream. The air inside the enclosed district was fresh and clean, and everything around her was brightly lit and richly colored in greens, reds, blues, and violets. She had never seen so many colors.

She tried to hide her amazement as she walked the hallways, mesmerized by the various assortment of plants she had never seen before. They grew edible and medicinal plants back in their garage apartment in the slums, but the plants inside Morbel were ornamental. She wanted to touch them, smell them, but she didn't want to give away her cover.

The diamond districts consisted of nine buildings arranged to look like a diamond from the sky. They were all connected on multiple floors by glass sky bridges.

An outer wall protected the perimeter, with a guarded fence beyond that. Her mother had entered the first day through one of four gates. Two days later, Elektra entered through another gate, and they met in the heart of the district on the lowest level.

Her mother had already found them new friends and a place to stay.

Everything seemed brighter and fresher on the inside, where there existed a fully sustainable system for the controlled population of residents.

No one foraged for food or fixed broken technology to trade for scraps here.

Denny, the young partner at the firm, proposed marriage after only a few months, and invited them both to live with him in his exquisite apartment.

Of course, Denny didn't know they were from the Sarda slums.

At first, everything was perfect. Denny was kind. He asked questions, but never pushed or teased. He never belittled her for being a teenager or just a kid.

He seemed to genuinely respect her and even told her that she was brilliant whenever he sat down to inspect one of her projects or inventions.

Her affinity for technology only grew stronger when she started building with new tech instead of discarded and broken pieces. Denny was always happy to give her money to go buy newer tech, and he didn't bat an eye when she completely dismantled something brand new.

"When the baby comes, we can't have all of these small pieces lying around," her mother said to her one day in the living room.

Elektra was sitting cross legged on the floor, an expertly dismantled drone spread out around her, a third of the way to being put back together.

"What baby?" Elektra asked, choking on the last word.

"Denny and I are going to start the process of creating a baby."

The artificial sunlight was streaming through the window, cast down from the long, massive lights that lined the metal rafters high above the enclosed diamond district.

The light across her mother's brown skin gave her a golden glow. Her smile was wide and her straight white teeth, the envy of the women in the Sarda slums, seemed to twinkle.

Her mother's hair was straight black now with a glossy sheen. She had begun having it straightened once they moved in with Denny. Before, it had always been short, with tight curls like Elektra's, and she missed having that in common with her mother.

"A fish-tank baby?" Elektra asked, incredulously.

"Shhh, Elektra, hush," her mother scolded. Zatia's smile vanished as she looked around the room, as if someone could have heard them. "They don't call them that here. We are going to see an L.E.E. specialist this week and bring home the equipment to setup. I'm expecting your help."

"Of course, mother," she had said, dutifully.

Loving Embryo Embrace, or L.E.E. baby, came with a tank on top and a cabinet on bottom to hide the equipment necessary to ensure the survival of your genetically created and potentially modified offspring.

No need for women to gain weight, get tired, risk blood loss, or worse. No pain and no deformities. You simply set your developing spawn up on display in the middle of your living room and watched it grow like a plant.

She stared at the thing in front of her now, in its personal bubble, on its special table. She wondered if it would have dark brown skin like her and her mother, or if it would be light skinned like Denny.

Elektra's stomach turned and her lip creeped steadily upward in disgust, but she couldn't look away.

She knew what her mom was doing, and it made sense.

Her mother had expressed numerous times how lucky they were to have found Denny, who was smart, employed with a home, and long-term intentions.

But a woman can never be too careful.

It's the artificial womb baby that really seals up that package. He wouldn't leave her or kick her back to the slums now that their bundle of joy was here.

Elektra sighed, shifting her gaze away from the fluid-filled tank. She pulled the straps of her bag up over her shoulders and took one last look around the small space that had never felt like home.

Her mother finally had the life she deserved, but it wasn't the life Elektra wanted for herself.

She left the apartment, hearing the automatic click of the lock behind her. Just two steps beyond the doorway and she was on a nearly empty, moving staircase.

The artificial sun hadn't yet started to shine, and so the district was quiet. The metal staircase lightly clanked as it carried her down to each level beyond her stepfather's apartment.

Small lampposts lit up the staircases and sidewalks, apartments and shops, and the glass walkways that connected the vertical buildings.

She watched it all in wonder as she descended, realizing that it could be last time she laid eyes on the pampered city.

Elektra knew what she was giving up, not just as a

teenager, but her future as a woman also.

In Morbel, women could avoid pregnancy with expensive devices no bigger than a toothpick placed painlessly underneath their skin. They never had to carry the weight of a growing fetus. They never had to endure a painful labor with a great risk to their lives and the lives of the babies.

Once approved to have an L.E.E. baby, the women could stay home to raise the small child while their husbands continued working. All the jobs in the district were created to sustain the community within, and a mother's job raising a baby was seen as vital.

Morbel produced the right amount of water and the right amount of food for everyone living within its walls. Everyone received similar pay and were required to work one of a few available industries that maintained the social structure of the district.

Life was easier on the inside. She wondered if any of the residents realized how lucky they were in their fabricated lives.

Zatia had endured and survived true childbirth. She had lived through carrying a child through starvation, pushed out a bloody baby, then struggled to find food and water for them both.

But now, Elektra's mother had a new partner, a comfortable apartment in the best part of the city, and a mutant fetus swimming in a tank of gel in her living room.

Elektra wondered if her mother had completely forgotten about all the struggles they'd gone through, about the struggles of so many other women still out there in the slums.

She knew that her mother would be upset about her disappearing, but she couldn't continue living this privileged life after knowing what was happening to the underprivileged.

She had to do something.

She had to help somehow.

The airwave news reported often on the increased rebel activity throughout the slums. Many experts on the subject would describe the rebels as unorganized, disjointed, thugs, and bandits stealing and causing trouble without any agenda.

They dismissed the idea that the rebels were trying to coordinate societal upheavals or improve slum conditions.

Elektra wasn't taking anyone's word on the rebels. She wanted to hunt them down and find out the truth for herself.

If they were legitimate, she wanted to play a part in making the slums a better place. If they really were just a disjointed band of misfits, she wanted to organize them into something effectual.

Either way, Elektra was going to heal her world.

On the lower, moving sidewalks, she looked up at the glass sky bridges that connected the eight housing towers to the middle, control district. The schools, offices, doctors, and grocery stores were all located in the central tower.

She hadn't cared much for going to the school or for the other teenagers. To say that she didn't fit in was an understatement.

"I may as well be from a different planet," she told herself.

The kids there had never seen any kind of hardship. They had been planned and then pampered. They hadn't had to search for or beg for food. They'd never traded hand-made goods for water. The only guns they'd seen were the ones strapped to the guards along the gates; guards who were supposed to keep 'her kind,' people from the slums, out.

The students' skills were regularly assessed against the skills needed within Morbel, and then they trained for those roles. You had to learn how to grow plants from seeds, how to connect pipes for irrigation, and prune plants.

Others were taught how to solve disagreements, how to melt down waste, and there were early medical classes for identifying various sicknesses and how to care for wounds.

Maintaining the machinery was the only thing Elektra had found interesting in the school. She could see herself toiling away fixing things like moving staircases and air filtration systems for the rest of her life—safe and sound in Morbel.

Although, she knew she'd hate that life. That life was boring. That life was controlled.

The self-sustaining communities stayed that way by imposing mandatory birth control measures. All 9-year-old girls were required to have the implant, so Zatia and Elektra had to convince separate doctors that their implants had been damaged due to injuries in order to get 'new ones' inserted.

After seeing other women die from childbirth in the slums, she didn't mind having one less thing to worry about. She had no intentions of ever partnering with a man, but it was comforting to know she was protected from pregnancy in any event. She also didn't want to experience the same thing her mother had. She didn't want to try to raise a baby on her own in the slums.

The food was all grown underneath the district, and it was heavily guarded. No one, not even the district leaders, were allotted more than their fair share of food or water.

That way of living was much easier, and it took her a while to come to the conclusion that a harder life in the slums would be better than a steady job and a consistent source of clean water and healthy food.

Back in the slums, she had found ways to grow small amounts of food in the garage where they had lived, but hustling had been the way of life. Although she wanted to make a difference, she was not looking forward to struggling for food and water again.

The moving sidewalk was coming to an end. As it rolled beneath the ground, she stepped off and onto the floor.

"Miss, are you lost?" A young man stood at one of the few entrances to the diamond district. He was plain-clothed and pale-skinned.

"I am on a community outreach assignment," Elektra stated.

"Which community?" he asked.

"Sarda," she answered, using the name of her own original home.

"Ouch. What kind of trouble did you get in to get stuck with that assignment?" he asked, chuckling at his cleverness.

"I punched a teacher when he caught me cheating," she said without cracking a smile.

He laughed loudly and then reigned himself back in. "Wow, well, that'd do it, I guess. Are you sure you are old enough to go out there alone, though?"

"I will only be counseling a few groups of women right out beyond the gates," she said.

"Alright, I understand. At least you dressed down. That'll put you at less of a risk. Stay close so the guards can keep an eye on you. I don't have to tell you how dangerous those people are."

She resisted the urge to roll her eyes at the offense. She was one of 'those people,' after all.

Elektra had made sure to dress casually in an outfit she made herself, so as not to look like a wealthy diamond district resident. She wore a long tunic made of synthetic dark brown animal hide, which would keep her comfortable, over brown pants. She wrapped more of the hide around her arms and hands to protect her skin from the sand and winds.

The material was breathable and flexible enough for her to run and fight in, if she had to, and the color matched her skin and would hopefully help her camouflage herself in the brown landscape.

"Do you have enough protection?" he asked, looking her over.

Elektra patted her pocket, although the gun was tucked into her waistband, hidden beneath her long tunic. She had a second gun in the top pocket of her backpack. The guard couldn't see what she was patting beneath the clothing, but she knew he would assume she had a knife. The week before, she'd snuck out and stolen two guns off of guards. With very minimal threats, the guards were soft and inattentive, especially when they were in crowds.

"Good," he said, nodding in approval.

"Why are you heading out so early? It isn't even light yet?"

"I couldn't sleep anyway," Elektra said, answering honestly.

"Well, don't go too far out there until daylight. The guards will need to be able to see you."

He unbarred a large metal door and pushed it open. She was immediately hit with a dry heat and the smell of dust and smoke.

It was the same smell she had grown up with. The sensation of familiarity overcame her and pushed away the last bit of hesitation. This was the world she knew.

Elektra walked through the door, leaving the city of Morbel behind. She stood in what they called the yard, a large, weed-infested area covered in gravel and cracked concrete. It was surrounded by twelve-feet metal fences.

Guards patrolled the area regularly, and two stood at multiple fence gates around the interior.

Traversing the space between the interior doors and the exterior gates required boots, as the yard was covered in broken glass, gun shell casings, trash, and dead rodents.

She walked toward the guards, who were dressed all in black, standing by the gate, each holding long guns with thick round barrels.

They lacked the charm and humor of the interior door guard. They had clearly seen things that had zapped away their humor and casual nature over the years.

Beyond the gates were miles and miles of dilapidated and crumbling buildings. Tents and tarps were strung up in between alleys and over broken-down vehicles.

Nobody used vehicles anymore, except on rare

occasions when someone had to travel between districts. She had heard the dictator and his soldiers would drive large rovers between districts, but she had never seen one.

She had also heard the dictator had flying ships, but again, she dismissed that as a rumor. If a man could afford to create flying ships, why couldn't he create more districts to house the people living in the slums?

Elektra made the long trek across the yard to the gate. The soldiers looked at one another first, then to her.

One man cocked his eyebrow up and said, "You want to go out there?"

"I have to minister, as punishment," she said, gulping.

She figured it best to stick with the story in case the guards airwaved each other.

"Armed?"

"Yes, sir," she answered.

"Know how to use it?"

"Yes, sir."

"Good luck, miss." The man sounded as if he didn't to ever expect to see her again.

The gate was opened, and she was released back into the slums. She smiled to herself, realizing the irony of those men being concerned for her.

This was her home. This was where she had fought alongside her mother to survive. What those gatekeepers didn't realize is that the people on the other side, the people they were so afraid of, were resilient.

The gatekeepers wouldn't last a day in the slums, but Elektra had lasted an entire childhood among the crumbling buildings and polluted streets.

She didn't want to look too eager, so she slowly walked toward a group of people camped out near a broken-down car between two nearby buildings. When she got close, she veered off and went down an alley.

There was one incredibly important thing she needed before she started on her journey to track down the rebels.

Elektra slinked through the alleys like a rodent, dodging

the men sleeping in doorways. In the slums, no one got up early. The nights were pitch black and the morning came much later, since the sunlight had to fight through the clouds and smog. She hoped that anyone who had taken their place in her old building would still be asleep.

At the back of her old building's alley, she climbed on top of a packed dumpster to reach a fire escape. She expertly climbed two levels, avoiding broken rungs in the dark, then slipped into an open window. In the loft above the garage, she froze and listened. She and her mother had been gone a year, so she assumed that it was no longer vacant.

A small, low, rhythmic breathing was coming from below her. She heard one person for sure but couldn't be certain there weren't more people sleeping down there.

The loft was just metal piping that crisscrossed below the rafters. She could walk across them, but they would squeak beneath her weight. She had to move carefully.

She took measured steps across the piping, stabling herself as needed. Her backpack, filled with water and food rations, made her feel off-balance and heavier than normal. Of course, she hadn't been on the piping in over a year, so it felt way more unfamiliar than she'd expected.

Just one step at a time, she told herself as she walked over twenty feet in the air in the dark with a stranger or two sleeping below her.

She was only a few steps from the edge when she heard a crack shake the pipe below her right foot. She knew the pipe was about to break away and lunged for the windowsill.

She grabbed onto the sill and found her footing right as the busted pipe broke loose and swung across the ceiling, crashing into another pipe.

"What in dragon's blood is going on?" boomed a loud voice from below.

A pipe hit the ground and a gunshot rang throughout the garage. Elektra muscled up the old window and dove out onto the ledge of the roof as quickly as she could, hoping that the man or men below hadn't seen her.

She stood with her body pressed against the outside wall of the tall building, feet on a narrow roof ledge. She could see lights now coming from inside the building and sighed.

That was close, she said to herself, and then she started creeping along the edge toward the exterior attic access.

When Elektra had been young, she explored every inch of their garage loft building. She had discovered an attic that only she was small enough to get into.

Once she'd grown too big to climb into it from inside the garage, she had to go searching for another way in and she'd found it, through an exterior hatch that looked at first as if it was just a vent. She used the vent as a handle to open a hidden door into the attic.

The door was on the edge of the roof, so she had to lean against the building carefully while opening the latch. She lifted the heavy section of the trap door leading into the attic with one hand, then slid inside and gently closed the door behind her.

In the dark, triangular shaped space, she reached out and touched cool metal gears. A feeling of relief filled her chest, lifting her spirits.

She pulled the metal wings down from the wall and dusted them off, running her hands along the synthetic animal hide stretched between the metal rods. She expanded and contracted the wings, listening to the clinking sound that the large, golden metal gears made.

"Hello, beautiful," Elektra said.

She took off her backpack and swung her wings around to her back, clipping herself into the harness. She looped the backpack straps into her belt and made sure everything was secure before testing the fans at the base of the wings. They purred to life, and she begin to lift.

"I can do this," she said to herself in the dark. "I can find the rebels."

She pushed the vent door back open and climbed up onto the ledge of the roof. She touched the controllers that were tucked into the harness, and the metal rods expanded, spreading the brown wings as far as they'd go.

A slight breeze caught the material and combined with the small fans hidden inside canisters at the base of the wings, she was almost lifted off the rooftop.

"I guess I'm a little rusty," she said to the pre-dawn night as she readjusted the wingspan slightly. She stood up straighter and took a deep breath.

"I may not know where I'm going, but at least I've got my wings to get me there."

She launched herself off the roof and flew out across the sky.

She flew over buildings and alleys, looking into the darkness below, banking around taller buildings. The sun was starting to rise behind her, casting a gray light over the dingy city slums.

She had never actually seen the sun. It had been hidden by a smoke-choked sky her entire life. Elektra had never seen the stars, the moon, or a distant planet called Naldash, that she'd only heard about in stories.

She wondered briefly about what life on a non-polluted planet would look and smell like as she drifted through the Denlerack skies.

Elektra's first goal was to visit someone sympathetic to the rebel cause, who might have information about how to find the rebels.

She headed for the professor's house. He was their only friend, and the one who had taught her how to improve her metal working and engineering. She hoped that he'd be able to tell her something or at least point her in the right direction.

A sudden burst of blue light, leaping up like flames between two nearby buildings, distracted her from her thoughts. Any form of electricity in the slums had to be run by physical force, like riding a stationary bicycle connected to wires. Most people used old fashioned fire to cook meals, which glowed yellow and red, never blue. The blue flames she'd just seen looked unnatural and almost magical.

Curious, she decided to go check it out. If there was some new technology or weapon being used in the slums, she wanted to know about it and if possible, figure out how to use it herself.

❧KaLeah☙

KaLeah's body was consumed by the blue flames. They licked across her boots and up her legs, climbed her torso and spread over her arms. Her skin was comfortably warm, and then the flames filled her line of sight.

All she saw was blue.

The phantom dragon, Anissa La Alani, was going to transport her from the planet Naldash to Denlerack. She had watched the dragon ignite Prince Nikolat with the same blue fire.

Had she also transported him to Denlerack? She asked the question in her mind, but there was no reply from the dragon. There was only silence. The flames made no sound.

Then, as quickly as they had spread, the flames left her skin. She blinked and watched the flames trickle down past her feet and into the ground.

KaLeah noticed immediately that the ground was different. There was some sort of solid gray stone beneath her feet. It was cracked and crumbled in places, and she assumed that it was a road of some kind, but of a material she'd never seen before.

"Am I on Denlerack?" KaLeah asked aloud, thinking that maybe the dragon would answer her as it had on Naldash. There were strange towers on either side of her and the grayness of the space left her confused on what time of day it was.

A young man suddenly walked out a few yards in front of her. He looked her up and down, but he said nothing.

His hands were covered in black oil, and his clothes were

filthy. His long, brown hair was matted against his skull, and he had dark spots under both eyes.

"Hey Chalk, come out 'ere," he called over his shoulder.

Another man walked out from an opening in a tower, wiping his hands on a towel. He stopped and tossed it aside, staring at KaLeah.

He had bright white hair and the palest skin KaLeah had ever seen on a man. His cheeks were sunken in, and his tattered clothing was also covered in stains. "What's this?"

"Beats me. Look at 'at sword." The first man nodded his chin at KaLeah, who had her sword sheathed at her side.

"Dragon's blood, what she doin' with a sword? You goin' to a costume party, sweets?" Chalk asked.

The men laughed and KaLeah remembered the kidnappers from the day in the woods that had changed her life forever; the bandits that she'd had to kill, and the princess she'd inadvertently rescued.

She did not want her first act on Denlerack to be spilling more blood. These were her father's people, after all. She would have to face him eventually. How would he treat her if she'd killed two of his people on her very first day?

She slowly reached for a dagger, strapped close, then readied herself to grab the sword.

"Don't be like that, sweetie," the first man said, taking a step toward her. "We just want to know what brings you to the alley outside our building, is all. You looking to trade that sword in for a real weapon? Might be we're just the right men to make you a deal."

She repeated the words alley, building, and gun to herself and took another quick look around. There were towers and structures in the Belarone kingdom, but the ones around her now seemed to touch the sky. The alley, as the man had called it, didn't look at all like the dirt and gravel alleys that ran throughout her small village of Erion.

The words were the same, but everything looked so different. She knew guns, though. She'd seen the one that had killed Prince Bylex. She didn't have one of those.

Everything was filthy. Trash was lying all around, the sky was filled with brown clouds, creating a thick, haziness to the air around her. The smell was … off, as if someone had been sick on top of the nose-piercing smell of pee and smoke so thick she could feel it in her throat.

"This is Denlerack," she stated.

"Where else in dragon's blood do you think you'd be?" the one called Chalk asked.

"This ain't no diamond district. Welcome to Sarda, sweetheart!" the brown-haired man boomed.

She furrowed her brow in confusion. The men took two steps closer, and she prepared herself to fight. She didn't know if there was a way to run, or even where to start running. These buildings were tall and all over, blocking any view of the landscape.

She drew her sword and the men laughed louder.

"No way, are you gonna use 'at? What are you?" the brown-haired man asked.

They both bent over laughing. Once they calmed down, they stood back up and stepped closer to her.

"Look little miss, I appreciate you beings all tough an' all, but *that* is not going to stand up to *this*." The brown-haired man patted something strapped to his hip. The handle was black metal, and she knew instantly that they had guns. The vision of seeing a bullet rip through and kill Prince Bylex came back in a flash.

How can I die this soon into my mission? I just got to Denlerack. I haven't found my father. I haven't done anything that I'm supposed to do. Where are you, Anissa La Alani?

Then KaLeah thought she heard the sound of wings beating in the air. She looked up, hoping the phantom dragon had come to her rescue.

Instead, two arms slid underneath hers, clutched around her chest, and lifted her up and over the men's heads.

"I gotcha, hold tight. And don't drop that sword." It was a young woman's voice, and the golden-brown arms wrapped around KaLeah were strong. She tried not to move, so as not to throw the woman off balance.

"Who are you?" KaLeah called up to her winged rescuer.

"My name is Elektra Dean. It looked like you were in trouble."

"I was, thank you. I am KaLeah Trapper."

She suddenly realized that she'd used Clegg's last name, the man who had raised her but who wasn't truly her father.

If the dictator was her father, then her true name was KaLeah Keldon. She thought that maybe she should keep that information to herself, for now. She didn't yet know who she could trust.

The woman swooped over to a roof and set the two of them down gently. KaLeah stepped forward and turned around.

"Wow, your wings!" she exclaimed.

Elektra smiled wide. The young woman appeared to be similar in age and height, but where KaLeah's skin was white, Elektra's was a dark brown. Her hair and eyes were also dark brown.

The wings she wore were large swaths of material connected by metal rods and gears. They made Elektra look part-dragon.

"They come in handy for traveling and for rescuing too, I guess," Elektra said, wings slowing to a stop.

"I don't know what I would have done if you hadn't seen me down there," KaLeah said.

"I didn't see you; I saw a blue light. What was that light?" Elektra asked, turning around as if the light could reappear at any moment.

KaLeah looked back toward the alley. She wondered why the dragon had dropped her there, of every possible place on the entire planet. Why hadn't she been placed right in front of her father's front door?

Do I tell her about the magical blue flames? Best not.

"I didn't see a blue light," KaLeah lied.

❧Nikolat❧

Prince Nikolat screamed out, knowing that he was about to die, but the pain never came. The blue flames just covered his entire body, blurring out his vision, and then they were gone.

He opened his eyes and found that he was no longer standing on the castle balcony with his sister and KaLeah.

The Belarone Castle, his home for eighteen years, was gone. The emerald dragon, KaLeah with her brown hair shining in the sunlight, his little bratty sister trying to steal the crown—everything was gone, replaced with mud as far as he could see.

It was dark, so he really couldn't see that far. He stood up and noticed that he was slowly sinking into the mud, stopping around his mid-shins. He had no idea where he was or what was going on, but he knew that it couldn't be good.

Did I die?

The last thing he saw was the dragon taking in a breath that seemed to suck his own breath out of his lungs, and then it had exhaled dark blue flames that spread over him without mercy.

The searing heat and pain didn't come as he'd expected, and he was pretty sure that he was still alive. He pulled his arms up to his face and for good measure, pinched himself.

No, he thought, *I can't possibly be dead.*

He looked up but couldn't see Denlerack or the moon. The sky was thick with clouds, something he wasn't used to seeing on Naldash. They had their storms and cloudy days, but mostly Belarone enjoyed mild weather with ample sunshine, and clear, moon-lit nights.

He was standing in a lake of mud as far as he could tell. He knew of no place like this in Belarone. If he was no longer in his kingdom, then he was somewhere on Naldash that he'd never heard of.

He decided that the only thing he could do was wade out

of the muddy lake as quickly as possible.

Once on solid ground, everything would make more sense, he told himself.

He lifted his legs and made the slow, laborious trek through the muck, grateful that his boots stayed on despite the tarry, sticky mess.

Nikolat walked this way for what seemed like hours. His muscles ached from the repetitive motions of lifting heavy, mud-covered boots out of the muck over and over. His stomach grumbled angrily, and his mouth was so dry that his throat was starting to hurt.

He could see faint dots of light in the distance and kept encouraging himself to keep moving.

There had to be water, food, and rest at those lights, he told himself.

He continued the slow trudge toward the few, twinkling lights. When he finally heard sounds of people, he started to feel relief. He heard the metal clanking of what he assumed were spoons and forks against plates, light chatter and laughter mixed with the faintest hint of music. His heart began to lighten, not only to be free of the mud, but to solve the mystery of where on Naldash he was so he could begin his journey home.

"What's that?" came a husky voice.

"Some beast coming out of the mud," answered another.

"Never heard of such a thing."

"Shoot it."

"I ain't gonna shoot it until I see it."

"Awe come on, shoot it."

"What if it's yer mother?"

"Then I'll shoot it."

Nikolat heard the confrontation along with laughter up ahead, and even though he didn't fully understand the context of the conversation, he knew enough to duck a little lower and walk a little bit more cautiously toward the voices.

"I mean no harm," he yelled, for good measure.

And even if he did, he couldn't cause much. He didn't

have his sword or any other weapon. He'd lost it all during the blue fire.

"Come on out of there, boy."

It was a man's voice, but he couldn't quite see how far away he was. More lights were lit and swinging, closer than he expected.

After a few more steps, he was surrounded by many men who grabbed at him and pulled him aggressively out of the mud. He was unceremoniously dropped onto hard dirt.

"My name is Nikolat Belarone," he said. If this were Naldash, the people would know him to be royalty based on his name alone.

"Never heard that name here," said a man who had hauled Nikolat out of the mud.

"I'm not from here," Nik said, standing up straight but wobbly, feeling as if he were still treading mud.

"Let me see them boots," a large, muscly man said, shoving some younger, thinner men aside.

At first, Nikolat thought that the men were going to assist him in cleaning away the caked mud. Instead, he was pushed down and held against the ground while two hands ripped the boots from his feet.

"Very nice. Just need some tidying up is all," the big man said, admiring his score.

The men laughed together.

Next, his soldier's vest was being taken from him and his pockets fished out. He watched the men take everything that belonged to him, including his royal silver dragon pendant. Nik was proud, but he knew enough not to say anything.

These men would not help him and would take everything from him, but at least they would leave him alive as long as he kept his mouth shut. So, he sat on the shore of the muddy lake, under an unfamiliar sky, in a strange new place, and watched as his belongings were divvied out among thieves.

He waited there until the men walked back to a scattered

group of wooden crates, thick tarps strung between wooden poles and rope, and pieces of what appeared to be metal scraps arranged as chairs.

The fire that burned there was the only source of light for miles. He knew better than to follow the men into their camp, but he wasn't sure about what direction to walk, either. He needed to know where he was, but he also needed to avoid the violent sport of thieves.

The sky became dark quickly, and a chill set in even deeper without his vest jacket or shoes.

He was embarrassingly exposed on the muddy shore and decided to give himself at least a hundred feet of distance from the mud and men. He stood up, feeling the mud that had started to dry on his socks crack with each step he took on the dry ground.

He walked away, painfully, tripping over sticks and sharp stones. Through the darkness, he saw a dark shadow in the distance. At first, he only walked toward it because it was the only thing that stood out aside from the fires he'd left behind.

Luckily, the shadow turned out to be a number of bushes and trees growing closely together.

He got onto his knees and crawled into a small space between a few of the trees. Once inside the alcove, he found a nature-made bed of old, dry leaves. He lay on his back, looking up through the branches toward the sky.

Where is the sky, he wondered? *Where are the stars? Where is the dead planet?*

The trees were not that mature, but he was thankful. His feet hurt, his muscles ached, he was lost and confused, hungry and thirsty. He crossed his arms and closed his eyes, silently wishing that this were all a dream.

2 TRAVELERS

KaLeah had never been easily intimidated, but this girl was fierce. Although she looked to be the same age, KaLeah sensed that Elektra had seen things beyond her years. She supposed they had that in common.

Elektra stood on the roof with her mechanical wings spread out behind her, staring intensely at KaLeah.

"Why do you have a sword instead of a gun?" Elektra asked.

"I don't know anything about guns," KaLeah said, automatically putting her hand on her sword's hilt, back at her side. "I only just learned about them. My father, the man who raised me, that is, taught me swordplay from a young age."

"So, you can really fight with one of those?" Elektra asked.

"Very well, yes." A smile curled up on KaLeah's lips, feeling proud. But then she realized how useless that skill would be here on a world covered with advanced weaponry.

"Maybe I should learn more about guns," KaLeah said, looking out beyond the edge of the rooftop, through thick haze and smoke.

"Maybe?" Elektra made a ticking sound with her tongue.

"I don't know how you have survived this long in Sarda without knowing how to use a gun. A gun is the only thing these thugs out here understand."

Elektra pulled a gun out of her hip holster and admired the black, metal object that looked like an odd-shaped hammer to KaLeah. KaLeah instinctively took a step back.

"When you're young, punching, kicking, and biting may work for a while, but these guns have saved mine and my mother's lives more than I care to think about," Elektra said.

KaLeah bit her tongue and kept looking out at the strange new planet. There were countless, gray metal towers spread out around the one they were standing on, all disappearing into the hazy landscape. That was the second time she'd heard the word Sarda, and she assumed it was the name of Elektra's village.

She wanted to know more about Elektra and why they needed guns so badly to survive here. But she hadn't considered a background story when the dragon had talked her into traveling to Denlerack.

She couldn't just tell the winged warrior girl that an extinct, magical, phantom dragon had blasted her from Naldash through blue flames to try and save her planet.

Not only did it sound completely crazy, but she also wasn't sure she could trust Elektra. The girl could be loyal to KaLeah's biological father, the dictator. If Elektra saw KaLeah as a threat, she'd never make it to the dictator's door.

On the other hand, if Elektra was against Dayne Keldon, she could still see KaLeah as a potential threat and kill her before she ever found her father.

"Where's your family?" Elektra asked, crossing her arms over her chest.

KaLeah thought for a moment. She technically only had one living family member.

"I've been separated from my family," she said, trying to make it sound truthful while her brain scrambled to come up with a story.

She found it ironic that she was yet again on a quest to find her father—just a different man this time.

"For how long?" Elektra asked.

"A long time. I am trying to find my father. I don't know where he is and I'm not sure where I am. I don't know my way around. And I don't know where I'm going." KaLeah shrugged, trying to appear as completely vulnerable as possible. She didn't want this girl to perceive her to be a threat, and she might need her help navigating this planet.

"What's your father's name?" Elektra asked.

KaLeah hesitated. Her instincts told her not to reveal that the dictator was her father.

"I don't know," she lied. Then she added, "I've never met him," which was the truth.

Elektra narrowed her eyes, seemingly inspecting her trustworthiness.

"Why don't you know your father's name?" Elektra asked. "I thought you said he taught you how to use a sword?"

KaLeah looked down at the sword hitched to her hip. "I thought the man who raised me was my father, but it turned out, that he was not. I am now searching for my real father," KaLeah explained.

Elektra turned away and took a few steps, pacing the rooftop as if mulling things over.

She finally turned back toward KaLeah and said, "I don't know my real father either. I don't know his name—nothing about him. I don't even know if he's alive."

KaLeah stayed quiet, giving Elektra the space to make up her mind about her. She knew the odds of her surviving alone on Denlerack with no gun and no guide were very slim.

KaLeah needed a gun, she needed to learn how to use one, and she needed someone to point her in the right direction. She needed to find out where the dictator lived.

She needed Elektra to trust her long enough to let her tag along until she could get a gun and proper directions.

"I am on my way to see a family friend," Elektra finally said, taking a step toward KaLeah. "He's a professor, a scientist, and an inventor. My mother and I used to visit him when I was a child. He may be able to help you out. He has maps and connections all over this part of Denlerack. Maybe he's heard of your family. He can at least guide you back to where you came from."

"I really appreciate the help, Elektra," she said, folding her hands in front of her, trying to appear as humble and non-threatening as possible—as if approaching a child or a wild animal. I know we are strangers. But right now, you're my only hope. Where I'm from, we don't have towers like this, or guns. I'm afraid that I am too far out of my element. I need your help."

"Towers? You mean buildings? How is it that you've never seen buildings? Where are you from, KaLeah?"

KaLeah didn't want to lie, but she wasn't ready to tell this young woman that she was a space traveler from Naldash. Elektra might just throw her over the edge right then, literally, and figuratively.

"I am from Erion village in Belarone," she said, looking Elektra fully in the eyes.

"There is no such place on Denlerack. There are no diamond districts by those names, not even beyond the mud lands."

KaLeah could hear her heart beating in her chest. It was now or never, she told herself. The girl was clever, but maybe not trusting. KaLeah could ask to be dropped off at a market to make her own way, but without proper weapons, she didn't know how she would survive the journey to find Keldon.

"Either this place exists, and nobody speaks of it, or you are lying," Elektra said, hand fingering the gun in her waistband.

"I truly am from a village called Erion," KaLeah said. "As crazy as it sounds, we hunt the woods, fight with swords, build huts, and farm."

Elektra erupted into laughter. "Farm? Nobody farms on Denlerack. Why didn't you just tell me you were from the underground?"

The young woman looked relieved and had a smile on her face. "I had heard that some people went underground to grow food like they do in the diamond districts. In fact, if I hadn't gotten my mother into Morbel, I would have found a way to go underground myself. I had a few growing operations in our garage when we lived here. Wow," Elektra shook her head in wonder. "You have to talk to me about the tech they used to accomplish a sustainable operation. I mean, with stolen or scrap tech, even then it would be challenging. You'd have to run alternative sources of power to keep from being found out."

Elektra shook her head, as if dumbfounded. KaLeah had no idea what she was talking about, but her plan to be honest appeared to be working.

"Listen, I'm going to take you with me to see my friend, Professor Wheelwright. I know what it's like to be out here alone, and I know all about missing a father you never knew. Wheelwright will be able to help you get back to your farming village and maybe help you find your father along the way."

KaLeah smiled in response. She pieced together that they were currently in a place called Sarda, that Elektra and her mother had lived there but now lived in a diamond district, which sounded cleaner and safer. Everyone had guns and nobody farmed above ground. And apparently, it was dangerous to even farm underground.

Denlerack was a confusing and frightening place, she concluded.

"It isn't too far, so I'll try my best to carry you for a little bit. We'll go from rooftop to rooftop. It's best to avoid the ground." Elektra wrapped her arms around her.

KaLeah closed her eyes as they slowly lifted off the rooftop, sounds of whirring and flapping filled her ears. Then they soared out into the dawn, the sun making the clouds and smoke look aflame as it struggled, fruitlessly, to break through.

Aside from the people, it seemed as if nothing on Denlerack was anything like Naldash.

❧Elektra❧

Elektra was uncertain about taking KaLeah with her. She had acted instinctively when she'd swooped down to rescue the girl, but after hearing KaLeah's story, she wondered if she should have hesitated before jumping to bring the stranger along.

KaLeah was clearly being elusive about where she was from.

Why hadn't she just said she was from an underground farming colony, Elektra wondered? *What was she hiding?*

Growing up in the slums had made Elektra a good judge of character, but she wondered if she could trust her own instincts in this situation. She wondered if KaLeah was as helpless and lost as she seemed.

Elektra tried to shake away the uneasy feeling.

KaLeah said she was looking for her real father, and it had caused a small pain in her own heart. She had turned away to conceal her emotions, in that moment.

They were both just two girls with no fathers. Fathers were supposed to protect their little girls. A vision of her stepfather holding her soon-to-be-born brother entered her mind and a jolt of pain shot through her chest.

She hated being emotionally connected to things. She wanted to be strong, disconnected, and untouchable. A true warrior, a true rebel, has no family. Elektra felt her calling was to sacrifice her chance at a comfortable life and family in order to fight for other families to have better lives.

Here was this stranger, this girl, who seemed to fall out of the sky, and she couldn't just dismiss it. They were both looking for something. They were both alone.

She sighed when she made up her mind and again when

she committed to the decision.

Elektra would take KaLeah as far as the professor's home, and then figure out what to do then.

The girl she carried had white skin and was dressed in a black leather, wraparound top, similar to her own, except instead of gun holsters, she had a sword sheathed to her side.

She knew that she wasn't getting the whole truth but hoped that Professor Wheelwright would be able to see what she couldn't.

One thing she knew for certain was that KaLeah was not an immediate threat. If Elektra had left her on that rooftop, the girl would have been as good as dead. Maybe she could use a sword, but it was useless in Sarda.

KaLeah seemed to be telling the truth about being lost. Nothing about Sarda seemed familiar to the girl, and that puzzled Elektra.

Denlerack was so over-developed that there were buildings and factories covering a majority of its lands. Some had even tried developing unsuccessfully in the mud lands.

Diamond districts were built by the previous dictator to house and protect the rich from the poor migrant laborers and farmers. It was a success for everyone except for those living outside of the walls. Families like Elektra's were left to fend for themselves.

All monetary systems had failed outside of the diamond districts. Anyone who was able to produce a good to sell, usually had it stolen away from them instead. Families had to learn how to survive and defend themselves at the same time.

That's what Elektra and her mother Zatia had done.

The only consistent friend they had throughout all their hardships was Professor Wheelwright. Although her mother had never explained their friendship, she had a feeling that he might be a distant relative. Growing up without a father, it could have just been wishful thinking.

They had to take frequent breaks from flying because Elektra's arms ached from carrying KaLeah from rooftop to rooftop. She had carried her mother short distances before, but never for this long in a single day. She was glad that she had kept up her workout routine after moving into the diamond district.

"What was it like growing up in Sarda?" KaLeah asked, calling back loudly over the wind, wings, and motor fans.

"When I was young, I was scared all the time that someone would break into our garage and hurt us," Elektra said. "We hung a hammock high in the rafters and tied a gun to hang within reach, so we could shoot at anyone who entered from below us. We found, fixed, and sold tech scraps. We grew most of our own food and were able to slowly secure the garage loft with bolts and chains on the doors, and bars on the windows. I learned how to fight and protect myself really young."

"The man who raised me taught me how to fight," KaLeah said. "I didn't really have to fight that much though, until recently."

Elektra thought it was interesting that the girl was trying to relate to her. She assumed the life of an underground farmer wasn't the same as growing up in the slums, but it probably hadn't been an easy life, either.

"Do you still live here?" KaLeah asked.

Elektra took a minute to answer. "I moved into the Morbel diamond district with my mom and stepdad, but I'm not living there anymore." Elektra put a firm edge in her tone, hoping that KaLeah wouldn't ask any more about why she left.

"What's a diamond district?" KaLeah asked.

"You've never seen a diamond district?" Elektra asked, surprised. "Have you never been above ground until now?" Elektra shook her head with confusion, not understanding how someone living on Denlerack, whether above or under the ground, couldn't possibly know about cities like Morbel. KaLeah didn't answer the question, but Elektra continued.

"The diamonds were built for the rich families to protect themselves from the rest of us."

"But you were in one? Are you rich?" KaLeah asked.

"No, but my stepdad is from one of the legacy families. I figured out a way to sneak my mom and I into the city. It was nice, for a time. But I didn't feel like I belonged there, and so, here we are."

"Why are you going to see this professor?" KaLeah asked.

Elektra let her wings beat a few times, gliding through the haze, watching out for tall buildings.

I don't know who this girl is, where she's truly from, or what she's after, Elektra told herself. *She's asking a lot of questions for someone who didn't give her a lot of answers,* she realized.

"Why are you asking so many questions?" Elektra asked.

"Just passing the time and trying to find out more about this place," KaLeah responded.

Elektra suddenly realized that this girl could be on the same mission to find a local band of rebels to join. She wasn't ready to trust her with that information yet, and let the conversation drop as they neared the home of Professor Wheelwright.

He lived beyond the edge of the Sarda slums, in what looked like two smaller buildings that had crashed together in a mudslide.

Elektra was relieved to set KaLeah down, blood rushing in and out of her arms all at once, making them throb painfully. She rubbed at them and KaLeah frowned.

"That was quite a feat of strength, Elektra. Thank you."

Elektra noticed that the girl looked genuinely grateful. Maybe her initial instinct to bring her along was correct.

"Don't mention it," she said. "Now, let's go see the professor."

There was a ten-foot, black iron gate stuck into the hardened dirt and chained together all around the buildings. Only one spot looked like an entrance and Elektra approached cautiously. It had been well over a year since she'd been there.

As she moved closer, two cameras whirred to life and spun to record her.

"Hi, Professor Wheelwright, it's me, Elektra Dean," she spoke loudly toward one of the cameras.

There was a loud clank and bang of locks and gears moving, and Elektra stepped back, feeling the tremors beneath her feet.

"What's going on?" KaLeah asked, hand on the hilt of her sword.

"It's fine, KaLeah. The trap door entrance is opening for us."

"We can't go through the gate?" KaLeah looked from the ground to the metal gates, the crumbling building in the background.

"We can't go through the gate, no," Elektra confirmed.

Elektra watched as the metal grate slowly slid open beside the front gate. The dried dirt cracked, broke, and crumbled down into the opening. "Follow me," she said. "You'll have to climb down."

She clicked a button on the edge of the fan canister to close her wings as tightly as possible. She hadn't been through the tunnels with them on, but she was sure they fit since the professor was the one who had made them.

She slid into the manhole and used a built-in ladder to climb down into the tunnels below the buildings.

She heard KaLeah climb down after her, and then the grating started to close once they were both safely underground.

The girls walked through long, dirt tunnels lit with lights strung together, until they came to a concrete staircase. The concrete was lopsided and cracked in many places, but a metal framing had been put around the concrete as an effort to reinforce the steps.

She wondered about how many visitors the professor received, and how many times the steps had been reinforced over the years.

The staircase led up to a wooden door that she had to nudge open with her shoulder. She walked through the door and into a large room with red rugs strewn haphazardly about, mismatched electrical lights hanging from the ceiling, and varying sizes of lamps sitting on tables.

She heard the sound of barking and clanking, and she smiled widely. The clanking got louder, and she spotted Rascal trotting toward them.

"Hello, you old Rascal," she said to the mechanical doquer as it trotted up to them, barking and snapping its metal jaws.

"What is that?" KaLeah asked in curiosity, without any hint of concern.

"All clear," said a robotic voice, and the doquer stopped barking, switching into a friendlier gear.

"The professor made him before I was born. This is Rascal. He is supposed to look like the doquers."

The doquers had long snouts, sharp teeth, and talons at the ends of their furry feet. They had evolved from dragons and were said to have roamed the lands in packs, hunting for food during the day and howling throughout the night.

"He's pretty small for a doquer," KaLeah said from behind Elektra.

She bent down to pat the creature on its head. "You say that as if you've seen one."

"I have," KaLeah said.

Elektra stood up and turned around, narrowing her eyes suspiciously. "The last living doquers died over a hundred years ago. They are extinct."

"I meant in a painting," the girl said, raising even more of Elektra's suspicions.

She turned back around and followed the metal doquer as it led them through the dilapidated buildings that had been refitted into a home. The little machine wagged its tail happily and trotted with its pointy ears facing outward.

She knew that Rascal had a camera in one eye and picked up audio with its ears. She wondered what the professor would have to say about this mysterious new traveler.

The doquer rounded a turn, out of a hallway, and into a workshop.

A tall man with skin much darker brown than her own, stood up from behind a table covered in scrap metal and broken technology. His beard was thick and gray, matching the gray hair on his head. He smiled widely, showing bright, white teeth behind large lips.

Nostalgia washed over her, remembering the days spent playing with his mechanical creations. He had taught her so much about electronics and had always been so kind and patient with her as she learned.

"Elektra, my child, how wonderful to see you again," Professor Wheelwright exclaimed.

He walked over to the girls, and squeezed Elektra's shoulders affectionately, looking her over.

"You've grown. You look more like your mother every day. I haven't seen either of you in over a year—ever since you told me your plan for sneaking into Morbel. I hope everything went well. Is your mother alright?"

"She's good, yes," Elektra said, casting her eyes away, feeling guilty all of a sudden for leaving her mother behind without a word.

"And who do we have here? In all the years I've known Zatia and Elektra, they've never brought along a guest. Hello, miss, I am Professor Wheelwright," he stuck out his hand toward her.

"Hello sir, I am KaLeah Trapper."

KaLeah bowed slightly, instead of taking his hand, and both Elektra and the professor cocked their heads, curiously.

"You aren't from around here, are you, dear?" the professor asked.

KaLeah smiled. "Is it that obvious?"

"Oh yes, but no need to worry. I accept all kinds of odd folks into my humble world." He stood back with his hands on his hips, looking like he was assessing the situation.

"Won't you both join me next door in the study for some tea? Then we'll talk about why you've come to visit me after so long. I expect this isn't a regular social calling."

He winked, kindly. The girls followed the man into a room off the workshop. The doquer clunked along behind them. There were old, mismatched chairs strewn about the room and a few worn-down couches.

Professor Wheelwright plopped down in what appeared to be his favorite chair by the amount of wear on the arms and seat. The green and purple pattern had long worn away into a frazzled brownish gray combination. The chair was nestled tightly next to a cluttered table and a fireplace with no wood.

On the table sat an old, metal kettle with a hose that may have once been clear coming out of the back. He pressed a button hidden underneath the tabletop and a tiny door dropped open from the table. Gears from beneath started to turn, bringing up teacups from under the floorboards, up and onto the tabletop.

The water kettle purred to life and deposited hot water from the hose into the cups, as they rotated on a spinning plate. The professor pulled tea leaves from a bag in his pocket, and using his fingers, just sprinkled them in each teacup before handing the first cup to Elektra.

She had never been a fan of the tea. Without much greenery on the planet, she wasn't even sure where they came from, and she hated the way the loose leaves felt in her mouth and stuck to her teeth.

She smiled and thanked him anyway while he handed a cup to KaLeah. Oddly enough, the doquer had curled up beside KaLeah, who calmly stroked its metal head.

After the professor had his cup in hand, he flipped another hidden switch that caused a metal box sitting inside the fireplace to start clunking to life. It whirred and banged until finally a small yellow light began to glow and a fan blew heat over them that smelled like burnt dust.

Elektra noticed that KaLeah kept smiling despite the

oddities. With each new clank and turn of a gear, she whipped her brown hair back and forth, tracking the machinery with her inquisitive, stormy blue eyes.

Elektra admitted that it was a strange house with marvelous mechanical creations, and she had always loved it. So many memories of time spent here came flooding back. She had once asked her mother why they couldn't just stay with the professor, instead of trudging back to their hammock high in the garage rafters.

"We are lucky that he is our friend and allows us to visit," her mother had responded. "We must never put him out or inconvenience him, or we may lose our friendship standing. Do you understand?"

Elektra had never brought it up again. She understood that even though the man was friendly and welcoming, that his hospitality had a limit.

"So," Professor Wheelwright said loudly, causing both girls to jump a little. "Why do you honor me with this visit? Do your wings need mending?"

"No, the wings are fine—perfect, really. I decided that it was time to leave my mother to her new life in Morbel and try to find…" she glanced toward KaLeah, still not sure if she should talk about the rebels in front of this stranger.

She turned back to the professor with a thought.

"I want to make Denlerack a better place," she said, opening her eyes slightly wider. "I want to find a way to help."

"I see," he said.

By the way he said it, she could tell that he'd caught her meaning. People did not openly discuss the rebellion against Keldon. Speaking against the dictator was a crime on Denlerack.

"And you?" he turned his wise eyes to KaLeah, who looked down quickly into her teacup.

"I am trying to find my father, but I don't know his name."

The words sounded truthful, but still, Elektra had a

feeling there was something else she wasn't saying.

"That is a mystery, to be sure, but do you also want to make the world a better place?" he asked, pointedly.

There was a long pause and KaLeah looked up to meet his gaze.

"I don't want any harm to come to Denlerack or Naldash," she said firmly.

"Naldash. I haven't heard that name in a long time." He looked up toward a high window, as if he could see all the way to the sky.

"She has been lost to us in the haze for many years now. Most your age have never even seen Naldash. Curious that you'd want to protect that one too."

He turned his eyes to KaLeah, and Elektra was puzzled by the mysterious exchange. She didn't know much about Denlerack's sister planet.

"Do you have a family name, KaLeah?" the professor asked.

"The man who raised me; his name is Clegg Trapper."

The professor held eye contact with KaLeah and took a slow swig of his tea. He set the cup down and then clapped his hands together, causing both girls to jump.

"Let's look at the maps, and see if we can chart your paths," he said.

He got up and headed toward a wall that was covered in pieces of various maps, all pinned over one another. The girls followed him.

Elektra looked more closely at the wall of maps, confused because they seemed to be different versions from different time periods, all cut out and then pieced back together.

She knew better than to ask the professor to explain the peculiar layout. He would end up talking about it for hours. Instead, she kept quiet and let him point out where they were.

"Here," he said, pointing to where they were on the outskirts of Sarda.

"And you want to head here." He trailed his finger across the map and tapped a diamond shape on the map.

"A diamond district?" Elektra asked.

"A failed one. It was the very first one and it collapsed. You won't find the people you are looking for there, but if you go there, they will find you. Do you understand?"

Elektra nodded. Head to the northeast, try to find the building in the general location he pointed to on the map, and the rebels would find her. A nervous knot began to grow and twist in her stomach.

"Thank you, Professor Wheelwright," she said.

He clasped her hands in his. "It is an honor to assist you. You have always been an ethical person. I know you'll do the right thing." His eyes seemed to bore into hers for an uncomfortable amount of time before he released her hands and turned to KaLeah, who was studying the maps very intently.

"And what about you?" he asked her.

"What is this?" KaLeah asked, pointing to a spot on the map beyond where he'd directed Elektra.

"That is Keldon's compound," Wheelwright said, a darker tone in his voice.

The drawing represented a mansion surrounded by factories.

"You girls will want to steer clear of the dictator unless you are ready to go in with an army."

"Why would we go in with an army?" KaLeah asked, sounding more inquisitive than confused. Elektra noticed that KaLeah's eyes didn't move from the compound.

Was the girl looking to join a band of rebels, she wondered? *Was she really lost?*

Elektra still didn't feel ready to ask the questions, just in case the young woman secretly supported the dictator. She needed a way to figure out if she could trust KaLeah.

The professor tilted his head, looking KaLeah over more closely.

"What do you know of the dictator, my dear?" he asked.

KaLeah shrugged and looked more closely at the map.

"Just that he is a bit of a tyrant and has caused a lot of hardship for his people on Denlerack," she stated, as if rehearsed.

"And what do you know of the rebels?" he asked.

She paused and had a far-off look in her eyes, as if lost in a memory.

"I was told that there was once a rebellion against him. People tried to oust him."

"That is correct," Professor Wheelwright said in a whisper, beginning to wander off toward another area of his study. Elektra watched him open a drawer, look into it for a few moments, and then close it again.

He took in a deep breath and then walked back toward them.

"If you want to get home, which is the safest thing to do, then I believe the underground farming communities are hidden beyond these parts here, here, and here."

He pointed to other areas of the map with broad strokes of his palm, maybe not knowing precisely where any of them were. "But, if you aren't looking for the safest thing to do for yourself, then perhaps you will go with Elektra to the ruins of the first diamond district. Maybe you both can do something together that no rebels have been able to do so far."

Elektra glanced at KaLeah, who was looking back at the compound on the map.

"Are you ready for an adventure?" the professor asked.

"I feel like I'm already on one," KaLeah said.

"Come then, let's get you both fed and rested before you head off."

❦Nikolat❧

Nikolat awoke at dawn. At least, he assumed it was dawn given the faint light coming through the hazy, low-lying clouds. In fact, he'd never seen clouds so low before and instead of white, they appeared yellow in color.

The small, thin bushes around him were much sparser than he expected, not offering much cover, but apparently enough to keep him safe overnight. They all appeared to be dying of thirst, with spots worn into their bark and large chunks of bare branches sticking through thin foliage.

He stretched and rubbed the aches in his leg muscles before standing. He came out from under the bushes and looked around. Even though the light was still dim, he couldn't make out any distant villages, people, animals, or even farms. The dirt was dry and brown below his shoeless feet.

The land surrounding him was truly desolate. There were small, sickly-looking, thorny bushes growing wild across the dirt landscape.

Nikolat was overwhelmed by thirst, as if the landscape itself had sucked the moisture from his skin.

Although the dragon hadn't killed him, it may have sent him to his death. He had no way of bartering for food and water, and if the men last night hadn't recognized him as royalty, then there would be no chance of an escort home under the promise of a reward. He wished he could at least ask someone where he was.

He suddenly noticed a short person standing in the distance as if the spirits themselves had heard his wish. It appeared to be a girl much younger than his own little sister.

The wind made her long, brown hair and clothing dance around her tiny body. She turned from him and took a few steps, then deliberately looked back at him as if waiting.

What danger could she bring, he wondered? *Surely where there was a child, there would be adults who feed her. There must be a place where they all get water.*

He looked down at the socks on his feet, caked in dried dirt, knowing that he really had no other choice but to follow this strange waif across the barren wasteland.

He walked toward the child until he reached the spot where he'd first seen her. There, on the ground, was a pair of shoes.

The quality was nowhere near as good as his own boots had been, and they looked to have been hand sewn with some very rough, natural materials. But they were the right size, so he removed his socks and put the clean shoes on quickly.

This can't be a coincidence, he realized, as he continued to follow the girl.

She had stopped up ahead and was looking back at him. She turned around and kept walking on. There was still nothing of substance in the surrounding landscape, so he couldn't tell if she was headed toward a particular destination. Whatever camp he'd stumbled upon in the previous night was nowhere in sight.

After walking more, he came across a canteen sitting in the dirt where the girl had momentarily stopped. He picked up his pace and grabbed the small metal flask. He unscrewed, smelled, tasted, and then gulped down warm water.

Once he started, his brain told him to save some of it, but his body couldn't stop drinking. Like a plant in springtime, he felt each of his limbs respond to the water.

Following the young girl was turning out to be the right decision. He wanted to talk to her and find out where he was, so after she turned to continue walking, he quietly began jogging to catch up, not wanting to startle her or scare her away.

He closed a lot of space between them but didn't get too close to her. To his surprise, she stopped walking and motioned to him for the first time with a wave of her hand, and then she disappeared into the ground.

He got closer and saw that she had gone into a small cave-like hole dug into the side of a thick, mountain of dirt. He couldn't see anything beyond the entrance and knew that it could be a trap. She could just be luring him, but he quickly dismissed the idea.

It's just a little girl, he reminded himself.

Nik got onto his knees and crawled into the hole. After a few feet in, the entrance opened into a dug-out den.

The brown-haired girl with bright, blue eyes, was sitting inside with her legs crossed. He awkwardly moved from crawling to sitting, trying not to hit his head on the dirt ceiling.

Once he was seated, the girl gave him a handful of red berries. He took them and looked them over, carefully. Would a child who gave him shoes, water, and invite him into her shelter, poison him?

The girl popped a few into her mouth, so he tasted one. It was tart but not disgusting, and it didn't immediately kill him, so he shoved the rest into his mouth.

The girl stopped eating and handed him the ones she had left. He took them without hesitation.

"Thank you," he said. "You've saved my life. What's your name?"

The waif didn't answer. She just stared out the front of the dirt cave.

"My name is Nikolat Belarone. Do you know where Belarone Kingdom is from here?"

The girl tilted her head upwards to the sky and then turned back to him. She shook her head no.

"Are you alone out here?"

She nodded that she was.

Nikolat had been rescued by an orphan vagrant roaming a nameless desert with no idea of how to get home. He sighed deeply. At least she seemed interested in helping him stay alive. He was grateful for that. He leaned back against the dirt wall.

"I need to find my way home. I was about to take back my kingdom when a dragon covered me with blue fire. I was standing in front of my people—my father's people. My sister was there. KaLeah... KaLeah was there and was going to try and fight me, but then this dragon appeared out of thin air. Dragons aren't even real. They're supposed to be extinct. This probably all sounds crazy but there was a dragon and then suddenly, I was here. I don't even know where here is. How do I get home from here if I don't even know where I am?"

He put his face into his hands, trying to contain his frustration and the anger that was beginning to resurface.

"Denlerack."

Nikolat opened his eyes and looked at the little girl.

"What did you say?"

He jerked up fast, knocking his head on the top of the cave. Specks of dirt crumbled down onto his shoulders.

"Denlerack is the dead planet in the sky over Naldash," he said. "Why did you say Denlerack?"

The little girl reached out a thin arm toward the cave entrance, toward the desert wasteland.

"Denlerack," she repeated.

Bile rose into his throat as he crawled back out of the cave. It seemed as if the sun was higher above now, but the dreary, yellow fog still lingered and covered the entire sky.

He couldn't see Denlerack out in the universe because he couldn't even see the sky or sun through all the haze. He looked around at the burnt dirt that seemed to stretch on for miles and shook his head in disbelief.

"No, no, no," he said. "You are wrong. You are just a child and you're confused because the landscape is so dead here. You only think we are on the dead planet. This is Naldash. I can't be on a different planet. The dragon could not have sent me across the skies."

The girl emerged and stood, pointing at the sky. "Naldash is there. Denlerack is here." She pointed to the ground.

"Oh, this is not good. Do those clouds ever clear? I need to see the sky. Denlerack is out there, and this is some distant part of Naldash that I've never heard about."

The girl was silent while Nik paced back and forth across the dirt in his fabric shoes. He looked again in every direction, just to be sure. Then he let out an angry, frustrated shout that echoed across the empty land.

"What in dragon's blood am I supposed to do now? I can't travel through the sky!"

"Yes, you can" the girl said.

He spun quickly to face her. She didn't seem to be fazed by his raised voice or anger. She stood there, looking at him with no expression in her blue eyes, light brown hair falling in waves over her tattered dress.

"Yes, I can, what?" he asked, slowly.

"Travel through the sky," she responded.

"I can travel through the sky… how?" he asked, slowly and clearly. "Like a dragon, like juliebees? I have to get all the way up there." He pointed again toward the sky, to clarify.

"Yes," she said, simply.

"How?" This girl was clearly dumb or confused about what was happening.

"In a spaceship."

Nik furrowed his brow and cocked his head. "A what?" he asked.

"A machine that flies through space," she said, using her hand to demonstrate a levitating motion.

He thought about what she was saying. The words were unfamiliar, but he had no other option than to accept what she was saying. If a craft existed on this planet that was similar to a ship but that floated through the space between planets, it didn't seem crazier than a dragon transporting him through cool blue flames.

"And you can take me to this ship?"

She nodded that she could.

"Show me. Let's go." Nikolat stood up taller, ready to travel, when the girl wrapped her tiny fingers around his arm.

"We only walk at night. We eat, drink, and sleep now."

Nikolat looked into her glassy blue eyes and at the small freckles along her cheeks and nose. She reminded him of his sister and yet she looked like a younger version of KaLeah. He found himself annoyed by her resemblance to both girls responsible for getting him into this situation.

He wanted to go right then. He wanted to get home and take the kingdom back from his sister, but he was lost in a strange, potentially dangerous world, whether it was Denlerack or Naldash.

This child, no matter how young, seemed to be more familiar with how to find food and water. She had managed to survive on her own, and so for that, he begrudgingly admitted to himself that he should listen to her recommendation to only travel at night.

"Yes, of course," he said. "What's your name, little girl?"

"I am Ash," she said.

"You can call me Nik."

Without a word or expression, she turned back to the dirt cave. He gave Denlerack one more look around, still not fully believing that's where he was.

He hoped that this spaceship wasn't just some fantasy and that the craft not only existed but could take him back home.

If the people of this place could traverse space, why hadn't they come to Naldash? Why have I never seen a flying ship in the Naldashian skies?

He shook his head, dismissing the thought. Of course, he was still on Naldash, and the girl was confused. He would follow her until he got to a kingdom he knew, or at least, where the people knew him.

He thought back to the previous afternoon on the balcony at Belarone Castle and how KaLeah, looking beautiful and intensely focused, would have killed him in an instant if the dragon hadn't done it first. He realized that his sister had probably resumed control of Belarone and wondered what kind of a world he'd be returning to.

Whether he returned in some sort of flying craft, if he found a draggot, or if he walked the entire way, he would have to convince the people to choose him over his sister. He would have to prove that the dragon spirit had not divinely chosen his sister over him.

Nik's skin prickled with anxiety and impatience.

Ash must have a good reason for only wanting to travel at night, he told himself again, trying to temper his desire to march off into the desert wasteland.

He wondered how long the journey would take and looked up into the hazy sky.

How could this even be possible, he wondered?

If he truly were on Denlerack, it went against everything that his people had always believed. Denlerack was the dead planet. Naldash, his home, was alive and thriving. But here he was, standing face-to-face with someone claiming to be an inhabitant of Denlerack.

Legends said that Denlerack and Naldash were once one planet until a dragon mystic divided the planet into two sister worlds to end a ruthless civil war. Nikolat wondered how much of that story Ash knew, as he crawled back into the cave.

"What do you know of Naldash?" he asked Ash.

She blinked and looked up toward the sky through the tunnel entrance.

"The world leader will save Denlerack by enslaving the sister planet Naldash," she said, as if she'd grown up reciting this as prophecy.

Things were even worse than he thought, he realized.

3 REBELS

For a few hours, Elektra felt safe and relaxed. Professor Wheelwright fed them and provided them with two clean, albeit odd, rooms.

Her room was small with a mismatched collection of assorted knickknacks, blankets, and bedding. There were colorful curtains hung over walls since there were no windows. She assumed the curtains and tapestries had been hung haphazardly over the many cracks and crevices in the walls from when the buildings had fallen into each other.

The entire space had a triangular feel to it. She unlatched her wings and hung them on one of the nails holding up a tapestry, then she took her boots off and climbed into a bed that creaked loudly as she made herself comfortable.

She jumped back up quickly to lock the door, just in case. Although she trusted the professor with her life, she did not yet know this young woman she was bringing along on her journey.

Back in bed, she closed her eyes and took a deep breath. Dust particles swirled around her, but she didn't care. It was better than sleeping outdoors or in a strange, abandoned building.

She fell asleep fast.

In her dreams, she was flying. The air smelled

different—fresh. Alive. She looked around and saw green grass, lush farmlands, and great forests of trees.

A cool breeze trickled across the hair on her arms and tossed her head of curls. It smelled like ice, she realized as she approached the snow-capped mountains. She started to feel colder and colder, and then she woke up in the bed in the professor's house.

A small light in a clock-like device across from her had started to come on, simulating dawn. She noticed that she was cold because she'd kicked off the covers and most of her clothing overnight. She quickly stood and dressed.

It was going to be another long day, but she was ready to restart her journey.

The professor had a breakfast of fried eggs, toast, and muffins ready for her. Of course, none of it was real. It was made of artificial and imitation ingredients that he himself had learned to make from who knew what.

People had found very strange methods of surviving. She figured that he had a small growth operation somewhere within his home, but she didn't ask too many questions. At this point, food was food.

"Good morning, Elektra," Professor Wheelwright said, just sitting down with a cup of tea and toast. "Come have a seat and enjoy the meal before it gets too cold." She noticed the robotic doquer lying in a small bed near his feet.

"Thank you so much for your generosity, sir, and for helping point us in the right direction. You have been invaluable to us."

She meant it. It wasn't often she encountered generous people, and he had always been that way for her and her mother.

"It is my pleasure," he said, smiling.

KaLeah walked in as soon as Elektra had taken a seat at the round table. A tiny sliver of light was sneaking in through a window high up that seemed to still contain glass in one piece. KaLeah stopped right in the path of the light and looked up, squinting. It only seemed brighter due to the refraction in the glass.

"This is a very fascinating place, Mr. Wheelwright," KaLeah said.

"It's *Professor*, KaLeah," Elektra corrected.

"That's quite alright, dear," Professor Wheelwright said, waving Elektra off. The dismissal stung.

"I like to think of this building a lot like this world," he said, looking up toward the bright spot in the ceiling. "It's broken but hasn't yet completely fallen apart. I guess most of us are like that too, it seems."

Rascal, the doquer, got up and trotted over to greet KaLeah, who reached down and patted its head.

Elektra felt a little jealous. The robotic doquer had never acted as if it had emotions in all the times she had spent visiting. She wondered if the professor had recently given it a response other than guard and alarm. And if he had, why was it responding to KaLeah so sweetly and not her, even though she had known it for most of her life?

What does that girl have that I don't, she wondered?

Smelling breakfast, KaLeah smiled and made a dramatic show of breathing it in deeply.

"Wow," she said, making her way to the table. "Thank you so much for this and for letting me stay here. Thank you both."

"It's my pleasure to help you out," the professor said.

Elektra forced a smile and took a bite of the imitation toast. It tasted a bit like cardboard, but at least she knew it wouldn't kill her.

"The butter helps with the taste," said the professor, pushing along a small tin with a yellow paste-like substance.

"What's it made of?" she asked without thinking.

"You don't want to know."

She cast glances at KaLeah, curious about how she'd respond to the food, but she just ate it without any expression or hesitation. It honestly impressed Elektra a little, having trouble with her own reactions to the mystery food.

After they helped clean up the dishes, which consisted of putting the chipped plates onto a conveyor belt and watching the dishes disappear through a small window, they washed up and accepted a few extra packets of dried food from Professor Wheelwright.

He gave them specific instructions on where to fly and for how long, and then at dusk, where it was safe to drop down and travel between buildings.

Elektra rubbed her arms, not sure how she'd be able to handle carrying KaLeah another long distance.

"There's just one more thing before you go," said the professor. "Come along."

The doquer and the girls followed him through a hallway and into a large, open workshop that looked as if it must have been an event space at some time. The ceilings were twice as high as in the other rooms, and tiny windows allowed just enough light into the room to guide their way across a dirty black and white checkered floor.

He walked to a wall and pulled a pair of mechanical wings from a hook.

The wings were black canvas, connected by metal rods and gears. There was a black harness across the front and two fan canisters on the back.

"Another pair of wings?" KaLeah asked, a hint of hopeful expectation in her words.

The professor laughed heartily, and Elektra looked from the professor to KaLeah and back again, feeling jealous.

"I've been holding onto these for a long time. I think it's time I let them go serve their purpose in the sky," he told the girls.

He carried the dark wings over to KaLeah, helping her get her arms into the straps, then buckling her into them.

"For me? Dragon spirits! Thank you," KaLeah said, beaming, a look of pure disbelief on her face.

"Here, under this strap, turns on the fans," he instructed. "This expands or contracts them but getting them to move and steering is all up to your movements. Elektra and I can give you a quick crash… well, non-crash course, to get you started."

"They are beautiful," Elektra said, jealous again of KaLeah as she watched this strange girl parading around in a new pair of mechanical wings.

"I stayed up all night cleaning and fine tuning them," the professor said. "I think you'll need them more than me." He was talking to KaLeah but turned to wink at Elektra. "Well, your arms maybe need them more. It can't be easy carrying someone that distance, and I know you'll want to make good time."

"Absolutely," Elektra said, trying to not sound bitter. "Thank you."

KaLeah turned on the fans and began to levitate. "I'm going to practice here," she yelled over the noise.

"Just stay low until you get the hang of it," Professor Wheelwright yelled back, so that KaLeah could hear him over the fans. "It takes a few hours to really get the hang of wings, but you may not want to take that long."

The professor stepped closer to Elektra and lowered his voice.

"She is a good person, I think," he said. "But she isn't telling you everything."

He placed a hand gently on her shoulder, looking deeply into her eyes. She felt a warm, almost fatherly, affection coming from him, and she realized he was the only man in her life she had ever looked up to.

"Maybe you already realize that," he continued. "You have always been clever. You are a survivor. A fighter. Be careful out there trying to save the planet."

"I will be," she said. "Thank you for everything."

He squeezed her shoulder once and released her, smiling thoughtfully. Elektra hoped that he realized that she was thanking him for all of the kindness he had shown her and her mother over the years, and for everything he had taught her.

She didn't know when, or even if, she would ever see

him again. A moment of sadness passed through her, but she quickly shook it off. She wasn't a woman of attachment.

She was a fighter now.

❧KaLeah❧

The purr of the fans vibrated against KaLeah's lower back, vibrating through her tunic. She opened and closed the wings, touching down and then pushing back off, going up only a foot before coming back to the floor again.

She tilted from side to side, testing out small turns along with her balance.

The black wings seemed as if they were out of a dream and made her feel as if she'd flown on the backs of dragons before. Of course, she realized it probably only felt familiar because Elektra had flown her over the rooftops of the crumbling city.

Higher, how do I get higher?

She took a deep breath and turned the fans up, opened the wings, and jumped. The combination propelled her up over Elektra and the professor's heads.

The room was cavernous, so she had plenty of space to fly in circles, inspecting the old walls and high windows that were caked in a gray layer of dust.

Flying was fun and exhilarating. For the first time in a long time, she forgot about everything happening and enjoyed studying this one thing in front of her: flight. She had wings like a dragon, and she was flying.

So far, nothing had gone the way she'd expected. KaLeah wondered why the dragon had paired her up with this strange young warrior woman.

Had it been the dragon's plan, or just a coincidence, she wondered?

KaLeah looked down at Elektra, who was staring back up at her, impatiently. Elektra's arms were crossed, and she was tapping one foot. KaLeah smiled at the girl's annoyance. She could have spent all day whizzing around the old room.

"Are you ready to go yet?" Elektra asked. "We need to gather supplies and make a plan," she said.

KaLeah landed softly, collapsed the wings, reluctantly unstrapped them, and then hurried to help Elektra pack up.

When they were ready, the young women followed the professor to the lopsided roof, where they reconnected their wings and strapped on their weapons and supplies.

A warm wind swept up and over the side of the crooked building, rustling KaLeah's long brown hair. She realized that she would have to leap from the roof, just as Elektra had done, and her stomach turned.

"You are looking paler than usual, KaLeah," Professor Wheelwright said with a smirk. "You'll be alright. You're a natural flyer."

"You think so?" KaLeah asked, her heart pumping blood so hard she could hear it in her head.

"Not sure how someone from underground could be a natural flyer," Elektra mumbled to herself. Then, to the professor she said, "Thank you again for everything you've done."

"You ladies just get to where you are going safely. I'll be asking the dragon spirits to keep you safe."

Elektra nodded and then turned for the edge of the building.

"Come on," she shouted back to KaLeah as she leapt off the side. Her brown and gold wings caught the wind and carried her effortlessly onward.

KaLeah turned on the motors, letting herself levitate for a moment. She knew that by jumping, the wind and air would help guide her, but she wanted to start out slowly, regardless.

Elektra wouldn't wait up, but after seeing the location of Keldon's compound on the map, she wasn't sure how much longer she needed her company. Elektra clearly had her own agenda that she wasn't divulging, and the professor seemed to be aware of what it was. But KaLeah had only needed to tag along until she had a clear path to the dictator.

That path seemed to run straight through where Elektra was headed, anyway. She was curious but didn't want to be distracted from her own objective, either.

For now, she assumed it was best to fly through the unfamiliar territory with a local guide.

"Go on, now," the professor nudged.

KaLeah nodded, took a deep breath, and then ran off the edge. She fell forward into the wind and the wings took over. The world of dirt, broken metal, and crumbled stone passed below her.

"Woo-hoo!" she cried, laughing to herself. She knew she wouldn't be able to catch up to Elektra at this point, but she kept her eyes ahead, making sure not to completely lose her. If anything, following Elektra would get her mostly to her actual destination.

She wanted to get close enough to at least talk to her. KaLeah had determined that the planet, ruled by her father, had fallen into almost complete ruin. Nothing seemed to be growing, everyone was in hiding and trying to survive, except for groups of wealthier families that lived in secured diamond districts.

It made no sense to her. How could a leader just let people starve and suffer? It seemed that a lot of those people had turned to crime. How could the wealthier families not care about the well-being of fellow humans living in squander?

The professor was a wonder. Clearly, he was smart enough to create contraptions and make his own food. He had found ways to survive on his own, but not everyone has the same skills.

KaLeah had been taught to hunt and cook, but the game was plentiful on Naldash. The lands were lush, and she knew how to plant around the seasons, when to harvest, and how to take care of the land around her so it would take care of her in return.

Denlerack was once exactly like Naldash. Both planets

had dragons. Both had humans and a lot of the same animals that had evolved from dragons.

What had gone so wrong here, she wondered? The only difference she could see was the proliferation of technology.

The professor had fascinating machines that could do all sorts of things, just like the wings she and Elektra were using to fly like dragons. She couldn't understand how the technology could have destroyed their world.

I'm not supposed to be concerned about this world though, she reminded herself. *I need to figure out how to protect my own.*

She needed to pry a little more and find out about the leader and his capabilities. *Did he have more ships like the one her mother had used to escape in? Did he have weapons? An army?*

"How do I make this thing go faster?" she asked out loud, grumbling.

"You're too slow," Elektra said, soaring at her from behind a tall building.

KaLeah had to angle to keep from bumping into Elektra as they passed. She was surprised she'd lost sight of the girl so easily. Elektra came around to fly beside her.

"Where are we going?" KaLeah asked, blurting out the question that had been on her mind since the professor had pointed out a spot on the map.

"We are looking for the first attempted diamond district. It was overthrown during its construction and torn down. It's symbolic to the rebellion."

"What rebellion?" KaLeah asked, and then she wished she hadn't. She realized that anyone from Denlerack would surely be aware of attempts to overthrow the dictator. She laughed to cover her mistake.

"I mean, how is it symbolic of the rebellion?" KaLeah asked.

"It's symbolic of what happened here," Elektra answered, eyeing her suspiciously. "The separation of the classes, the desiccation of our lands, the authoritarian dictatorship, the pollution of the skies. Everything."

"Why are you going there, though?" KaLeah braved the

question, not sure she would get an honest reply.

Elektra was quiet. They flew in silence past a few more crumbling buildings before she responded.

"There may still be rebels out there," she said. "And if there are, then I want to help them. I don't want the next generation to experience this—" she motioned to the world below them.

KaLeah looked around more as she flew, feeling a strange sense of guilt for having a healthy planet and wondering if her true father really was to blame.

"Was it the king's fault?" KaLeah asked.

"What's a king?" Elektra flew a little further, putting distance between them and then called back loudly. "Why do you act as if you know nothing about this place, KaLeah? If your people went underground, they went for a reason. How do you not know about the dictator? Have you never heard of Keldon? You need to tell me what's going on right now or I'm leaving you behind."

A loud explosion filled the air, echoing throughout the hollow buildings beneath their wings. KaLeah recognized it instantly as the same sound she had heard in the throne room on the day Bylex was shot.

Two more loud bangs rang out.

"Duck, dive, get out of here!" Elektra screamed as she tilted herself and flew off at a sharp angle between two buildings.

KaLeah tried to follow her, but froze, blinded by the memory of seeing Bylex dying from a bullet wound in the throne room on Naldash.

Snap out of it and go, she told herself. The fans were keeping her moving, but she knew that simple momentum wouldn't be good enough. KaLeah knew she had to fly away, to hide behind a building, on a roof, in the clouds, something, but she didn't want to lose Elektra either.

She took more evasive measures right as the sound of two more gunshots filled the air. She couldn't see where they were coming from or whether or not they were aimed at her, but she had seen the damage that just one bullet could do. It was more important than ever to get someplace safe and out of sight.

KaLeah headed in the same direction Elektra had gone, bringing her wings in to propel her faster down and across the landscape.

Another shot and she felt something hard slice through her left shoulder. She curled up from the pain and it sent her spiraling. She tried to recover but her body kept involuntarily bending toward the injured shoulder. The wings were failing, flapping against the wind as her body twisted.

She was falling fast. She had to do something, or she was going to die.

KaLeah clenched her teeth and straightened out both of her arms, laying her body straight into the fall, expanding her legs back and willing the wings to level out.

Miraculously, she stopped spinning and regained control just in time to bring her legs down for a hard landing. She let her knees buckle so that she could fall forward onto her hands and avoid breaking anything. Pain still shot up through her legs, paling in comparison to the pain in her shoulder.

KaLeah reached up to her shoulder, pulled her hand back and saw blood. Lots of blood. She remembered holding red-hot bullets in her father's cellar before she'd known what they were. She remembered how quickly just one of them had killed Prince Bylex back on Naldash. *Am I going to die too?*

"Spirits," she said out loud.

Like a calling to them, she heard the guttural growls start to creep into her thoughts. She hadn't heard the familiar dragon spirit warnings since arriving on Denlerack, so it was almost a surprise. It wasn't that she'd forgotten about them, she just hadn't expected the spirits to communicate with her on this planet too.

"Alright, I get it. I have to go now," she said, responding

to their warning. Whoever had shot her down would be looking for her. She had her sword, but she knew it would be useless. These cowards would never face her honorably.

KaLeah started walking through the alleyway, not knowing where she was going except to find a place to hide. She hoped that the dragon spirit growls would keep guiding her.

She checked to make sure she wasn't leaving a trail of blood along the way. She pressed her gloved hand over the wound, trying to keep all the blood at bay, and kept walking.

The alley was dark, even in the light of day. The yellow haze did little to permeate around the decaying buildings. She tried to step quietly around shards of glass, trash, and what looked like human feces. There were sounds of boots running somewhere and she knew that whoever was looking for her was close.

There was no other choice but to duck into one of the abandoned buildings. Most were boarded up, some with boards torn off shattered windows. Nothing looked safe or inviting but she was running out of time.

KaLeah turned a corner and saw what looked like a giant metal box. She gathered that it was for trash, but since nobody actually picked up their own trash here, she figured it might be empty inside.

She was wrong. It was filled with trash, but it was still a place for her to hide in plain sight. She climbed in and was hit with a sour, putrid smell that made her instantly nauseous. KaLeah tried not to look too much at what she was lying down in, feeling bad that her beautiful wings were being subjected to such filth.

Pinching her nose, she looked up into the hazy sky and waited.

More running. A few yells and a shout. Another gunshot. Running.

KaLeah waited for the sounds to pass while she bled into the garbage. The dragon growls had subsided in her head, so she assumed that meant she'd done well, and that the danger was passing.

She may have drifted off for a moment, because she could see Prince Nikolat. He was standing in front of Belarone castle, smiling. Then a wind drifted in and began to blow him away. His smile vanished as he tried to keep his balance. The wind just kept pushing him further and further from KaLeah. When the prince was gone, the wind grew stronger. It flew Captain Daven into her path. The wind dropped him like a gift in front of her, and he smiled.

She realized she could hear wind blowing, it wasn't a dream, and she thought faintly that a storm was coming.

"I think they're gone now," Elektra said.

KaLeah slowly opened her eyes and saw Elektra floating in place above her.

"How did you find me?" KaLeah asked.

"The advantages of flight. I never would have found you if you'd gone into one of the buildings. Now come on, we need to keep moving. Do your wings still work?"

"I hope so," KaLeah said, trying to pull herself up to standing, the wings making movement awkward in the tight space.

The smell of dead animals and mildew rushed into her senses as she pushed herself up from the trash pile, making her feel sick all over again. "Dragon's blood, it smells in here."

"No one in their right mind climbs into one of those," Elektra said. "But that's why the men ran right by it without looking for you there."

KaLeah lifted herself out of the bin, cringing at the pain in her shoulder that ran all the way down to her fingertips.

"Is that your blood? Were you shot?" Elektra asked, her eyes wide in surprise.

"I believe so," KaLeah answered.

"Huh, you're tougher than I thought, then." Elektra inspected KaLeah's arm while helping her climb down. "You're lucky it wasn't a heater.

"What's a heater?" KaLeah asked, hesitantly, not sure

she wanted to know.

"It's a fire bullet or a poison dart. They have different names, but they basically burn red under your skin and spread a poison that kills you after only a few heartbeats. They belonged to Keldon's army, but a few got out into the public. I haven't seen any in a long time. Seems like you were hit with an iron bullet, which are still deadly if they hit you in the right organ."

KaLeah was relieved to still be standing. She realized that the bullets she'd found under her house in Naldash were these heaters and was the type of bullet that had killed Prince Bylex.

"I have a patch, and I can stop bleeding, for now," Elektra offered. "Do you think you can still fly?"

"As long as the bullet didn't tear through a wing, yes."

"Come on, let's take a look." Elektra moved closer and inspected the black wings, determining that they were still in working condition. She pulled a bundle from her pack and dabbed something onto KaLeah's shoulder before sticking a large patch over the wound. KaLeah bit her tongue to keep from making a sound.

"I can't tell if the bullet is inside you or if it just grazed your arm. I think it just ripped off a layer of skin. Once we are in a safer place, I'll take a closer look."

"Thank you, Elektra." KaLeah looked at her black-gloved hands, which were now covered in dried blood. She couldn't do this alone, she realized. This fierce woman had already saved her twice. KaLeah took a deep breath, realizing that the dragon spirit had paired her with Elektra on purpose. It was clear the young woman wanted to join the rebels, and she saw the dictator as a threat to Denlerack.

But if she saw KaLeah's father as a threat, there was no safety in telling her about that relationship.

Maybe it's time to trust her with a little more information, KaLeah thought.

"Elektra, I haven't told you the truth about who I am. I wasn't sure who I could trust on this planet," she started.

Elektra stood up a little straighter, giving KaLeah her full attention.

"I'm not from an underground farming community. I'm not even from Denlerack. It might sound crazy, but I'm actually from Naldash."

"Naldash," Elektra repeated. She looked up into the clouds. "The sister planet, Naldash?"

"Yes."

Elektra crossed her arms, looking doubtful. "If that's true, then how did you get here?"

KaLeah hesitated. She didn't want to lie, but how would Elektra believe that a dragon phantom can transport people through space with blue flames, even if the girl *had* seen the blue flames for herself.

She remembered her hesitation about telling Clegg, the man who raised her, about seeing the dragon in the woods. If she had just told him from the beginning, he would have told her about how the dragon spirits were said to call to the great warriors. She could have saved herself so much trouble.

She decided to stick with the truth—most of it, at least.

"Back on Naldash, a dragon spirit called Anissa La Alani, transported me here through blue flames. She said that I am to try to stop this world's leader from invading Naldash."

Elektra studied her face for a few moments and then turned and began walking down the alley. KaLeah slowly followed.

"I saw the blue flames," Elektra said, speaking more to herself than to KaLeah.

"And everything has been so unfamiliar to you. You had never seen buildings. You don't know how to use a gun. You have a sword. You didn't know about the rebellion."

Elektra stopped and scanned the area. KaLeah froze too and listened for any other sound besides their breathing. Elektra turned to face her.

"Dragons are extinct, but I've heard stories of spirits

interfering in our lives," she said. "It doesn't make sense, but you haven't done or said one thing that makes sense since I met you. We don't have time to talk about it now. We need to keep moving."

"Yes, of course," KaLeah agreed, relieved.

Both girls turned on their propeller fans.

They flew straight up to the clouds for cover, then continued their trip slowly, dropping down to see where they were as infrequently as possible.

Elektra said nothing and it made KaLeah nervous.

Does she believe me? Is she trying to figure out how to get rid of me? Would I believe a story about a dragon spirit transporting people through blue flames?

KaLeah's mind buzzed with doubt for the rest of the flight. She tried to keep as level as possible, avoiding too much movement, but the wind battered her wings, jerked her injured arm up and down, and back and forth. Worrying about Elektra's silence was the only thing keeping her distracted from the pain.

The sun was starting to set when Elektra finally spoke up.

"There it is," she said, pointing through the clouds.

Below them was a foundation of what would have been an enormous structure. There was a giant square shape that contained nine squares within it, all connected by what would have been bridges. Scaffolding still stood, walls, and even some doors. The gate that had once surrounded the compound was lying flat around the exterior, with large chunks of it missing.

"Where do we go?" KaLeah asked.

"To the control district, the center. The heart of the diamond," Elektra said, leading the way.

KaLeah looked again and realized that from another angle, the square that contained the nine squares, did look more like a diamond.

"And who exactly are we meeting there?" KaLeah asked, trepidation flooding her body.

"The only people who could possibly stop the dictator from attacking your planet—the rebels."

Elektra descended toward the heart of the structure and KaLeah followed. Things were starting to make sense now. The professor had pointed Elektra to the original diamond district, the one rebels had destroyed, in the hopes that rebels would still be around the area, as it was symbolic to their cause.

Her shoulder was throbbing now, and she was starting to feel light-headed. *Almost there*, she told herself. *I'm almost on my feet again.*

Of course, she had no idea what to expect once she was on her feet.

Would there be more flying after meeting with the rebels? Would they walk? Are they underneath the abandoned foundations?

She watched as Elektra touched down in almost the exact middle of what she had called the 'heart'. It looked like she was on an interior floor, a few floors up from ground-level. KaLeah landed a little harder than she'd intended, sending pain throughout her shoulder, back, and arm. She wasn't used to landing, let alone while being injured. She gritted her teeth and tried not to grimace, not wanting to look weak in front of Elektra.

"So, where are they?" KaLeah asked.

"I don't know how this works." Elektra seemed to be inspecting the stability of the floor they stood on.

"Are they the ones that shot at us?"

"Doubtful," Elektra said, shaking her head.

"How did the professor know about this place?" KaLeah walked around, careful of her foot placements on the unstable flooring. There were areas where weather had worn away the wood and only beams remained.

"People have been rebelling against the Keldon family for a couple of generations," Elektra said.

"Family?" KaLeah's curiosity peaked, since she was technically family.

"Yes, as the family wealth grew, they passed it down

from son to son, each one taking over the companies that continued polluting our air and water. That family legacy blocked out our sky."

"Why were they ever in charge in the first place?" KaLeah shook her head, confused at the idea of her original family members causing so much damage.

"As the gap of wealth grew, they were able to pay armies to protect them from people who tried to steal from them or rebel against them. Eventually, they bought the favor of all the other wealthy or well-off families by building them their own secure cities. Diamond districts." Elektra kicked a piece of broken metal off the edge of the ruins. It clanked as it hit a pile of metal and concrete on the ground.

Elektra took a few moments to canvas the entire area, looking for signs of what, KaLeah didn't know. She felt useless standing there. She realized that Elektra probably didn't need her peppering her with questions right now. This wasn't the time for questions or conversations.

They had just flown a great distance after being shot down and were now in a strange new place with potential dangers lurking everywhere. They needed to pay attention to their surroundings, ensure they had cover, and weren't targets out in the open, especially with the sun setting.

Maybe it's the pain or the loss of blood that's keeping me from thinking straight, she assumed. She hunched down and tried to help Elektra by assessing the environment.

The floor they were on did not seem completed or sturdy. There were frames all around the edges but only half built or torn down walls. She had never seen structures quite like this. It appeared that the process had been to frame out the entire foundation and then build up. It was all amazing to KaLeah.

Belarone castle had been huge and beautifully constructed, built stone-by-stone in elaborately rounded columns, grand staircases, and rich, dark wood. The buildings she'd seen so far on Denlerack were also equally impressive, just different, and not beautiful at all. She hadn't seen a diamond district city, but she wondered if it was much more lovely than the castle or just cleaned up versions of these tall, crumbling rectangles pointing to the sky.

All that she saw of it now were ruins.

"Here," Elektra called. "We don't want to stand out in the open," she said. "We can sit here next to this wall."

The wall would be barely tall enough to hide them if they both sat side-by-side with their backs to it. "We can check around the side to make sure no one is sneaking up on us."

"Aren't the rebels supposed to be here?" KaLeah asked, feeling dumb.

"They may or they may not. We'll find out soon enough."

They sat in silence for some time. Finally, KaLeah took a deep breath. "Can you tell me more about the rebels and the dictator?" she asked.

"Might as well, since we're in this together now," Elektra started. "But you are going to have to tell me about Naldash, too."

"Absolutely," KaLeah said with a smile. That was one thing she knew.

❮❮Elektra❯❯

Elektra sat in the heart of the abandoned diamond district and told KaLeah all about how Keldon had made himself a dictator. He was not born a king, as KaLeah had mentioned earlier. She still couldn't quite believe that this girl was from Naldash. She definitely acted like she was from another planet with her word choices, sword, and lack of knowledge.

Elektra explained how Keldon had no great intelligence. The only reason he rose to power was because he had been born wealthy.

"Our king was also wealthy, along with a lot of families in the kingdom," KaLeah said, comparing stories. "But they still led the kingdom and tried to make sure that it was protected, that people were fed, and that everything ran as it should," KaLeah explained. "Although we never had much money in the village I grew up in, we were able to take care of ourselves and each other. Food and water were plentiful; you just had to be taught where to look."

"Food and water were once plentiful here, also. At least, that's what I was told," Elektra said, having no experience of anything other than the desolate state of the planet. "But Keldon's family began to build factories and manufacture a lot of the kinds of technology that the professor learned to create himself. Keldon's family mass-produced it all. They spent generations creating things that nobody even needed. Conveniences. When illness befell a few of Keldon's family members, killing most of them, he inherited an enormous amount of wealth at a young age. And then he began buying more power from other men who also wanted to become rich."

Elektra kept her wings attached, just in case she needed to make a quick escape. But she stood up and walked the low walls of the ruins, keeping an eye out for who she hoped would be rebels.

"Keldon bought things just to own them and make money off them, not to make the businesses better or make improvements to the world around him" Elektra continued, repeating the stories she'd heard growing up. "He dismissed any notion that his manufacturing and factories were creating more pollution, speeding up the cycle of destruction that his family had started. The changes were so gradual, at first, that he dismissed the conditions as natural within the environment. He wanted all cities to have buildings, but when they became too expensive for common people, he decided to move the wealthy into elite, custom created, and internally sustainable mini-cities, or diamond districts."

Elektra rolled her eyes, mostly to herself. Although she'd lived in one of these self-sufficient cities, benefiting from the food and shelter and safety, she still found herself despising their origins and the people born within them who knew nothing of the external struggles.

"The poor people, the ones who were too sick or injured to work in his factories, or the ones who worked but still couldn't afford to pay rent in the buildings he owned, started to rebel," Elektra felt pride in this portion of her storytelling. Her chin lifted and her shoulders dropped back, elevating her stature. "In response, Keldon increased his army and had protestors killed. The current-day rebels are the children or grandchildren of many of those protestors."

Elektra continued explaining how things had already been falling to pieces even before Keldon came to power. There was a great divide between the poor and the wealthy, with no one in between. The rich profited off their legacies of wealth and the technology they had access to, which became more and more complex, and more out of reach for the lower working classes.

Pollution had put the farmers out of work, and they couldn't afford the new technology needed to set up underground or in-building growth operations. Energy and utilities were too expensive. Only the rich within the diamond districts could afford to grow food on a larger scale.

People rebelled and attacked the districts. Keldon's army put them down and they scattered as fragmented gangs. Some learned how to fend for themselves, others became criminals, and some set up underground communities.

Elektra told KaLeah about the rumors of rebels still trying to infiltrate Keldon's armies or the districts. She had heard that the rebels were trying to overthrow Keldon. Some said that they were trying to find sustainable methods of large-scale food production. They were supposedly recruiting in areas all over Denlerack and waiting in hiding until the perfect time to strike.

Elektra stood up straighter, quickly crossed to KaLeah,

who was still sitting with her back against a wall, and placed her hand on KaLeah's arm to alert her. Someone was coming. She had heard what sounded like a piece of glass underneath a boot. She reached for her gun slowly, not wanting to accidentally shoot at a rebel she was there to find.

"Who's there?" Elektra called out into the dusk.

"I should ask you the same thing," a male voice called back.

She could tell that he was young, about their age, and was approaching from behind them. She dropped to her knees and carefully spun around to peer up over the wall.

"My name is Elektra Dean, and I am from Sarda. I am searching for people who want to make Denlerack a better place for all."

"Well, there are a lot of different opinions out there about how to accomplish that goal," the young man shouted back. "And who's with you?"

"KaLeah – what's your last name again?"

"Trapper," the other girl whispered.

"KaLeah Trapper!" Elektra chose not to add any more details than that. The sun was setting behind the gray sky, but there was just enough light to make out the silhouette of a man coming through the rubble.

"Do you think he's a rebel?" KaLeah asked.

"He should be," Elektra said, feeling confident. The professor had directed her here. Everything inside of her hoped that this was a rebel.

"But what if he's not? What if he's one of Keldon's men?" KaLeah asked, a note of concern in her tone.

Elektra's pulse quickened. She pulled her gun up a little higher but did not aim.

"No need for that," the man said, coming closer toward them. "Although, it is your right to protect yourself, I am not a threat. But, I guess, no one should ever lower weapons out here. Woah, are those wings?"

The young man was very tall, lean, with brown skin, brown eyes, and black hair buzzed short. His smile spread across his face and Elektra surprised herself by almost smiling back. He was disarming in a spirited, casual way.

"I have never seen anything like that!" he exclaimed like an excited child. "And she has them too? Where did you say you were from? How did you get wings like that? Can I get some?"

Elektra found herself smiling for the first time in a long time, unable to resist his charm. He did not seem to be a rebel, however. There was nothing that said fighter about him.

"My friend, Professor Wheelwright, made them for us," she answered.

"You know the professor?" he asked.

Elektra furrowed her brow. "Yes. I've known him my whole life," she said.

"That man is a legend. We didn't know he was even still around." The boy walked around them, keeping distance and inspecting them, but still friendly and enthusiastic.

"He's a legend to whom?" Elektra asked, trying in investigate this strange boy further.

He didn't seem to hear her, as he was now looking over KaLeah's wings and mumbling to himself.

"That is so cool," he said, clearly wanting to get his hands on the flying contraptions. "So, anyway, I'm Rustin. What are you ladies looking for out here? Are you lost?"

Elektra's smile dropped, and she looked him in the eyes. Either he really was a rebel, and the professor had directed them to the right location, or he was just some stranger who may try to steal from them, hurt them, or worse.

She couldn't tell if he was armed, from looking at him. He hadn't made any threatening statements and didn't look to have a mean bone in his body. He seemed sweet.

Still, she had to tread carefully. He could turn on them at any moment. She kept her own gun in her hands, lowered slightly so it wasn't pointing directly at him, but she could quickly rectify that angle if necessary.

"How do you know Professor Wheelwright?" she asked,

trying to assess the situation they were now in.

The boy shrugged as if this question was no big deal. "The word is that he helped arm and equip a few rebellions over the years. Nobody has heard from or seen him in some time, but we all know about him."

Elektra was shocked and a little hurt. All this time, the professor had helped the rebels but never told her? He never tried to recruit or encourage her? He didn't even tell her that he was clearly directing her to their hideout.

She tried not to get upset by this and focused on the task at hand. Although the young man did not look tough, at all, he was clearly connected to the rebellion in some way.

Now or never, she told herself, taking a deep breath.

"I want to join the rebellion against Dictator Dayne Keldon," Elektra said.

He stared at her for a few long moments, looking her over.

"Very strong words," he said. "Dangerous words on Denlerack. And what about you?" He nodded toward KaLeah, slumped even lower against the wall, her wings spread out to the sides of her like blankets. Elektra wondered if the girl's pain was getting worse.

KaLeah tilted her head. "Elektra has saved my life a couple of times, so I'm with her. If she trusts the rebellion, then I trust the rebellion."

"I like you ladies," Rustin said, smiling that big grin again. "But I can't let you come with me without knowing more about you. I need details, information, family names, where you grew up, why you hate Keldon enough to want to risk your life in the rebellion. You know, all the stuff."

He casually shrugged his shoulders, kicked a foot up against a nearby wall, leaned into it, and crossed his arms.

Elektra swallowed back an angry protest. She had come a long way to find a group she inherently belonged to, and this kid was going to waste her time. She clenched her fists.

"Elektra has suffered," KaLeah said, surprising her. "Her mom raised her alone in a garage, hiding out in a hammock hanging from the rafters every night. She grew up fighting to survive in a world that Keldon destroyed. I don't know much about the rebels, or much about this place, but Elektra dropped down from the sky to save me from being shot twice. Well, the second time I was actually shot, but she mended me."

Rustin kicked off the wall and came toward KaLeah in one smooth motion.

"You've been shot?" The boy's expression changed in a heartbeat from inquisitive to passionate concern. He was at KaLeah's side in a breath, bending down to look the girl over. He inspected her bandaged arm with one hand and placed the back of his other hand against her forehead. "Dragon's blood, girl, you're feverish," he said. "We have to go. Colt isn't going to like this, but I can't leave you out here. I'm going with my gut on you two."

He dipped low and put his arm underneath KaLeah's, wrapping around her back despite the awkwardness of the extended wings. He lifted her up to her feet. Elektra said nothing. She was surprised at the sudden change of events, expecting to be interrogated.

"I'm not sure I can help you walk with those wings on. Can we take them off?" Rustin asked.

Elektra stepped in to help. She didn't want the wings to get damaged, and she also wasn't sure if Rustin was the type of kid to run off with a fancy new toy.

She unfastened the straps and helped KaLeah out of them while Rustin held her steady. KaLeah grimaced only when the strap came off from around her injured arm.

"Is that a sword?" Rustin asked, noticing the object sheathed at her side. She laughed but must have run out of energy because she didn't say anything in response.

Elektra thought about what KaLeah had told Rustin. She was being complimentary, but was it just to get access to the rebels? Maybe it had been the fever talking.

What does this girl really want, she wondered?

"Here we go; hold on." He swept KaLeah up into his

arms and headed out of the ruins toward the direction he'd come from.

Elektra should have been happy and excited. She was getting what she wanted. She was following a rebel through the darkness to join the others. But she was nervous, which wasn't like her. She shook away the feeling and raised her head high.

Here we go, she told herself.

4 GUNS VS. SWORDS

They hadn't been walking for long when Rustin stopped and scanned the darkness around them. He seemed to be making sure there was no one lurking or watching them. He disappeared behind a crumbling building and Elektra followed carefully, trying to see her way in the darkness.

"Where are we—"

"Shhh," Rustin cut Elektra off. Then, in a whisper, he said, "We're here. It's a secret entrance. We can't let people find it. I'm supposed to blindfold you both, but there's no time. I'm just going to have to trust you."

He set KaLeah down gently on the ground, then he went to work quietly sliding over a manhole cover on a sewer drain.

"There's a ladder leading down to the tunnel. You go first and I'll lower your friend. I don't think she has the strength to climb down."

He was being very quiet, so Elektra nodded. She'd been talking to KaLeah for what had felt like hours, so him noticing a weakness in KaLeah that she had not, sent a wave of guilt through her. She also wondered if there could be people lurking in the darkness around them above ground and tried not to think about what might be waiting below.

He was already on the move, ushering KaLeah back to her feet. Elektra looked and reminded herself that she'd been in worse locations before looping her arm through the black wings' straps and stepping down onto the first rung.

She was pleased to see that the tunnels beneath were not shrouded in pitch darkness. There were electrical lights strung and flickering around the tunnel, heading off into three different directions underground.

Looking back up the ladder, she prepared herself to support KaLeah's full weight as Rustin lowered her down. She clasped the young woman's back and tried to guide her down the ladder, while pushing KaLeah's weight toward the ladder at the same time.

Elektra could feel how hot the girl was through her clothing. She hadn't realized how bad it was and started to worry. She didn't trust the girl, and hadn't known her for long, but she didn't want her to die.

Rustin slid the manhole cover back into place and climbed down, taking KaLeah back into his arms.

He started heading into one of the tunnels, and Elektra readjusted her hold on the black pairs of wings and followed him. They walked for even longer than they had walked above ground. The ground was wet and muddy, and all manner of critters clung to the walls around her. It smelled like mold and wet dirt, but she was almost there. She was almost with the rebels. She was almost with her people; people who cared and wanted to make a difference.

The anticipation filled her with excitement and nervousness.

They finally reached a large metal door. Rustin placed his finger on a rusty looking button affixed to the side of the door and spoke into a speaker.

"Rustin's home with two guests. One needs immediate medical attention. High fever and a bullet wound."

Then he turned to Elektra, "That's so they don't shoot us when we walk in." He was smiling but she assumed he was telling the truth.

"You're going to have to help me here," he said. He nodded at the door and a loud grinding sound began emitting from it.

"That's the gear unlocking. Once it's done, lower that lever by pulling it down hard. Then turn that knob and pull it open as hard as you can. It's pretty heavy."

Elektra waited for the gear to stop turning and then she did as he'd said. In the middle of the massive door was a black metal lever. She used both hands to pull it straight down and back to flush with the door. She then grabbed a knob at the opposite side as the speaker box, turned it, and pulled the door open.

The electric lights continued running along the tunnel on the other side of the doorway. Rustin went through first and then she pulled the giant door closed behind them. She heard the gears turning again, automatically locking.

"Pull the lever up on this side," he instructed.

She did and then followed Rustin further down the tunnel, which seemed to grow more and more lit until she could see people standing at the end of the hallway. There was a small group of teenagers standing in front of two metal doors hanging wide open.

"Alister, this one was shot out of the sky. I'm not sure if there's a bullet in her shoulder or not, but she's burning up," Rustin said, approaching the group at the doorway.

A man with honey-hued skin, black hair, and soft features stepped up and took KaLeah into his arms. "Lina, Lainie," was all he said, and he whisked her off. Two blonde twins with very pale skin followed quickly behind him.

"This is Elektra," Rustin said, motioning to her. She was standing in the entryway with a dumbfounded expression on her face. "They are from Sarda and are escaping the slums. They want to join us. I would have quizzed them longer, but I didn't want the girl to die." Rustin motioned toward where Alister had taken KaLeah.

Another tall, brown-skinned young man stepped up from the group. Elektra was immediately struck by how handsome he was, but he also carried an air of calm authority. She assumed he was in charge.

"Hi, Elektra, is it? My name is Colt."

He stuck out his hand and she looked down first before taking and shaking it with hers.

She wasn't used to formal greetings, especially since she'd tried to avoid making new friends in the diamond district.

"Hi," Elekatra said, feeling small. "Thank you for taking us in. I've been searching for a group like yours, wanting to join, for a long time."

"Why don't you come in and we'll all meet and discuss who you think we are, exactly." He smiled and she noticed dimples in his smooth cheeks.

She followed Colt past the other people standing in the doorway, through the doors, and into a massive, round room with high ceilings. There were no windows, so she assumed the entire facility was underground.

The room was furnished with mismatched couches and oversized chairs, a few scattered small tables, and two long, rectangular ones. There were books overflowing from shelves and stacked throughout the room in corners, on tables and chairs. There were screens on the walls of varying sizes showing black and white images, with one showing a colored news program that she was familiar seeing within the district. She assumed it was completely run by the dictator.

Two iron staircases on either side of the room led up to an open loft that contained more furniture and books.

Even though it was a cavernous space, it felt cozy. They had obviously turned the basement of the deserted building into a home.

Elektra followed Colt to an assortment of worn sofas around a low table in the center of the room. The rest of the group joined them. Colt motioned for her to sit on a burnt orange fabric sofa, so she shrugged out of her wings and took a seat, sinking deeply.

Rustin sat across from her on a green sofa, and the rest of the rebels filed in and took their seats around her, staring intently.

"Is this wise?" A young man who had just sat next to Colt asked in a low voice. He was pale, thin, and had shoulder length wavy black hair.

"It's too late either way," Colt replied, smiling at Elektra.

"This is Von." Von looked at her but did not smile.

"Where is she from?" A young woman with dark hair, creamy white skin, and sharp, pristinely pointed eyebrows stared hard at Elektra, although she hadn't addressed her directly.

"Easy Felisha, we'll get there. Let's finish with introductions." Colt kept smiling warmly but Elektra felt like her stomach was being squeezed from the inside. She looked from one new face to another, nervously.

She felt unwelcome and she was starting to feel concerned about not being with KaLeah.

Could she even trust these people, she wondered? *How could those young girls she'd seen earlier be healers?*

"That's Felisha. You've met Rustin. That's Zuri." The young man named Zuri sat on the green sofa across from her. He had thick dark hair standing on disheveled ends on top of his head and his skin was the color of a young sapling tree. Colt continued with introductions.

"Alister studies medicine here and the sisters, Lina and Lainie, are healers. They will take care of your friend while we get to know each other."

Colt sat on the arm of a chair, and leaned toward her in a friendly way, although she knew an interrogation was coming.

"So, what brings you and your friend here, Elektra?"

"How did she get shot?" Felisha interrupted, this time her question was directed at Elektra in accusation. "Rustin said something about being shot out of the sky?"

"We were flying, and we got shot at," Elektra spit back, holding the woman's glare. She realized that she'd been clutching both sets of wings so hard her knuckles were starting to look white against her brown skin. She focused on loosening her grip, then set the wings beside her on the couch.

"I'm sorry, flying?" Von asked, blinking rapidly.

"Those wings are mechanical!" Rustin said, clearly still in awe of the contraptions.

Everyone leaned forward, trying to see without touching, or getting too close to the new girl.

Everyone except Felisha. She sat back with her arms crossed over her chest, scowling at both Colt and Elektra. "I can't believe you all," Felisha said. "This puts all of us in danger. Colt, do you not care about our safety at all? And Rustin… I'm ashamed of you."

Rustin stood up fast, stricken. His face was twisted in pain, as if he didn't know whether to be hurt or angry.

"That's enough, Felisha." Colt leaned forward and everyone shrank back, watching him. "We will handle this as a team, and as a family. These young women do not pose any threat to us, so far as I can tell, and Rustin did the right thing by bringing that girl here to help her. Don't lose track of what we are doing and who we are."

Colt rubbed his hands together in a contemplative way, or maybe, Elektra thought, in a way that helped him maintain calm control over a nervous crowd. "Yes, Denlerack is a dangerous place right now, but we are standing up for its people, for our people. Elektra and her friend *are* our people, and we are fighting *for* them. They have a right to be here with us tonight. We have a duty to care for them. Does anyone here have a problem with that?"

He looked around the room, making eye contact with each one of them.

It was strange for Elektra, being the center of attention and a point of contention. She'd never experienced having a man defend her. It was uncomfortable but slightly exhilarating. Here was this tall, handsome man welcoming her into his home and standing up for her to his friends.

But then guilt crept back in remembering that KaLeah had said she wasn't from Denlerack at all. Technically, she wasn't their people.

Elektra swallowed down a dagger in her throat. She didn't want to lie to this new group, to Colt, but she wasn't sure how to explain KaLeah's claim to be from Naldash.

She decided to keep the information to herself for now.

"I apologize, Elektra," Colt said, turning his soft eyes to her. She found herself surprisingly transfixed and unable to speak for a moment.

"Please, tell us more about where you are from and why you sought us out."

"Yes, of course," she said. Then she told them her story, keeping her eyes mostly on Colt.

She told them how she'd seen KaLeah being attacked and flew her to safety, and how the professor had gifted KaLeah a set of wings to carry them to seek out the rebels. She expressed her desire to improve their world, but that she didn't know how to do it alone. By the end of the story, she was starving and exhausted.

"Rustin, will you please get some food for our guest and show her to a guest bed?" Colt asked. "I think we all need some rest."

Elektra watched as Colt's eyes wandered over to the wings lying next to her.

"Those seem oddly familiar, like I've seen them before. Quite fascinating. And you say that Professor Wheelwright made them for you and KaLeah?"

"Yes, that's right. I've known him most of my life."

"He has been in hiding for most of mine," Colt said with a sad undertone in his voice. "Perhaps you can show me how they work tomorrow?"

Elektra nodded but didn't have the energy left to smile. She grabbed both pairs of wings and followed Rustin to the kitchen where she ate some warm bread before being shown to a room up a set of stairs. The room was long and had single size beds lined up in a neat row along a wall. KaLeah was resting in one of them with the girls Lina and Lainie standing watch over her.

"Will she be alright?" Elektra asked them.

They nodded in unison.

"I'm Lina."

"I'm Lainie."

Elektra smiled, knowing she wouldn't be able to tell them apart. "I'm Elektra. Thanks for looking after her."

"Her fever has gone down, so by morning, she should be strong enough to eat and drink," the one who had introduced herself as Lina said.

"If she wakes in the night, please try to get her to drink water and change the washcloth on her head. The bandage on her arm is clean and won't need changing until morning. Alister got the bullet out."

Elektra shivered involuntarily. She hadn't realized the girl had been walking and flying around with a bullet in her arm. There must be more to this young woman than she realized.

"Thank you," Elektra said, genuinely meaning it. She climbed into one of the beds and the girls left the room. She was asleep in the blink of an eye.

❧KaLeah❧

KaLeah didn't know where she was, but she could see Prince Nikolat walking toward her from out of a thick gray fog.

"KaLeah? Is that really you? Are we home?" he asked, his voice sounding both distant and nearby at the same time, as if carried on a breeze across a pond.

"What do you want?" she asked, immediately on edge.

"I want you to know that I miss you," Nikolat said, taking a step closer to her. "I can make everything better. Everything can go back to the way it was —back to that day in the library when we kissed."

She scoffed. "What about back to the balcony where you tried to kill me and your sister?"

"I was angry!" he yelled back, defensively. "You were both trying to take something from me that I'd been planning to get my entire life. Amirra had no right to the throne. Belarone should have been mine by rights when Bylex died." He shrugged, stepping even closer, and tried to calm down his tone. "I was angry at you both for that. But I realize now that I was wrong. I never should have attacked her. Because of that one stupid mistake, I've lost everything. I lost you."

KaLeah took a step back and shook her head, distrusting his words. "Don't try to convince me that you care about me. You never have."

"That's not true, KaLeah," he said, his face swirling around her, dizzyingly. "I have loved you since the moment I first saw you enter the throne room in that red dress. I cared about you so much that it scared me. We are meant to be together. Nobody has ever made me feel the way that you do. I would do anything to win you back. I would do anything to be back on Naldash with you again."

"What do you mean, back on Naldash?" KaLeah asked, her curiosity peaking as emotions swirled in her gut.

"The dragon sent me to Denlerack," he said. "I know it sounds crazy, but I'm still alive and I'm on Denlerack."

"You're here?" KaLeah looked around her, but all she saw was fog and glimpses of Nikolat's face as his words came from all directions.

"What do you mean? KaLeah, are you here too?" he asked.

"I'm on Denlerack," she stated, the blue flames coming back to her vision. Realization started to sink in. She hadn't been thinking about Nikolat over the past couple of days, but he'd been swallowed up by the same blue flames that had transported her to Denlerack. It made sense that he would be on the same planet.

"KaLeah, you're here? You're on Denlerack? KaLeah?"

She kept hearing him repeating her name over and over as it faded into the fog and light started to enter her mind again.

She awoke, sweating, and breathing hard, afraid that she might open her eyes and find him in the same room with her.

Why was he in my dream? she wondered. Worry flooded her mind.

Elektra was standing over her, holding a washcloth to her head. "KaLeah," she whispered. "How do you feel?"

As the dream faded away, reality started to come back. She was in a building underground with a bunch of strangers on a strange planet.

"You're being…nice," KaLeah said, the words sticking in her dry throat.

Elektra laughed and KaLeah realized that was the first she'd ever heard the girl laugh.

"Yeah, well, I figure we're in this together now, whatever this is. They don't all like me out there. And you were literally almost dying, and you didn't complain once. I'm really curious about how you did that."

KaLeah smirked. "Being shot was worse than being stabbed with a sword, I admit."

Elektra shook her head. "Dragon's blood, lady. I don't want to admit it, but you may be tougher than me."

"You're the one who wants to join up with rebels," KaLeah said. Her throat was parched, and she realized she wouldn't be able to speak again without water. She tapped her throat, and Elektra handed her a glass.

"Listen, I told them my story," Elektra said. "I told them how I rescued you, but they are going to want to know where you are from and why you're here. I wasn't prepared to tell them your story for you because I'm not sure I believe it myself."

"I wouldn't believe it either," KaLeah said. "But don't worry about it. I'll figure something out."

"Figure out how to tell them the truth, you mean?"

Elektra raised an eyebrow.

KaLeah paused and slowly started to lift herself up into a seated position on the narrow bed. Her body ached all over, but especially her left shoulder down to her elbow and up throughout her neck.

"Right," KaLeah answered, hoping that Elektra would drop it.

She wasn't sure who all was here, who these rebels were, and what they would make of the dictator's daughter dropping in from Naldash through the magic of dragon flame. She hadn't even told Elektra the entire truth and she wasn't sure she should.

The truth was that she had been living a fantasy ever since the phantom dragon had appeared to her and showed her the spaceship buried in the woods near her village. Her entire life had changed, and she had to learn how to embrace it and trust that the people around her would be able to help guide her somehow.

She had never been very good at trusting anyone other than the man who had raised her. But even he had lied about being her father. Her entire life felt like a lie, but instead of feeling sorry for herself, she had to figure out a way to protect all of the people on her planet.

After being shot from the sky and haunted by Nikolat, she wasn't in any position to walk into a room full of rebels and convince them of anything.

Her head suddenly felt heavy, and she lay back down.

"You alright?" Elektra asked.

"It's all just too much to carry right now," KaLeah answered.

"Rest then. Come out when you're strong enough."

She watched Elektra leave the room and then fell back into a light sleep.

When she awoke later, she did feel stronger. She was able to sit, drink the water by the bed, and then stand up on her own. She took slow steps across the room and out into the hallway, following voices down a staircase and into a large open room filled with sofas and bookshelves.

The talking stopped as soon as she started walking down the stairs.

There were a handful of young adults sitting around the room. A couple were inspecting unfamiliar equipment in a corner, and she saw that Elektra was buckling a tall, dark brown skinned man into her pair of mechanical wings.

They both turned to watch KaLeah walk in. She walked over and a few of the men stood. She recognized Rustin and he helped lead her to a sofa and helped her sit down.

"Thank you," she said. He smiled big, with his friendly brown eyes and teeth shining brightly.

"I'm glad to see that you're doing better," he said to her.

And then to the room, he said, "Everyone, this is KaLeah." He sat down beside her.

The man wearing the wings stepped closer. He had black hair and kind eyes.

"My name is Colt," he said. "You are welcome and safe here. That is Alister who took the bullet from your arm. Lina and Lainie, who bandaged you up and brought your fever under control. Then there's Von, Zuri, and Felisha."

KaLeah looked around the room at the new faces. Felisha seemed to be the only unfriendly one, sitting with a scowl and crossed arms. Lina and Lainie seemed to have no emotions at all in their glassy blue eyes, their disheveled blond locks hanging loosely around their shoulders. The young men held stoic expressions, seeming cautious. Colt was clearly in charge.

"Why have you come to us, KaLeah?" Colt asked her.

She had been thinking about how to answer their questions all morning.

"I am a stranger here," she started. "Elektra rescued me from danger, and not knowing where else to go, I stayed with her."

"Where are you from?" Colt pressed.

Even if she pretended to be from Denlerack, she wouldn't know anything about the place she pretended to be from. She had decided to tell them at least the truth about being from another planet. Even if they didn't believe her, it was better than being caught in a lie and being distrusted immediately by the only people who may be able to help her.

She turned to the group.

"My name is KaLeah Trapper, and I am not from Denlerack. I am from the planet Naldash."

"You have got to be kidding me," Felisha said, recrossing her arms even tighter, as if containing herself. "Colt, what is this? You've brought some space-nut into our safe house. Have you gone completely mad?"

But Colt just ignored her. He looked to the man who was introduced as Alister. He had light brown skin, dark black hair, and eyes so dark they looked black. Alister started drumming his fingers on the book in his lap.

"How can you prove this?" Alister asked KaLeah.

"I can tell you about Naldash," she said, "but I can no more prove that I am from there than I can prove I am from here. I know none of your village names. I do not know what kinds of food you eat. I do not know your history or legends."

"Well, maybe you just can't remember anything from being shot," Felisha said.

"Why do you have a sword and not a gun?" Alister asked.

"I travelled with it," KaLeah said, feeling hopeful. "We don't have guns on Naldash, only swords, and I can fight very well. Can anyone on your planet swordplay?"

She asked Alister directly but looked around at everyone. No one said a word, which meant she wouldn't really be able to prove her skills.

Rustin suddenly sprung from the couch and ran from the room. KaLeah looked to Colt questioningly.

"Oh, he does that," Colt said.

The young man ran back into the room moments later with two long, thin poles. He tossed one at KaLeah and she caught it with her right hand.

"I watch the really old slate shows," he said, a big toothy grin on his face. "Let's do this."

A smile came easily to her own lips. She liked this young Rustin.

She moved to an area of the room that was relatively free of furniture and clutter, and then she took a stance. Rustin was obviously not a sword fighter, but she appreciated that he was brave enough to be her sparring buddy. He mirrored her but his stance was sloppy.

"Um, maybe you should try to hit me first," KaLeah said, thinking of some of the training she'd provided to others in the past. She turned her right side to him, keeping her left shoulder out of harm's way. She knew that moving would be painful, but she didn't expect him to be too aggressive.

"As you wish, my lady."

He moved forward and brought the pole around from his side to hers. She easily swatted it away. He tried to stab her with it and again, she diverted him. With every failed shot, she took a step closer to him. Then she began tapping him with her make-shift sword.

She lightly tapped his shoulder after he missed her. Then she sliced his thigh. Finally, she moved in and placed the tip of the pole against his chest. He was out of breath and laughed deeply.

"You've gotta teach me some of that," he said. He held out his hand to her and she took it, happily, shaking his sweaty palm in hers.

"Oh, please," Felisha said, rolling her eyes.

"Don't be jealous," Rustin teased, moving back to the sofas.

KaLeah leaned the pole against a nearby wall and then walked back to the group. Her arm and shoulder ached a bit, as she expected, but it was worth it to see the young man so pleased to try something she loved so dearly.

Zuri, the young man with the disheveled dark hair,

leaned forward.

"KaLeah," he said. "I think you'd better tell us all about Naldash. We've heard rumors that the planet is within reach of the dictator's spacecrafts. Is that why you are here?"

KaLeah sat down, trying to be careful not to lean into her shoulder. She knew that she had to weigh what she said carefully, not willing to completely trust the band of rebels quite fully yet.

"I grew up on Naldash but recently discovered that my parents travelled there on a space craft they had stolen from Lord Keldon. I have come back to find out why."

"I'm not buying it," Felisha said. She stood and left the circle of sofas with her fists clenched and started pacing the room.

"We have heard rumors that Keldon is planning on invading Naldash," Colt said, defending KaLeah's story.

"She could have easily heard the same rumor, Colt," Felisha shot back, walking toward a cluttered bookshelf at the back of the room.

KaLeah's mind was racing. How could she prove to these people that she was truly from another world? They looked similar and spoke the same language. There was nothing drastically different that set them apart.

Felisha returned to the circle with a gun in her hands. "How do you know what this is if they don't have them on Naldash?" she asked in an accusatory tone.

KaLeah took a deep breath, recalling the memory. The sight of the gun made shivers crawl up her spine and the wound in her shoulder ache more. "Back on Naldash, my father was kidnapped by men from Denlerack. He managed to take a gun and escape from the men. But then, he was captured by soldiers and brought to the castle where I was staying. The soldiers weren't familiar with guns and handled one carelessly. It exploded and killed the prince. It killed him with one shot. I understand how dangerous they are, but that's all."

Colt began to pace with the wings still attached to his

back. There was something about his movement and his profile that felt familiar to KaLeah. She realized that she'd seen this man before; she'd seen him in the woods after assassins had attacked Amirra.

"I saw you on Naldash," KaLeah said to Colt. Everyone looked between her and Colt, confused.

"I saw you walking in the woods near the castle. I didn't know who it was at the time. I thought I was chasing an assassin in the woods, but he had strange armor, and I could have sworn I saw wings. He kept disappearing behind trees—as if he weren't there at all."

Colt turned and searched KaLeah's eyes.

"I did dream that I was lost in some woods," he said softly, but loud enough for the others to hear.

"The trees were taller than this building and bigger around than these couches put together. We do not have woods like that anywhere on Denlerack anymore, that I know of. I thought that I was dreaming about the past," Colt looked off, dreamily, remembering the experience.

"There was a time we had forests, before drought, fires, and deforestation. But no one in our generation has ever seen anything like the tall, thick trees that I saw in that dream. Everything was so clear: the layers of bark, moss growing along the ground and up the sides of the trees, the sounds." He snapped out of his memory and back into KaLeah's eyes again.

"The sounds," he said. "I heard someone calling out to me as if chasing me."

KaLeah smiled, remembering. "I thought you were one of the assassins that had just attacked the princess. I was tracking you."

"I can't believe this," Colt said. He put his hands to his head. Everyone was quiet for a long time, not wanting to challenge the validity of their leader's dream.

"If Keldon was aware of intelligent life on Naldash, he wouldn't necessarily let information like that get out," Alister said. He then turned to look sincerely at KaLeah.

"It is possible his men have been able to travel to Naldash for some time and that they've been gathering information about the planet and determining weaknesses prior to a full-scale invasion. It could take ten or more years to plan the takeover of an entire planet. That might explain how she is here now."

"We believe her," said one of the blonde twins.

"But why is she here?" asked the other.

"Did her parents work for Keldon?" the first one added.

Everyone started talking at once, asking if KaLeah's parents were spies and if she was a spy returning to report to Keldon. Alister and Colt had begun an argument of some sort and KaLeah's head was beginning to spin.

"Stop it, everyone. Quiet!" KaLeah yelled as loudly as she could manage without straining herself.

Through the dimming murmurs, she said very sternly, "I am not a spy. I just found out that my parents were from Denlerack, and the dragon sent me to try to stop Lord Keldon from invading my home."

The room grew very quiet. Everyone turned to look back at her, and she had their undivided attention. She realized that she'd mentioned the dragon and wondered if they all thought she was crazy now.

Just then, a slow, familiar sound began to fill her mind and shoot dizzying stars across her eyes. She heard the dragons calling, sounding out their alarm.

"Something is wrong," KaLeah said to the group of young adults, still staring at her. When no one moved or said anything, she repeated it with more urgency. "Something is wrong."

Von quickly jumped up from the couch, sweeping his long dark locks back from his face, and went to the nearest screen hanging on the wall. He touched it and made some movements along the surface until pictures began to appear in individual windows. While he was looking at the screens, a high-pitched, repeating sound began to fill the air.

"Intruders in the south tower," Von said. "Bandits by

the look of it."

"South tower fish in a barrel strategy; scare mode," Colt said. Everyone had moved to various locations in the large, round room to collect guns and bullets.

"Too bad, because I'm really in the mood to shoot something," Felisha said, casting a look toward KaLeah while she quickly loaded a couple of guns.

"KaLeah, Elektra, please stay here," Colt said.

"What? Colt, what if these men are with them? This is probably a trap. We can't just leave them in our headquarters unguarded." Felisha's knuckles were white around the gun she was clutching.

"KaLeah will go with me, then," Alister said, calmly. "Rustin, take Elektra with you."

Alister strapped weapons into a holster hanging across his chest, then plugged something black into his ear. "Let's go." Alister motioned for KaLeah to follow him.

Everyone filed out of the room and down a long hallway. Von stayed behind, moving his hands across screens, and reporting to the others through devices that transmitted their voices. She heard his voice come faintly through the black plug that Alister had put into his ear.

KaLeah was fascinated by all the strange technology and wanted to ask questions about every single thing she saw. She bit back her curiosity for now, wanting first to win the trust of the group.

"You are to keep low. We will fire scattered warning shots to let them know they are facing multiple, hidden opposition. We shoot as few bullets as possible."

"To not hurt anyone?" she asked.

"That and they are in limited supply."

Alister explained the plan to her as they separated from the group and went down a hallway in the deserted building.

The hallways were barren, with paint and paper peeling from the walls. She wondered what was behind the numerous doors they passed and what this place used to be.

"How did you know about the intruders?" he asked in a

way that did not insinuate any suspicion.

"It's crazy," KaLeah said. "You wouldn't believe me."

"Let me be the judge of that," he said, not making eye contact. He was focused on quickly navigating them through narrower passages that he called air ducts.

They emerged over a large courtyard, long overgrown. There were five men picking through the courtyard, perhaps for food. Alister aimed a weapon and looked around him. The courtyard was surrounded by other buildings.

"In position," he whispered.

KaLeah heard responses from his earpiece.

The rebels peppered the ground, sending sprays of dirt and dead foliage into the air around the intruders. The men called out, drew back, and pointed their own guns at the shooters they couldn't locate.

More gunshots were fired and KaLeah tried to hang back, despite wanting to see the action. The loud boom from Alister's gun made her jump every time. She was embarrassed by the unfamiliar sense of fear and danger the sounds stirred up in her.

The melee didn't last long. The men withdrew into the shadows of another building. After a few moments of silence, KaLeah spoke up.

"So, now what?" she asked.

"We wait," Alister said. "Von will keep us updated. In the meantime, I think you were about to tell me something that I won't believe."

"Right."

KaLeah pictured the ancient phantom dragon in her mind. The shimmery green dragon had spoken to her many times and called herself Anissa La Alani. She had claimed to be the dragon sorceress who had created the sister planets Naldash and Denlerack.

KaLeah felt crazy remembering, as if it had happened in a dream. But she was here, sent by the dragon's blue flames.

She took a deep breath. She had nothing to lose.

"I can hear the voices of dragon spirits in my mind

whenever danger is near."

She wasn't sure what kind of reaction to expect. Alister didn't seem like the type to burst out into laughter. He was serious and calculating.

"I thought as much," he said.

"Excuse me?" KaLeah asked, stunned. Alister didn't seem to be surprised, or even curious. Was this strange ability somehow common on this planet?

"There was once a rebel leader named Huntra," Alister said.

KaLeah's heart stopped in her chest at hearing her mother's name.

"She was said to have the same ability and was destined to be our savior. But she risked infiltrating Keldon's inner circle, was discovered, and killed. Keldon sought revenge on many of our groups after that and vowed to kill us all.

"Most of our people escaped, but we were torn between running and fighting and ended up as scattered groups instead of an organized rebellion. Keldon eventually stopped tracking us, but we are still cautious. Some rebel groups have begun recruiting again. Colt is the son of one of the original rebels who fought alongside Huntra."

Hearing about her mother made her seem more alive than she ever had. Tears pricked and pierced her eyes. The people, the rebels, they all knew more about her mother than she did. She wanted to find out more than what her father, what Clegg, the man who had raised her, had told her.

What the rebels didn't seem to know was that Huntra had done more than just infiltrate Keldon's ranks. She had created a child with him.

KaLeah wasn't sure what they would think about their beloved savior procreating with their worst enemy. She swallowed back the information, deciding to keep it to herself just in case.

Alister's dark eyes grew unfocused as he stared out over the courtyard.

"Many of us thought that all hope died with her. Perhaps, KaLeah of Naldash, you are a relative of hers. Perhaps, if you carry the same gift, you also carry the same destiny."

"A different destiny," KaLeah added.

"Ah, yes. Not just to save our planet, but yours as well."

KaLeah tried to picture her mother, even though she had no idea what she looked like. She imagined brown hair, like her own, and sharp features. She envisioned a strong woman who spoke her mind.

But then she saw her mother together with the dictator.

"She failed," KaLeah said. "How will I do any better than her?"

"Hopefully, the dragon spirits will tell you more than they told her," Alister said.

5 RUNNING IS THE PLAN

"Dragon's blood," Prince Nikolat said, waking from a dream. He had seen KaLeah so clearly and heard her voice as if she had been right in front of him.

His cheeks burned as he recalled what he'd told her in that dream. He confessed that he loved her.

Two involuntary emotions entered his gut. One was a sense of longing, as if he really did love or at least miss her. The other feeling was one of embarrassment. Even though it was just a dream, he'd tried to win her over and he'd lost.

She rejected him.

I wonder if she's actually here, on Denlerack?

He shook his head and ran his hands through his dark, disheveled hair. It was a ridiculous thought, he knew. He was the only one trapped on this pile of dirt planet.

He looked around at the dark, cold burrow Ash had miraculously located in the pitch blackness of the night before. She seemed to be driven by dragon spirits, knowing how to find food, water, and shelter. He had no doubt that he'd be dead or dying by now if she hadn't been guiding him.

After a couple days of traveling, half-starved, and digging out burrows to hide in for one night at a time, he'd given up hope that he was still on Naldash.

The sun rose but he never saw it beyond the clouds. He never saw any trees taller than his knees, and the familiar rivers and lakes of his home were nowhere on this desert planet.

None of the people knew him or Belarone Kingdom. Although it seemed unbelievable, the dragon flames must have shot him across the skies and onto Denlerack, as the young girl had said. He had no other viable explanation for the world that surrounded him.

If his only way home was following the child to a spaceship, then he only functioned every day to achieve that goal. Whether KaLeah was really on the planet was of no concern to him. In fact, it would be preferable to leave her behind, so he could get back to Naldash and take his kingdom from his sister without KaLeah getting in his way again.

Sure, he was attracted to her and was intrigued at the possibility of being with her once, but he was still angry at her for helping his sister steal the throne from him. There was no going back to being nice.

Since the moment she'd rescued his sister from the kidnappers, KaLeah had been the reason every single plan he formed had fallen apart. She was the reason that he wasn't sitting happily on his throne. The fact that he woke up in a hole in the ground on another planet was entirely KaLeah's fault, and he hoped that he never saw her again.

Ash dropped down into the den, and he jumped, hitting his back and head on the side of the dug-out hole.

"Don't scare me like that, kid."

He had automatically reached for a dagger at his side that he no longer had, realizing the challenges of not having any weapons. How was he supposed to continue traversing this desolate and dangerous planet with nothing but a child and his own hands?

He had always had a sword. He had never had to fight with his hands. If he was ever un-armed, he had hordes of armed men around him for protection.

"How much further do we have to go to get to these spaceships?" he asked the girl, who was busy bundling a blanket and other supplies into a make-shift pack.

"Many more days," she said.

He groaned and sat up, rolling up the cloth that he'd slept uncomfortably on. He wanted to be there already. He wanted to be back on Naldash, tossing his sister out onto the street, and taking back his throne—his kingdom.

KaLeah popped back into his mind again. He knew that if she was still at the castle with his sister, then he'd have to deal with her. If she didn't come around to his side, then he would kick her out to the streets too.

She and Amirra could go back to the farming village for all he cared. He started to smile again, knowing that he would get back to his kingdom, and he would get revenge. Little girls were not going to take his kingdom from him and get away with it.

He looked up and saw that Ash was staring at him, waiting.

"Alright kid, I'm coming," he said, crawling to follow her out of the tunnel entrance. He wondered if she would go back to living in burrows after she led him to the spaceship.

It's a strange way to live, he mused. But it wasn't something he would waste time or energy thinking about. He had one focus and that was to get home. Ash was on her own after that.

They walked for most of the night. There was no moonlight or starlight to guide them. He had no idea how the little girl knew where she was going. With no choice, he had to believe that she wasn't just taking him in circles.

The air was dry and chilly, but after walking for a while, Nikolat started to sweat. He wasn't used to walking in such simple shoes, so his feet ached after only traveling for a little bit. They had found and stolen various objects along the way like food scraps, blankets, and a pair of cloth shoes with holes but enough sole remaining to lesson the strain on the bottom of his feet.

To keep himself sane in the pitch-black landscape, and marching after a child who barely spoke, he began counting his footfalls. With each number, he imagined being closer to home. It lulled him into a mindlessness that kept him moving. It was a trick he'd used many times when marching with soldiers, and it helped melt away most of his stress and worries.

After a while, he saw yellow flames rising ahead of them in the distance.

"Hey, it's a camp," he said. "Should we stay clear?"

It was dark, but Ash was close enough that he saw her shake her head no. In fact, she veered toward the camp instead, causing Nik's heartbeat to tick up in speed.

There were two options, as he saw it. Either she knew them, and they'd be welcome, or she didn't, and they would be in danger. He was not used to trusting children with these types of decisions.

"Who are they? Do you know them? What are we doing here?" he asked, but she said nothing and kept walking.

"Spirits," he cursed under his breath, following the child.

He could smell the smoke from the fire, and then what might have been smoked meat. His stomach rumbled. The girl had fed him fruits along their way, and they were able to suck water from a few leaves and roots, but he was starving and thirsty.

When they were close enough to see the camp clearly, Ash dropped down to her knees.

"Spirits," he cursed again, realizing that these were not friends of hers. They were going to steal supplies.

One half-starved, unarmed man, and a little girl against how many armed men in this camp? he wondered.

What would death be like? Would they torture them first or end it fast? He hoped for a quick, honorable death. He dropped down to his own knees behind the girl, staying low for whatever she had planned. She circled around and hid behind a short, spiny bush.

Saying nothing, she motioned to him that she would sneak over and steal something. He was to stay put and be quiet.

At first, his ego was insulted. Stay put and be quiet is what you instruct a child to do, not a soldier, and certainly not a soldier who is also a prince.

He bit his tongue, though.

He had no weapon, and this child was used to slinking around without detection. He was bigger and more likely to make noise. He nodded back and she scrambled off without a sound.

And then he waited.

It was another thing he wasn't good at doing but he crouched there on the hard dirt behind the thorny bushes and waited for the child to save them.

It wasn't right. It wasn't natural.

He started to grow antsy and wanted to at least stand up and get a better view. Right before he stood, Ash came around the corner of a bush.

"Spirits!" he gasped.

Her eyes were wide, and her hands were full. She handed two pouches of water to him, and she held onto a sack of food so warm that he could feel the heat coming off it.

"Run," she whispered loudly, and then she took off into the darkness.

He followed quickly and heard loud shouts from behind him.

"Well," he said to Ash's back as they flew across the sandy land, "at least we're moving faster now!"

↾Elektra↽

"So, your friend is a little weird, right?" Rustin asked.

Rustin and Elektra were sitting three floors above the courtyard, watching from a window.

"First, she isn't exactly my friend, and second, what do you mean by weird?" Elektra raised an eyebrow at the young man.

Even though he was taller than her, she assumed that he was younger. He seemed a bit too happy all the time to have seen some of the same kind of traumatic life events that she had seen.

"You saved her life, didn't you?" he had a gun in his hand, still pointed down at the courtyard, and she realized that nobody had tried to take her guns from her. She wondered if it meant that she was trusted, or if they hadn't been concerned because they could protect themselves?

"Sometimes, you have to look out for people in trouble, especially other women. This world is not easy on women. But it doesn't mean that we're friends. I hardly know her."

"I think you are more of a friend than you realize," he said. "You don't have to know someone for your entire life to be a friend. I think you and I will be friends soon."

His grin spread even wider across his face. He was quite charming, and Elektra couldn't see how he could possibly be a fighter in a rebellion.

She couldn't resist smiling back at him. He had a positive energy that just seemed to fill the space around him.

In a way, she guessed that he was right. She was closer to KaLeah than anyone else here.

"And weird like… she was still joking with us when she had a bullet in her arm. She says she traveled here through space because a dragon sent her. And how did she know that there was someone in the courtyard before the alarms went off? I'm just saying, there is something odd about that lady."

Elektra didn't say anything.

He was right. From the very beginning, she noticed something off about the girl. Even when she'd assumed that she'd just been living underground in a hidden farming community, it hadn't really felt right.

She was a fighter, a warrior, and tough, but she'd never held a gun. It didn't make any sense until KaLeah started opening up and telling them things about her. They seemed so far-fetched, and yet, held that tinge of truth that only a girl who'd grown up on the streets would recognize. If KaLeah had been lying at all, Elektra would have known immediately. But she hadn't lied; she just hadn't told her everything yet.

"Got it," Rustin said into an earpiece. "Colt says we are cleared to go back down now."

Elektra followed Rustin back through the building. She was glad they had alarms and video wired up and was surprised she hadn't actually noticed any of the devices. She hadn't even considered their safety when she'd arrived, and that concerned her.

Was she slipping? Or was she just trusting this band of rebels because she wanted to be a part of their group so badly? She didn't want to ask questions or test boundaries. She wanted them to accept her.

They went down many sets of metal stairs, past floors that looked hauntingly empty and frightening without light. She felt shadows watching her and the hairs on her arms stood on end.

They went back inside the safe house through a large, locked door on the lowest level. Inside, she saw that everyone else was already back in the central living area. People were sitting on couches, but no one was saying anything. They all seemed to be staring at KaLeah.

Elektra sat down on a couch next to Rustin, across from KaLeah, who was sitting alone.

Colt stood up and paced for a moment. "Now that we are all back, I'd like to continue our conversation. I'd like for you to tell me how you knew people were approaching our hideout, KaLeah."

Colt sounded sternly serious, but without any hint of distrust in his voice. He seemed genuinely curious, and Elektra found a sense of relief in that.

He didn't see them as a threat—yet.

"Colt, are you blind?" Felisha smashed her fist into the palm of her other hand. Her eyes were burning at KaLeah.

"We never should have let them in here. She obviously led those guys right to us," Felisha yelled.

Elektra wanted to defend KaLeah, but she was also curious. She looked to the screens on the wall, wondering if KaLeah had seen movement in one of the security cameras. The slate flashed an image of the dictator above the figure of a talking head, and she was glad she couldn't hear what propaganda they were spewing. The anger mixed in with the current curiosity and frustration, but she turned her eyes back to the group.

"KaLeah? How did you know?" Colt asked.

KaLeah looked at Alister and then to Elektra. Finally, she turned her stormy blue eyes to Colt to answer his question.

"Back on Naldash, I started hearing a warning in my mind whenever danger was nearby. It starts off like whispers mixed with low growls. If I ignore it, it just gets louder and louder until my head is pounding. Every time it has happened, some sort of threat was present. Every time."

The room was silent.

Elektra narrowed her eyebrows in thought. It was a strange thing to say, and an even stranger thing to believe. But it sounded familiar to her, and she couldn't place why.

She slowly looked from face to face, and thought she saw a level of recognition there too. So far, the young woman had withstood a bullet, took to metal wings like she'd been born flying, knew swords over guns, and had warned them about the intruders.

She was having a hard time not believing the young woman every time something new was revealed.

Maybe she really was from another planet. She didn't seem to fit into the norm on this one.

Suddenly, the brunette called Felisha stood up.

"I'm not buying it," Felisha said. She left the circle of sofas with her fists clenched and began pacing in front of the bookshelves that lined the walls.

"I don't think I'd believe it either," said KaLeah. "I didn't ask to hear dragon spirits. If I could go back to that day in the woods, maybe I never would have followed the sound."

"What do you mean?" Colt asked.

"I was in the forest near my house hunting, and I heard loud, repetitive sounds. I followed the sounds and there was a dragon digging at a small mound in the clearing. Buried beneath a thin layer of dirt was a black metal, circular ship. It was a Denlerack spaceship. I saw a phantom dragon and a spaceship on the same day, and it started me on this entire journey. I'd like to just dismiss it all and go back home, but it's too late. My friend, Queen Amirra, is like a sister to me, and if Lord Keldon invades Naldash, then her life is in danger. I can't let anything happen to her or to our planet. I can't let him invade Naldash. I can't let him do to Naldash what he did to Denlerack."

Her eyes flashed with defiance and commitment. Elektra felt a small pang in her chest. She believed KaLeah's story, as strange as it was.

"Huntra," Alister said from his spot on the couch, catty-cornered to KaLeah's.

"That's just a story," Colt corrected.

"A legend," Alister said, defending KaLeah. "We are all here because we believe in legend. We believed in Huntra, who led the original rebellion against Keldon. And it is said that the dragon spirits spoke to her."

A silence fell once again over the room.

"Felisha, don't!" Colt yelled, and Elektra looked up just in time to see the woman stalking toward KaLeah with a gun pointed at her face.

"Did the spirits warn you I was going to do this? Did they?" Felisha stalked closer but left enough distance so that her friends couldn't get to her. The barrel was pointed directly at KaLeah, and Elektra was frozen.

She remembered the first moment that she'd decided to drop out of the sky and rescue the strange girl. Maybe there were things about KaLeah that didn't make sense, but she wasn't a bad person. She definitely did not deserve to have a gun put in her face.

Elektra had grown up in fear of people with guns threatening her and her mother, robbing, abusing, bullying, and other monstrous things.

It wasn't right.

Elektra didn't think; she snapped into the protective mode that had driven her all her life. She cared about people—all people. Everyone deserved a chance to be heard and nobody deserved violence. There was always a better way.

She leapt from her seat and crossed the space to Felisha quietly, coming up on the girl before she'd noticed her movements. Elektra used her forearm to knock Felisha's arm upward, then dislodged her grip and took the gun into her own hand. She hit the latch and let the clip fall to the floor. Then, to make her point, she threw the gun across the room.

Elektra took her time looking around the room before she spoke. "What a bunch of children," she said, boring her eyes into Felisha's.

"This is why men like Keldon can come in and destroy us. Although KaLeah didn't tell us everything at once, she is not the enemy here. Is this how you treat people who are coming to join you, to help you, to help our world? You give them distrust and violence in return? If this is how you welcome people looking to make the world a better place, then you're no better than the bandits and gangs of thugs out there stealing to survive. Maybe we made a mistake by coming here." Elektra spun slowly, making eye-contact with each one of them.

"You sit around with your cameras protecting your own space, but you haven't done anything to protect your own people. This is not how you rise above the challenges holding us all back. This is not how you take back our world. Shame on you."

She walked to KaLeah and held out her slender, brown hand. KaLeah's white one was cold, but she grasped it tightly and rose from the couch. They were in this together more than ever before.

Although she said nothing more, KaLeah went with her, following her toward their room. In her mind, Elektra was set on collecting their things and leaving. They would take on the dictator alone. They would find another band of rebels.

"What's your plan, Elektra?"

It was Colt. His smooth voice sent a curious shiver down her spine, and she didn't want to admit that she found him attractive. Instead of answering, she kept walking with KaLeah's white hand in hers.

"Are you going to keep running forever?" he asked. "Is that your plan? We do want to take back our lands from Keldon. Honestly, we have hit so many roadblocks and lost so many people, that our temporary pause has stretched on far longer than we intended. We attacked and we lost many, many times."

Elektra stopped walking halfway up the stairs, releasing KaLeah's hand to turn around. Colt had followed them and was standing at the bottom of the staircase.

"We've lost focus and motivation, he continued. "I don't want to see any more of my friends die. It's hard for me to admit, but I can't see the way forward. Keldon is only a day's walk to the south, but I'm afraid. I can't see these kids die. I'm not ready to die. We need more help. We need more people like you on our side to pick up guns to make this work. We can't do this alone. We do need you."

Elektra said nothing. She turned and followed KaLeah up the stairs.

They walked to the room with their beds and gear, then Elektra closed the door behind them. She let out a frustrated yell and then plopped down onto her bed. KaLeah, much calmer, sat down across from her.

"I don't really want to leave," Elektra admitted.

"I know you don't," KaLeah said gently. "You've been wanting to find these people, and here they are. But they are people. They have had hardship. They have lost friends and possibly family. That Felisha… I don't want to think about what she must have lost to be so angry and distrustful."

Elektra sat up and looked at this stranger who had become a friend. She was so mad at Felisha for putting a gun to KaLeah's head and yet, KaLeah didn't seem angry at all.

"Why are you not upset about this?" she asked.

"I am mad, but less so," KaLeah replied. "I guess I don't really blame them. I can see how hard it must be to accept a total stranger, someone who doesn't fit in, someone who hasn't had the same experiences they have. You found a way to look at me and feel like my life was worth something. You came back when you could have kept flying. We take risks every time we allow someone in. That person could hurt you or get you hurt. I think this group of friends has just seen so much loss they are broken."

"Broken," Elektra repeated the word, connecting to that feeling all too strongly. She saw Colt's dark brown eyes in her mind.

What had he lost, she wondered?

"Are you broken?" she asked, looking into KaLeah's blue eyes.

The girl looked away for a minute and let out a long sigh.

"I never knew my mother. The man who raised me turned out to not be my real father. My first true friend is on another planet trying to rule a kingdom alone. And the first man that I thought I loved, tried to kill me. I guess I have a few issues," she said, and then she laughed a little. "Did I mention the dictator wants to invade my beautiful planet and turn it into this one, and I have to figure out some way to stop him?"

"*We* have to figure out a way, together," Elektra corrected. KaLeah smiled and continued.

"But I don't feel broken, just empty sometimes." KaLeah took another deep breath. "We create a path and start to follow that path, only to be knocked off it again and again. It's hard not to feel like each time you are knocked down that you break a little bit. I'm not sure if finding the dictator and saving my planet, or even getting back to my planet, will ever fix those broken places within me. But if I don't at least make the path to follow, then I will be lost."

Elektra sat quietly and absorbed KaLeah's words. She found herself relating to this strange alien more and more.

"I understand all of that more than you know," Elektra admitted. "I guess all the people under this roof are suffering somehow. Maybe they just need stronger leadership. They need a reason to band together, to be a team, to find a way to make this world better together. They need someone to set a new path for them."

"Colt seems like a good strong man, but maybe he needs someone to encourage him," KaLeah said. "I think you and Colt could lead these rebels, Elektra. You can give them a renewed sense of motivation and direction. We can't just keep running. You have been trying for so long to get here, to find this group of people, and they are all we have now."

Elektra nodded and motivation started flowing through her veins. She always believed that there was more to live for and that she had a bigger purpose in life.

She couldn't just live a comfortable life in a diamond district while the people around her suffered. Hearing those words from KaLeah helped ground her. But who was this insightful and mysterious person, she wondered?

"Why are you really here, KaLeah? Was that true, what you said about hearing and seeing dragons?"

KaLeah smiled and looked Elektra in the eyes. Elektra held her gaze and listened closely.

"I honestly do hear spirits, yes, and a dragon sent me here to stop an invasion," KaLeah said. "I think that you are supposed to protect Denlerack, and I am supposed to protect Naldash. We are both here for the same purpose;

two sides of the same mission.

"Of course, I have no idea how you and I are supposed to be successful at this. Denlerack is ... so bad, and Naldash is so far away. But I have to believe that we made it this far for a reason. We can't give up. We can't keep running. We have to fight."

Elektra was quiet for a while. The words rang true. She could feel the truth in her heart, even if it did sound crazy.

Why were dragon spirits only talking to this one girl and not her? What made KaLeah more special?

She tried to push down the jealousy as it started creeping up.

They sat on their beds in that room in a dilapidated building halfway underground together in silence for a few moments.

Elektra did want to do something. She wanted to be a leader. She wanted to achieve a goal of truly making the world better, even if the dragon spirits weren't guiding her the same way that they were guiding KaLeah.

Maybe, she realized, she would be the one to guide them all to a victory, even without spirits' help. Taking on the dictator meant she would need each and every last rebel she could get, including KaLeah.

"Alright, we're staying," Elektra decided. She stood up from the bed. "I am not giving up. I am going to rally that troop into a fighting army. We will take this world back!"

"Yes!" KaLeah said.

Elektra bent down and hugged the girl. Although she had held the girl in the sky, this was different. She was starting to trust this stranger.

Maybe they were friends, after all. They were both broken, and both wanted the world to be a better place. Their destinies and their futures were intertwined now.

She let go and stood up.

"I'm going to go tell Colt and the others that we're staying, and they better get used to it," she said with a smile. "Felisha and the others are going to need to get on board with accepting who we are, even if one of us talks to dragons."

KaLeah smiled and Elektra gave her a wink. She was relieved knowing she wasn't going to be leaving Colt and his friends behind.

They just needed to know there was hope and that they could do this together.

She took that sense of hope and walked out of the door with it.

❦KaLeah❧

KaLeah's heart sank in her chest watching Elektra walk out of the room. She knew she'd tried to give the young woman hope, but she didn't feel that same sense of optimism herself. It was obvious to her that this rebel group had given up on the idea of ever making any kind of impact.

The dictator's rule was absolute. She didn't know how many kids had already died, but she imagined that these halls and rooms had once been full of smiling, hopeful faces.

The anger that boiled through Felisha's veins was probably just pure fear. She had seen death, as KaLeah had. She had seen so much loss and was trying to protect herself and her friends from anymore.

She didn't blame them at all. She didn't feel angry toward Felisha. She fully understood that need to protect the ones you love.

There was a time when it was just her and the man who raised her. But then her world had expanded to include the blonde-haired princess of Belarone. She pictured Captain Hilip Daven also, with his soft, caring expression.

She didn't want them to be in danger. She didn't want them to have to face the terrible consequences of her failing at this mission.

Back in the living area with all of them, she had almost told them her mother was Huntra in order to win them over. But she was scared someone would find out Huntra had made a child with the dictator, and her cover would be blown.

Maybe, if she decided to stay and fight alongside them, she'd tell them the truth, but something Colt had said kept replaying in her mind.

The dictator was only a day's walk to the south. Her true father was closer than she realized. It was the clearest direction she'd had regarding her father's whereabouts.

The group knew she was from Naldash, whether they believed her or not. But they didn't know her mother was Huntra, the apparent leader of the past failed rebellion. They didn't know Huntra had infiltrated the enemy closer than anyone else. They didn't know the dictator was KaLeah's father.

She was afraid it was only a matter of time before someone made the connection. What would they think if they found out their precious Huntra had created a child with the most hated man in the universe? Would they give up the rebellion completely? Would they assume KaLeah sympathized with her biological father?

She felt a great pull to find out more about him before casting complete judgement. She had never known any of her own flesh and blood. What if she could just convince him to take better care of the planet? What if she could get him to promise to never invade Naldash?

The dragon could have had that plan in mind all along, she realized.

Wouldn't the man be happy to see the daughter he lost so many years ago? What if his interest in Naldash was simply to find her and be reunited? Her heart fluttered at the possibility.

The entire thing was a mystery, and she was curious about this world leader who had made so many enemies.

He was her father. She was a part of him, connected to him, and she wondered what she had in common with him.

Could she have something in common with someone who had done so many terrible things? He was the reason so many of this group's friends and family were dead.

KaLeah had to know more. She had to know who this man was. She had to know if he was responsible for the terrible things that had happened to this planet.

And if she stayed here, this group would never understand. They would not allow her to go to her father. They would convince her he was bad and tell her she could never trust him.

But she had to find out for herself.

She looked around the room and made her plan. She would wait until nightfall, and then get the wings and sword, find her way to a window on a high floor where she wouldn't trip an alarm, and fly off toward the south.

She would find her father and present herself as his daughter. It was the only way to go straight to the source.

Maybe she would be heading into danger, but she was done running.

6 IN THE DARK

Nikolat ran as fast as he could through the pitch-black darkness without falling. The jugs of water he held sloshed, and he wanted to stop and drink so badly, but he didn't dare.

Men's heavy footfalls and yells chased closely behind him. He assumed they had lights and was glad he and the girl did not, since it would make them harder to follow.

Ash was fast and ran so quietly that he had to keep calling out to her to make sure he hadn't lost her.

"This way," was all she called back to him.

He didn't know how she was able to tell where she was going. The child seemed inhuman in her ability to survive out in the desolate wasteland.

"We can stop now," she said, finally slowing down to a walk somewhere in front of him. He could barely make her out. He was breathing hard but couldn't hear anyone pursuing them any longer.

"Sit, eat," she commanded.

He sat down across from her, and they exchanged food and drink. The drink was dirty tasting warm water, and he didn't recognize the taste of the cooked meat. He wasn't even certain that it was meat, but he ate and drank without complaint.

"Is this how it's going to be the entire way there?" he asked.

"Yes," she said, without any additional information.

"Where are you from?"

"Here," Ash said.

"Do you have any parents?"

"Dead."

"Mine are gone too," Nik said, not feeling any sense of remorse or grief. It was just a fact. "I guess we are alone out here too. How have you survived this long? How did you learn how to do all of this out here?" He nodded to the food in his hand as he shoveled it into his mouth.

"Think like an animal; act like a man," Ash answered.

Nik washed the dry meat down with a swig of water. It was an interesting comment coming from a child.

He had never thought about the need to survive before. He had always had the castle, and even when he was out in the field for a battle, there were always ample supplies of food and water. He had never had an uncomfortable experience outdoors, always sleeping in shifts on the best mattresses in the king's tents.

His life had been easy and comfortable, and he wanted that life back. He saw no value to living any other way.

Just a few more days and I'll be living that life again, he told himself.

"Must keep walking," Ash said, standing up.

"How long are we going to walk?" his muscles and feet ached.

"All night," her voice was already getting quiet as she moved further into the night.

"How do you know where you're going? How do you know you're going the right way?" He scrambled onto his feet to follow her.

"I know," was all she said.

❧KaLeah❧

KaLeah felt guilty all throughout dinner, but she tried to hide the guilt from behind a sweet smile. Living in Belarone castle had taught her how to conceal her emotions behind pleasantries.

Whatever Elektra and Colt had said to the group seemed to have gotten them all fired up again. She could tell by the lively banter at the dinner table that a certain level of hope had been restored. There was still a cloud hanging over the group, and no one talked about specific plans, but things started to feel lighter than they had before.

The kids were laughing together and KaLeah understood what they had all been fighting for. This was their family.

She knew it wasn't enough, though. High hopes, ideology, and a few weapons would not protect them from the dictator's army and deep down, past their smiles and pleasantries, they knew it.

The planet was ruined. The people were suffering. Well, the poor people were suffering as the rich sat within their protected palaces, relying on population-controlled labor to grow their food. They were too comfortable to care about taking care of anyone who may be suffering.

It made KaLeah sad. She understood why Elektra had left the comforts of the diamond district in order to seek out a way to bring a better life to others. Elektra had seen both sides and the girl knew what her world could be.

While the situation for those outside the diamond districts got worse, the people on the inside had stopped caring—if they had ever cared at all. No one was building sustainable diamond districts for the poor.

Buildings had crumbled. Industries had failed. People had lost so much. And KaLeah's true father, the dictator, did nothing to help. He perpetuated the polarization by ensuring that poor people were criminals by simply trying to survive. It wasn't that they weren't trying; it was that they had zero resources to start from.

KaLeah saw no way for this small band of rebels to make any lasting improvements. All she could do was try to save Naldash from the same fate.

That night, she made a point to thank Colt directly for taking them in. She thanked Rustin for rescuing her and carrying her back to their hideout, knowing that not everyone would welcome them. She thanked Alister, Lina, and Lainie for removing the bullet and helping her heal. Her arm and shoulder were healing fast.

They didn't know that she was saying goodbye, but she felt better knowing she had at least shown them gratitude before deserting them.

She wasn't the type to leave the battle, she reminded herself as she headed back to the room she shared with Elektra. It was a long room full of empty beds, and she wondered about the kids who used to live and sleep there.

How and when had they died? Would she be able to help save these remaining kids by going to her father?

"What a day," Elektra said, coming into the room and falling onto her bed. "I think I got everyone back on the same page here. I'll get them out in the courtyard doing exercises early tomorrow morning, and then we'll start assessing the situation. I just need to know the state of things, and then I have no doubt Colt, and I can come up with a strong plan to get this rebellion going again. I think getting more guns and more recruits will be vital to our success."

KaLeah sat on her bed a few beds over and nodded.

"Why are you being so quiet?" Elektra asked, turning toward her.

"Just tired," KaLeah said, smiling to assure Elektra that everything was fine. Neither one said much else as the evening wore on. They eventually turned out the lights that were kept dim in the evenings to avoid attracting attention to the higher building floors.

KaLeah was worried about staying awake, but before long, she heard Elektra snoring softly. She grabbed her boots and sword and then crept out into the hallway toward the end of the hall where no one slept. She had stored her wings and a bag of supplies there earlier that day.

Instead of climbing out of a window, she'd found a door that led to the roof. Hoping that the rebels hadn't placed any sensors on higher levels, she took a staircase up many flights until she reached a metal ladder that was badly rusted from years of rooftop leaks.

She put on the wings and boots, tied the satchel of supplies around her waist, and then carefully climbed the ladder. The latch to the rooftop entrance nearly snapped off in her hand when she forced it down, popping the door open barely a hand's width. She put her hand into the gap and pushed up with her good shoulder until the door swung open, falling back onto the roof.

The wind that hit her in the face was warm and dry, and smelled of metal and dirt. She climbed up through the square trap door and onto the rooftop.

The city was pure darkness around her. There was no moon and no stars to help her determine direction. She tried to envision the map from the professor's home, but she couldn't connect the image to where she was currently standing.

She turned slowly, seeing what she could make out in her line of sight. As she turned, she'd see a flicker of a light or two, but nothing more, until she noticed a dim glow in the distance. She stopped and let her eyes adjust. The glow was comprised of many rows of lights, seemingly in an organized pattern that denoted civilization.

"That must be it," she said out loud, hoping that she was looking at her father's compound and not at a diamond district.

She scanned the rest of the horizon, but only saw faint, scattered lights. There were brighter glows coming from further away, but she assumed those lights belonged to the diamond district city of Morbel. She could smell smoke in the air and thought that other specs of light were coming from fires of people struggling to survive in between the diamond districts and the dictator's compound.

For a moment, she longed for her village back on Naldash. That life hadn't always been easy, but it was simpler. There were lands to grow food, there were forests and fields to hunt, there were markets for trade, and even though there were the occasional tricksters and bandits trying to take advantage of someone, for the most part, people just wanted to eat, love, and play. If you worked hard, you had a comfortable life. If you fell on hard times due to illness, the village helped you out.

KaLeah shook the thoughts away. She wasn't on Naldash anymore. She was standing on the roof of a metal building, staring out into the darkness of a damaged world. Maybe she'd be able to do something to make it better and hopefully protect that simple life back on Naldash for others. For now, though, she had to soar over the despair and follow the lights to her father's compound.

KaLeah flipped the switch to stir the fan engine to life. The machine vibrated against her back, and she started to levitate. She bounded to the edge of the building and launched herself into the dark sky, her black canvas wings catching the wind.

It was exhilarating to feel fearless, although she remembered the fear of falling and the pain of being shot. Her shoulder ached when she tried to turn or when a gust of wind jerked her up, but she gritted her teeth and kept her course steady.

She needed to get to the compound before daylight so she could avoid being shot out of the sky again. She had no doubt that Keldon's men would see her as a weapon of some kind headed straight for them and take action before waiting for her to shout out her intentions.

The flight was quiet for a long time with just the soft

whirring of the fans and shifting of the canvas against the wind. She grew more and more tired, and her arm throbbed. The lights of the compound were getting closer, but she didn't think she had it in her to make it the entire way before sunrise. She needed to stop and rest or risk falling out of the sky.

A building suddenly appeared in her path, and she had to veer to keep from hitting it. The wind caught her wings and carried her up higher and around the side of the building.

She corrected course quickly and aimed for the roof, landing as softly as possible. It appeared to be the tallest building around, but being so dark, she couldn't be sure. Her vision had become blurry from lack of sleep and the wind constantly batting against her face.

Even though she wanted to keep going, she knew that it was time to stop. She found a corner between pipes and a maintenance shed on the roof and wedged herself in, hiding herself as best she could. She closed her eyes and was asleep instantly.

It was odd waking up to dim light without the sound of juliebees or any other animal already up and greeting the day. It was uncomfortably sad and lonely.

She blinked and opened her eyes to a hazy gray light coming from an unseen sun. She was on the tallest building for as far as she could see, and to the south, she could see the compound clearly.

The dictator's compound was only a few stories high all around, surrounded by a tall wall. In the middle was a large box-like structure that looked like a building within the building, like a castle keep in the middle of a fortress. It was taller than the wall and surrounding building, but nowhere near as high as she was.

Outside of the wall were rows and rows of black metal spherical spaceships.

Her heart pounded faster in her chest at the idea of taking one of those back to Naldash. She could leave this world behind and leave it to its fate, but she knew that eventually she'd see those spaceships invading the Naldash skies.

"No, I have to take care of this here," she told herself.

Faint noises drifted across the land and sky, but she couldn't make them out. There was movement, but she couldn't see the faces of the army. She had to get closer. It was too dangerous to fly in the gray light, so she'd have to soar downward and then walk the rest of the way.

Far beyond the compound were cylinder towers shooting plumes of black smoke into the air. Other than forest fires that happened back on Naldash from time to time, she had never seen so much smoke in one place.

Are they creating smoke, she wondered? It definitely explained the condition of the hazy skies.

She quickly ate and drank from her supply satchel, then started up the fans to begin her descent. She took a slow arch to try to fly as far as possible without being seen. Then, she hit the ground and turned off the engine. She considered drawing her sword but realized that it would be useless on a world teeming with guns.

She drew it out anyway, needing the nostalgic feeling to calm her nerves. Holding her sword was familiar and put her at ease.

As she got closer, she saw the soldiers. At first, she thought they were machines until she saw how fluidly they moved. They were covered from head to toe in metal armor and their faces were covered with masks. Some marched, some appeared to be exercising in the yard, and others were tinkering with the spaceships.

They all had guns holstered at their sides. The guards standing around the perimeter held the guns in their hands, waiting. She came out from between buildings, stepping onto a sparse expanse of dirt that surrounded the compound.

She walked toward an iron gate held up by two walls that grew taller and taller the closer she got. KaLeah held her chin up high. She had already made up her mind to tell the guards the truth and see if they took the message to Keldon.

It made no sense to lie; being Keldon's daughter was her best chance at getting to see him. She imagined what she would look like to the guards: a young woman walking out from the deserted city with black wings spread out behind her.

"Halt!" One soldier yelled, and she heard hundreds of them begin charging her way, their metal armor rhythmically clanking. She stopped walking but kept her eyes on the one in front of her—the guard at the front gate. He would be the one to grant her passage. He was the one in charge.

The mask covering his face had a clear shield over his eyes, and a black curved piece over his nose and mouth. Attached on each side was a canister with permeations that she assumed allowed air to pass through.

She didn't look, but she could see guns pointed at her out of her peripherals and felt dozens more surrounding her.

"State your purpose here before my men lay you to waste, dragon woman!" His voice was muffled, but still very loud and clear.

"I am the daughter of Lord Dayne Keldon, been missing, stolen away from him over sixteen years ago."

The soldiers were silent but began to slowly murmur amongst themselves.

"Attention!" the main guard yelled, and silence fell once again.

He then pressed a button on the mask and said something inaudible. She saw a handful of other men in her peripheral view do the same.

A few uncomfortable moments went by, and then he pressed and released the button again.

"At ease, the young lady may approach," the main guard commanded. The guns all dropped and KaLeah waited one breath before sheathing her sword and stepping forward.

"Follow me," the guard said when she'd come within a

few steps of him. He eyed her sword suspiciously as he checked her for guns but said nothing. He turned back to the gate and ordered it to be opened. She watched the black metal gates slide into the thick, gray concrete walls, and then followed the soldier into the compound.

The rest of the men fanned back out and returned to their posts. They crossed through a dirt yard toward the center building she'd been able to see from the rooftop. She followed him through two sets of tall metal doors, to the right, down a long corridor, then straight down a very long hallway. The hallways were lit with electrical bulbs, and the walls seemed to be made of metal, with a simple, concrete flooring beneath her feet.

Her heart raced with anticipation of meeting her real father.

Will he like me? Does he know what happened? What if I have to prove that I'm his daughter? How will I do that?

They turned left down another hallway and through another set of guarded metal doors. Each doorway required audible confirmation that the men checked on the hand-held communication devices. KaLeah was fascinated by the guards and technology but said nothing.

She couldn't help but remember the first day she'd been escorted through Belarone castle to meet the king. She had felt nervous that day, also, but in a different way. Although the worlds were different, the compound was cold and uninviting, where the castle had been ornately warm and made for entertaining and impressing guests.

The dictator's compound seemed to exist only as a command center. Their footfalls echoed through the empty halls.

"Your entrance, my lady," the guard said, stopping at another metal door. There was nothing that distinguished this door from the others they had passed. For all she knew, there was nothing but a jail cell on the other side.

She was caught slightly off-guard by his use of 'my lady.' Even though she'd earned the title of 'favor' on Naldash, and had sometimes been called a warrior, she didn't feel like a fancy lady. She started to wonder if her standing on Denlerack would be similar to Princess Amirra's back home.

If my father accepts me as his daughter, will I be seen as royalty on this planet?

There were two guards standing at the door. These men did not have on masks, but they did wear armor. The men did not greet her or give her any information on what to do next, so she stood awkwardly in the hallway for a few moments.

Finally, she took one step toward the door and one of the guards spoke up.

"I must take your weapon, my lady," he said.

The command startled her, and she jumped.

"Right, yes."

She unlatched her belt and handed him the scabbard. She was so curious about meeting her father that her safety didn't even cross her mind as she turned over her sword.

The other guard opened the large metal door for her, and she stepped into a high-ceilinged, sterile room with a cold, black stone floor. There was a long, simple gray rug running from the entrance, so she followed it into the room, looking all around. There was no decor and nothing that said anybody lived there.

She looked up and saw that the rug led to a wide, metal staircase. There was a man standing at the top.

He was handsome with high cheekbones, graying hair on his head, and a closely trimmed black beard, showing hints of gray along the edges. He was lean and his shoulders were draped with a large royal blue cloak fastened at the throat with what looked like an actual diamond brooch the size of her fist.

They stood still, inspecting each other from a distance.

"No one has ever shown up here claiming to be my daughter," he said. His voice was smooth and calm, but loud enough to reverberate throughout the cavernous space. "You are taking quite a risk telling such an outlandish story."

"It is not a risk. I am your daughter." She noticed that the previous nervousness was waning. She didn't feel as scared in his presence as she had expected. She didn't know him as the dictator that everyone else did.

She didn't know him at all.

She had a strange need for him to believe her, and then, to approve of her. He began to slowly walk down the staircase toward her, and she stood up straighter, more confident than ever.

"My mother was Huntra. Clegg raised me on Naldash."

He paused at the bottom of the staircase, looking at her face and eyes very carefully.

"I have not heard those names in over sixteen years. How do you know those names, child?"

"Clegg told me everything," KaLeah said with a shrug.

"Oh, I highly doubt that he told you everything, child. In fact, how do I know that you knew the man at all?"

KaLeah furrowed her brow. She hadn't thought about how to prove she'd known Clegg, the soldier from Denlerack who had raised her.

He stalked closer, his shoes making very precise taps on the floor.

"What is your name, child?"

"KaLeah," she said. "KaLeah Keldon."

Using his last name triggered a small twitch in the left corner of his mouth.

"I will not doubt that you look a little like the lovely rebel they called Huntra," he said, studying her face. He reached out and took her chin in his hand, turning her from cheek to cheek. "What do you know of her? I assume that her flock of rebels sent you." He looked her dead in the eye, still clasping her chin. "My men will eventually find all of them."

He dropped his hand and turned, walking toward a metal cabinet standing against a far wall.

"Clegg told me he was a soldier for you," KaLeah said, absently wiping at where his fingers had held her chin. "He became friends with Huntra and flew her to Naldash in a stolen spacecraft. She was pregnant with me, at the time, and didn't survive after my birth."

"She's really gone, then?" Keldon pulled a glass and bottle from the cabinet and poured himself a drink that he took down in one gulp. "That's a shame," he said, while refilling his glass. "Of course," he said loudly, spinning around to face her again. "This could all be an elaborate scheme to get close to me. You could be working for the rebellion, just like your supposed mother was. She tricked me, you know? Came into my home, into my life, into my bed, all to get close enough to destroy me."

"I only came here looking for my real father," KaLeah said, truthfully.

The dictator stared intently into her eyes, as if he could read her mind. She stared right back, refusing to blink or flinch in the slightest.

Keldon may consider himself a stern man, but KaLeah was raised by a soldier. Whatever nervousness she had felt when she'd arrived was gone, replaced by a fervent desire to prove her purpose for being there.

"You look more like my mother, anyway," he said. "I can see my stronger genes dominating in your features. Come, you must be weary. Let's have tea and you can tell me all about your journey back home to me."

KaLeah was relieved that he seemed to be accepting her story.

He motioned her out of the entryway and into a small seating area beside a fireplace with no wood. A fire burned there, but it seemed to be a light and not a real fire at all. She went to sit and then, realizing that her wings were still attached, began to unbuckle them.

"That is a very fascinating contraption you have there. Did you build those?"

"No," she said. She almost said they were a gift, but she

didn't want him to know that she had made friends among his potential enemies. "I found the wings in one of the buildings I slept in one night."

"How resourceful of you," he said.

He pressed a button on a table, and a machine on four wheels rolled into the room. It was a cylinder shape, no taller than a table, and pieced together with black and brown metal components.

On its top was a large circular tray carrying two cups and a pot of hot water. It reminded her of the contraptions that were in Professor Wheelwright's house, and she assumed that this sort of technology was common.

She wondered if he'd begun preparing for her arrival from the time she'd first crossed through the entrance gate of the compound.

"You'll have to excuse me, KaLeah," he said. He poured water into the cups and handed her one. She was only one soft chair away from him and the closeness of this stranger made her uncomfortable.

"I find myself quite speechless in your presence. For years, I wondered about the child that Huntra had stolen from me, but I did not know whether you'd lived or died."

He paused from taking a sip and looked up. Bright blue eyes that did not match her exact shade of stormy blue but matched in severity caught her own.

"Is your mother well?"

KaLeah was confused. She had clearly told him that she had died. She cocked her head to one side and raised an eyebrow. She replied to him very slowly, thinking that his question was either a trap, or he hadn't believed her the first time.

"I never met her. She died shortly after my birth."

"Yes, so you said. How did you come to know of me, then?"

"Clegg raised me as his own and only recently told me the story of how Huntra left the planet with him. I started to ask questions, and he decided to tell me the truth."

She watched as Keldon's lip raised slightly in disgust.

"That man stole many things from me that day. He was a liar and a fraud; of that you should be certain. I am sorry that you didn't grow up where you belong, child."

He looked at her for a long moment and then off into the imitation fireplace. "I am truly honored that you have come to me, finally, and so sorry that I was not able to find you sooner. I wish that I had been the father to raise you."

Tears started to sting her eyes. The emotion surprised her. She wasn't used to crying. She hadn't cried when she was stabbed on the battlefield. She hadn't cried when she was shot and fell out of the sky. It just wasn't something that she did, and yet, there they were, tiny tears trying to form and a sharp pinch inside her nose.

She blinked fast and took a sip of the tea. It was notably better than what she'd had at Professor Wheelwright's place. She could taste something floral, but there was still a tinge of metal. She wondered if everything on the planet was tainted.

"Do you know what happened that day?" KaLeah asked. "Do you know why my mother left and how? Clegg didn't tell me much."

Her father looked away from her, and she followed his gaze toward a faint light coming from a row of high windows. The room was spacious but wasn't adorned with any pictures or personal artifacts. There was nothing on the high walls or any furnishing besides the handful of chairs and a few tables around the fire-less fireplace.

"I haven't thought of that night in many, many years," he said. "Your mother was beautiful, but you don't have her red hair. You possess the same dark brown hair from my mother and me. In the beginning, we were so happy about you. I had a room prepared right beside ours. But then Huntra started to change."

The man paused to take a drink and crack his neck. "She started to pull away from me and no matter what I did, I couldn't seem to get her back to the person she had been.

She changed. She hardened. But I had no idea that she would take you from me."

He paused and took another sip of the tea. "I suspected that Clegg recruited her back over to the rebellion's ideals."

"What do you mean?" KaLeah asked, trying to play ignorant.

"Well, my dear, some people cannot bear to watch others succeed. When a man like me comes into power, our list of enemies grows. Jealousy for being in the place that I am in drove some to start rumors and rise up against me. I took over all the diamond districts and expanded into other territories. I expected more from the people of this world and most of them failed me. I only have this army because of the rebels who rose up against me. If the lazy, entitled rebels would just go off to live their own lives, then I wouldn't need to defend myself."

His demeanor suddenly softened, and he turned his eyes to hers. "Dear child, I don't want to bore you though with my troubles. I want to hear all about you. What was it like growing up on Naldash? Were you well taken care of?"

A flutter of excitement appeared low in KaLeah's belly. It was another strange feeling that she wasn't used to. She smiled slightly.

"I had a good childhood, yes," she started. "I learned how to farm and hunt, and sword fight. At the castle, I learned how to ride draggots."

He sat up straighter. "The castle? Was Clegg working with the kings then?"

KaLeah hesitated before answering. "No, I happened to stumble into a situation that put me at a castle for a few days. While I was working, I rode a draggot."

"Ah yes, draggots. We haven't had those on Denlerack since before I was a boy. I am afraid the sad state of this planet is not a place ripe for sustaining wildlife."

"What happened to the planet? Why is it so different than Naldash?"

"The decay started long ago," he said. "The more

technology we created, the less attention we paid to air and water quality, or the disappearances of seemingly inconsequential animals. We created engines that could take us from place to place, so we didn't need draggots. We created conveniences, so we didn't need to work as hard. Life was good and a lot of people, our family especially, became very, very wealthy." He took a deep breath and sat up taller, looking proud.

"I was born to a world already on the trajectory to death," he continued. "Now, the diamond districts have found methods of sustaining food and water for a controlled population. As long as they maintain that order within those boundaries, they can continue to survive. I also have the same mechanisms here to sustain myself and this army."

"What about the poor people in the slums outside of the diamond districts?" KaLeah asked, taking another sip of tea to hide any hint of empathy toward their plight.

Her father turned his blue eyes to hers and she sensed disdain, and even anger, behind them.

"They must find their own way to survive, and many do. As long as my armies protect the diamond districts from them, all will be well."

"Kids are still being born in the slums, though. There is no population control there."

A smirk crossed his lips. "Oh, but there is. Nature is its own population control. The air and water are tainted. There is not enough of it to go around. Without advanced medicine, disease runs rampant. They will not be able to live beyond a few more generations."

KaLeah didn't know what to say. This man was basically dismissing the lives of those he was able but not willing to help. She needed to press him for confirmation. "Do you have the resources to build them their own diamond districts, or at least provide the technology so they can create sustainable communities?"

"The families who are in the diamond districts come

from hard working lineages who have all paid into their ability to live there. No one is there for free. They all have required functions within the districts based on skills they learned there. The people in the slums are hard-worn criminals; thieves who have no skills or education. We would have to start at the very beginning with them, and they don't have the desire to be anything besides criminals, at this point. If I build them a district, they would have it in ruins in less than a year. I won't waste resources on people like that." Keldon scoffed, as if he couldn't believe the question.

"Besides. I am not responsible for fixing a world I did not damage, just because I have more resources than others. If they want a better life for their families, it is their responsibility to create that world themselves."

KaLeah couldn't help but understand his perspective. Although he didn't know those people, he also didn't know who he could and couldn't help. If he gave resources to men like the ones who had tried to hurt her when she first landed on the planet, or to the men who had shot her down for no reason at all, then he would be throwing his resources away.

She realized that she herself was angry at those people. Those men were dangerous. They had tried to rob her in the alley on her first day, and they had shot her out of the sky, nearly killing her.

Maybe Keldon was right; maybe it was too late to help them, and nature would need to run its course, she thought.

"I am so glad that you've decided to come home, KaLeah," Keldon said. "I'd like to show you around the mansion. I left your room exactly the same, but I did not keep it clean. I'll send in a service bot to tidy it up for you today. It is where you should have been, with me, all these years. You are lucky. You are now the richest girl on Denlerack. You will have everything you could ever need and want. Well, maybe you won't be riding draggots, but I can get you a rover and teach you how to drive it."

"What's a rover?" she asked, confused.

He laughed heartily.

"They were popular when I was a boy, but now, nobody travels outside of their diamond district. The army has a few larger ones they use, but I saved a few for myself. I can teach you to drive them on my property. It's like a draggot on wheels but a hundred times faster."

Keldon winked at her and KaLeah couldn't help but smile. It sounded fantastic. She took to the mechanical wings easily and was excited about the idea of another machine that she could master. Denlerack was full of all sorts of new mysterious things for her to learn and do. And Keldon could provide her with access to everything.

"I have only loved your mother and no other," Keldon said, leaning back in his chair. "Now that you are here as my heir, all of these lands, this mansion, and rule of Denlerack will be yours someday. I am looking forward to getting to know you and teaching you many things."

She took another sip of the tea and thought about the possibilities.

What if the rebels showed up to attack, she wondered?

She knew their small band would never stand a chance against such a massive army. And even with her here inside, she saw no way of tricking her father into giving up his rule.

KaLeah felt guilty leaving Elektra behind. The young woman had been so full of hope and eager to lead another rebellion against this man. KaLeah hoped that Elektra wouldn't hate her for abandoning them. She really did want to find a way to help Denlerack, its people, and Naldash.

Naldash.

"What about Naldash?" she asked.

"Ah, a rich planet indeed," he said.

He stood up then and walked to one of the tables. He pressed a button, and a large image appeared against a wall. It looked like two orbs in rotation around a sun, with moons orbiting each of them.

"I sent scouts a couple of years ago and they have

reported back to me the things you must have seen and taken for granted. Animals to hunt. Lush and bountiful farmland. Clean rivers and streams. It is everything that we have lost. I have been working on a plan to get it all back."

"But those things are all on Naldash," KaLeah said. "How would you get them here?"

"We wouldn't get them here—we would go there. I will lead my army in a fleet of spaceships and take Naldash by force. We will land at the various kingdom locations and overwhelm them with our advanced weaponry. It will be quite easy, really." He nonchalantly waved his hand through the air.

"Then I'll send for the highest bidders from Denlerack to join us. The wealthy families may come and start over, and we'll leave this planet behind, selling Naldash's resources back to it. Of course, I would still rule Naldash, and you would eventually rule both planets. Our legacy will rule the sister planets. I knew that I would rule until I died, but with you finally at my side, I feel as though I can now live and rule forever through you."

KaLeah set down the teacup. She had never thought of herself as being the ruler of anything. If he ruled Naldash, then he ruled Belarone.

"What will happen to the current kings and queens?" KaLeah asked, worried about young Queen Amirra.

"They will have to surrender or be killed, of course," he said. "And no one ever gives up their lands willingly. We will most likely have to take everything by force. And we will."

7 TRAITOR

Elektra woke up feeling refreshed the next morning and ready to restart the rebellion. She sat up with a smile. She would rally the team and get them out to conduct drills and exercises in the courtyard. They would rest, eat, and then talk strategies for recruiting.

She had every bit mapped out in her mind. She would recommend they split into teams and head in different directions to scout out others willing to join with them. She would set a date for them to stand together at the gates of Keldon's compound. They would be ready to fight his soldiers and take back Denlerack.

She saw that KaLeah's bed was empty and wondered how the girl had gotten up without waking her. She washed her face with the cold water sitting in the bathroom sink from the previous night and looked at herself for a moment in the chipped bathroom mirror.

Her brown skin looked darker in the dim lighting, and she tried to smooth down a few of her unruly curls.

Even though she'd given up the chance to live a comfortable life, she was finally feeling as if the decision was truly the right one. The people around her had already lost so much and now she hoped that she could help motivate them into fighting for their lives back.

She walked down to the main room with a bounce in her step. She was ready to exercise. There were a few kids already sitting downstairs and she clapped her hands together loudly.

"Alright, folks, let's get back into shape. Where's Colt?"

"Right here," he said, coming in from another room. His voice was slightly rough with sleep, but she turned and saw that he was smiling.

An unvoluntary trickle of excitement at seeing him spread through her body. She smiled back at him.

"Ready?" Elektra asked him.

"I honestly haven't been exercising lately, so thank you for kicking our butts. I'm ready," Colt answered. "Come on, let's get to the courtyard."

Lina and Lainie came in from behind Colt, Felisha slowly came down the stairs with her arms crossed. Alister, Von, and Zuri got up from the couches, and Rustin bounded over from checking the camera screens.

"Everything is all-clear out there," he said, beaming with his loving grin. "Where's KaLeah?"

A shiver ran up Elektra's spine. She looked around and shrugged, acting nonchalant and trying to ignore the strange feeling in her gut.

"I'm sure she's around here somewhere," she said. "Let's go ahead and head out and she can join us later."

"Oh, is this optional?" Felisha asked, shooting one eyebrow up high.

"No—" Elektra and Colt both said at the same time. Elektra's cheeks burned. "She's coming."

"We all need to get into better shape, and you know it, Felisha," Colt said. "We may have guns, but so do they. We are going to need to run and crawl and jump and maybe even fly if we are going to take this world back, and we need to be strong enough to do it. All of us. Now let's go."

Elektra felt some of her earlier gusto fading away.

Where was KaLeah?

She looked into the kitchen as they passed and into other rooms while they walked through the deserted building and out to the courtyard.

They spent an hour running laps, doing pushups, and shadow boxing. She discovered that they didn't do shooting drills above ground so as not to draw unfriendly attention to their location.

Sometimes they target practiced in the tunnels below ground, but not much because they needed to conserve their ammunition. The bullets weren't easy to get, and they didn't have a proper setup or materials to make their own. The ammunition they had was left over from when their parents had led attacks in years past.

Everyone was sweating and breathing heavily by the time they finished. KaLeah never joined them. Instead of facing questions, Elektra ran ahead of the others and back into the building to look for her.

She ran to their room and noticed that the small bag that usually sat beside KaLeah's bed was gone. She did a quick scan of the main areas and realized that the black wings were gone too.

"No, no, no, no, no," she repeated as she ran to the nearest set of stairs that she thought may lead her to the roof.

She ran up them quickly and then climbed a ladder, seeing that the door to the roof was wide open. She stepped out into the haze of the day and walked out, looking around.

She turned in all directions until she faced the south. Even in the morning fog, she could make out the dictator's fortress. It was closer than she'd realized.

If KaLeah had taken her wings and come to the roof, she could have set a course to fly there easily overnight.

Elektra stood and stared, disbelieving, but everything in her body told her that KaLeah was gone. She had seemed strange, in a heavily thoughtful mood, but not sharing those thoughts because they were traitorous.

She heard noises behind her like the shuffling of hands

and feet on the ladder.

"Hey, we're looking for you."

It was Colt. She didn't turn around. She kept staring out toward her enemies.

"What are you doing up here? Where's KaLeah?"

She took a few breaths, not wanting to say the truth out loud. She clenched her fists tighter in anger and embarrassment. "She's gone. I think she took her wings and flew off this roof last night."

Colt walked closer to her, and her nervousness mixed with her frustration caused her to hold her breath.

She didn't understand why she was attracted to Colt. She had never been attracted to a boy or a young man before. She'd always been focused on protecting her mother and surviving. She had known better than to trust any of the boys or young men back in Sarda growing up, and she hadn't tried to make a connection with any of the entitled rich kids back in the diamond district.

Colt was different from all of them. He had come from the same situation, the same desolate places, but hadn't joined some gang in order to take from others. He was trying to make a difference, even if he had failed. At least he had tried and was still willing to keep fighting for what was right, no matter the risk.

"I'm sure there is some explanation," he said. His tone was calm and his voice smooth. "Why do you think she left? Did something happen?"

Elektra rubbed her temples. "I don't know."

"How well do you know her?"

"Not well enough, it seems," Elektra walked closer to the edge of the building.

She was drawn to the compound. It was surrounded by an army and the dictator was somewhere hiding within its complete safety, cloistered from the damage he'd done. They would never make it to him through the army and his fortress. If KaLeah had come for the same reason, would she go there and try to take him on alone?

"That's crazy," she said, answering her silent question out loud.

"What's crazy?" Colt asked, his eyes boring into the back of her neck.

"I'm trying to figure this girl out," Elektra said, beginning to pace the rooftop. "She said she came to save her planet. What if she decided she would have more luck getting to Keldon without us?"

"How could she possibly take on Keldon's men by herself?" Colt asked, standing stoically, and watching her pace.

"It sounds too crazy, I know. She can hear dragons, but they aren't helping her fight. She couldn't possibly take on Keldon's army, so why would she leave? All I can assume is she is going to try to save her planet on her own, she ran off scared, or worse. I'm concerned…" she trailed off, not wanting to say it aloud.

"Concerned about what?" he pressed.

"What if this was her plan all along?" Elektra asked, stopping and looking up at his brown eyes. "She knows where we are. Everyone knows that the dictator wants to invade Naldash. What if she made up this story and played the victim in order to earn our trust? What if she was trying to find this hideout, find your rebels, the whole time? What if she is heading to tell Keldon's men how to find us?"

Colt was quiet for a few moments. He looked off toward the dictator's compound to the south. "Those are our options, then?" he asked. "She either went off to kill the dictator, gave up completely, or she was a spy for him this whole time?"

Elektra let out a loud, angry cry, then kicked a rusty pipe that was sticking up out of the roof. It snapped apart and bounced off the edge of the building. She heard it hit the concrete below.

"This is all my fault. I never should have brought her here. I should have made her go her own way after I rescued her in the alley." She reached up with clenched fists and started pulling at her own hair in frustration.

She felt warm, soft hands gently pulling her hands away from her head. He pulled her arms down to her side and put a hand on each arm, looking directly at her.

"You did the right thing, Elektra," he said. She opened her eyes and looked into his brown, golden speckled ones. "If we don't stop to help one another, if we don't trust each other, then our world is truly doomed. We need to save ourselves and others, no matter what."

"What are we going to do, Colt?" Elektra's voice cracked and her body was so tight with tension that she thought she might collapse. To her surprise, Colt pulled her into an embrace.

"Take a deep breath," he suggested.

She took a breath, and on the exhale, tears came to her eyes. She was exhausted and frightened. For the first time in days, she missed her mother. But as soon as the thought entered her mind, it was replaced by anger.

Her mother was living comfortably while her very home cast shadows on the people starving below her. Her mother and those people of the diamond districts didn't care about anyone other than themselves. And now, after saving her, trusting her, and getting to know KaLeah, she'd lost her too. It was another treachery.

Colt smelled like sweat after their workout, but he also smelled like grass and heat. She felt more comfortable in his arms than she realized was possible. But the hug was starting to last too long for her comfort, and she pushed herself back.

"What are we going to do?" she asked, trying not to look directly in his eyes, concerned she might forget about the situation at hand.

"We'll figure this out together, but it doesn't have to be right at this moment," Colt said, reassuring her. "Let's get cleaned up and then come back up here to put together a plan. KaLeah hasn't been gone long enough to alert an army to our whereabouts. Let's take a little bit of time on our own to clear our heads."

She looked up at him then and felt a flutter low in her stomach.

Does he feel something between us too? she wondered. *No, of course not. He is just being a leader,* she told herself.

"Thank you," she said.

He swallowed and let go of her arms. His voice cracked when he said, "I'll see you back up here in a few."

She nodded and headed to the rooftop doorway but then stopped and turned back toward Colt.

"Do me a favor?" she asked.

He gave her a smile that made her feel warm all over again.

"Tell Felisha and the others not to talk to me about KaLeah. I'm not sure I'd be able to stop myself from punching Felisha in the face right now."

His smile faded and his eyes grew large, but then he nodded. She disappeared down the ladder before he could say anything else.

She did not want to see or talk to anyone at that moment. Anger was bubbling up inside of her and she wanted to fight. She knew she'd take any excuse. If she hadn't just worked out, she might consider running in circles around the courtyard or even heading out onto the streets for a run. Adrenaline flowed through her veins and the last thing she wanted to do was sit down and talk.

She ducked around corners on her way back to her room, not wanting to run into anyone. Colt was the only one she could stand at a time like this. He made her feel calm, despite her anger.

Back in her room, she closed the door behind her. The long room was filled with empty beds where people ready to battle the dictatorship once slept in the comfort of knowing they all shared one purpose. Even though KaLeah's purpose was saving her own planet, she'd still felt a kinship, a sense that they were on the same team. They were going to save both of their worlds together.

And now she was gone. Could that young woman really bring an army down on them? So many lives had already been lost; would KaLeah be the reason all these remaining kids were killed too?

If they come here, if they kill these kids, it will all be my fault, she told herself again.

She sat down heavily on her bed, feeling defeated and desperate.

"I can't let that happen," Elektra said out loud. "I have to keep them safe."

With newfound determination, she got up, cleaned herself with some stagnant, cold water, then dressed in fresh clothes. She took her time, and when she was done, she could hear yelling coming from the main room downstairs.

She realized that Colt must have told them what happened. She hoped he could break away and meet her on the roof to come up with a plan. She didn't want to face the others without a fully thought-out, solid, and survivable plan.

Elektra crept back through the hallways and up the side staircase to the roof. The sun that she had never seen had moved across the sky. She could tell because the clouds in front of it were the brightest. Staring too long hurt her eyes, so she looked out over the city and let her gaze fall to the dictator's compound.

She wondered if KaLeah had really flown all the way there. The professor told her KaLeah was hiding something. Had she really been a spy for the dictator this whole time?

Elektra tried to think of other scenarios. Maybe KaLeah had gone out exploring and been captured by bandits. That scenario didn't make sense.

Why would she have taken her wings to just walk around?

Maybe she'd intended on flying around to explore the area and been shot down again. Elektra wanted to believe any alternative scenario to KaLeah being a traitor.

But she knew in her heart that people couldn't be

trusted. She had never trusted anyone; she couldn't even trust her mother with her own safety.

Elektra shook her head back and forth, releasing tension in her neck as her curly black hair bounced from side to side.

"Sorry it took me so long," Colt said as he stepped onto the roof. "How are you feeling?"

"I'm not really sure," Elektra said. "How did the rest of them take it?"

"Well, they're mad. They asked a lot of questions we can't answer."

"So, what now?" she asked, trying not to look at him for fear of losing her thoughts. She was already having trouble focusing through her own frustration.

"I think the safest thing would be to lay low somewhere away from here, to make sure we aren't around if Keldon does send his men." He paused and the unspoken reason hung heavy in the air between them.

"Just in case KaLeah is a traitor and sends Keldon's men here." Shivers ran up her entire spine saying the words. She cringed at how the rest of Colt's people would see her now, as the person who brought in a traitor. It was almost too much for her to bear.

"Hey," Colt said, his voice smooth and soft as he walked toward her. "This isn't your fault. You're a good person and you were trying to help her. We will be alright. I think we need to round everyone up, get some supplies, and head out of here for a while to be safe."

Elektra looked out over the dead city.

"Where will we go?" she asked.

"We'll figure it out together," Colt said. He stretched out his arm, opening his hand in front of her. She looked down at his long, brown fingers, realizing that she hadn't touched many other boys or men in her life.

There was no hesitation. She placed her hand in his and he wrapped her small hand up tightly. Tingles went from her forearm, through her body, and into her belly. Her cheeks flushed as she smiled. He smiled back and led her to the ladder back inside.

Together they walked hand in hand to the main room where the troop was gathered. Though she felt strangely vulnerable, she knew that she was protected at the same time. He cleared his throat, and everyone turned.

"We need to pack up essential items and head out for a few days, to make sure KaLeah isn't sending the dictator's army here."

The entire group started groaning at once. Colt squeezed her hand, and she started to sweat with a mix of adrenaline and excitement. Although she felt ridiculous, she didn't let go of his hand.

"But why is she still here?" Felisha yelled across the room. "She brought the traitor! She could be a traitor too!"

"Felisha, stop. I trust Elektra." Colt took a small step in front of her and released her hand. It was protective, but the sense of loss was immediate and struck her deeply.

"Listen, Elektra was trying to save the girl, just like Rustin was trying to save her when he carried her through the tunnels and into this safe house. For all we know, KaLeah could have gone back to her own planet scared at the possibility of fighting Keldon, or she could be on her way there now. Maybe she is ingenuous enough to think that she can talk him out of invading her planet." Colt his place in front of Elektra as he spoke, but looked each one of his people in the eyes.

"We may never know what happened to KaLeah or why she left. What we do know is that Elektra is from Denlerack. She wants to work with us to help save our planet. I don't want to hear any more about what may have happened with KaLeah. I don't want to hear any blame directed at Elektra. We need to focus our energy on figuring out how to protect each other right now."

Colt's voice had risen in volume and grown deeper with every word. He pointed firmly to the ground, the veins popping out of his forearm. Elektra found herself speechless and transfixed.

Nobody had ever stood up for her. She was always the lone fighter. It was a strange, new, and humbling experience.

"So, what do we do?" Rustin asked, still oddly chipper despite the dramatic tension in the air.

"I think we gather a few supplies and head out of here."

"But where do we go?" Lina and Lainie asked in unison.

"Alister, any thoughts?" Colt asked.

Alister smoothed back his thick black hair. His dark eyes drifted upward in thought.

"Without any surveillance setup, it would be best to be up higher, where we have a better vantage point," Alister said. "We can try to find an unoccupied building and climb as high as we can. We'd still have to keep watch around the clock and in multiple directions. No fires. No loud noises. We can't draw attention to ourselves."

"Have we scouted out any of the surrounding buildings lately?" Zuri asked.

"I have!" Everyone turned their gaze back to Rustin, who was sitting on the arm of a couch, his long legs reaching the floor. "I have a few ideas."

Colt smiled. "Good. Let's start gathering supplies and move out in less than an hour."

Elektra turned quickly to head for her room before anyone could make eye-contact, and before Colt could distract her with his gaze. She went into warrior-mode, gathering essentials, her wings, and her weapons.

She was sad to be moving again so quickly, but the momentum was also comforting. She knew better than to get too comfortable. Even though they were leaving the hideout before they were ready for actual battle, at least they were doing something.

It was strange pulling her brown leather and metal wings on again, thinking of how KaLeah had used the wings that Professor Wheelwright had given her to fly off without her. The betrayal of being left behind, and in the dark, burned her on the inside. It took all she had to bury the anger trying to rise like bile in her throat.

She strapped on her gun holsters and a knife. At least she knew that if she ever saw KaLeah again, she'd be able to take the traitor out quickly. The girl's sword would be useless. She wondered if the sword had just been a ploy.

Was KaLeah actually from Naldash? she wondered.

She left the room and headed down to join the others, who were stuffing rations into bags and passing them out. Rustin brought one to Elektra with that infectious smile on his face. At least he wouldn't be mad at her about KaLeah.

"Thank you, Rustin."

"Chin up, kid," he said. "We're going on an adventure." Then he winked and walked away.

Felisha was standing behind him with her arms crossed.

"Are the wings so you can fly off at the first sign of danger?" she asked.

Elektra tightened her lips into a thin smile. "I'll be able to fly ahead to ensure the path is clear if we have poor visibility on the ground."

Felisha huffed and turned away.

Elektra realized she'd been digging her nails into her palm. She forced herself to take a breath and unclench her fists.

Colt came down the stairs and Elektra's vision turned to slow motion as she watched every muscle in his body flex as he walked, carrying a heavy-looking bag. He caught her eyes and smiled, though she could see an uneasiness in him.

Elektra had always felt like a leader but had never led anyone other than her mother. She was impressed with how Colt stood by her and then rallied his people behind his suggestion. She loved how effortless he made leadership look.

"Are we all ready?" he asked the group.

Everyone had reassembled with their weapons, layered clothing, and satchels of supplies. The girls had pulled back their hair into braids and the men had strapped extra imitation animal hide to their shoulders. They all sounded off that they were ready to go.

"Do we know where we are even going?" Felisha asked.

"I believe our best course would be to find some high ground and keep an eye on the hideout," Colt said. "We will follow Rustin's lead. There aren't many gangs in the area, but every building carries that potential danger. We should head away from the direction of the compound, just in case Keldon has sent scouts to locate us."

"We aren't going to walk out into the open, are we?" Alister asked.

"Why don't we go out through the tunnel?" Von added.

"We need to stay away from any entrance that KaLeah has seen," Colt said.

"Technically, she didn't see the tunnel because she was nearly passed out with a fever," Rustin said.

"I don't think we should just head out into the light," Alister said. "Anyone could be watching out there, and that jeopardizes our ability to come back here safely."

Colt nodded and narrowed his brow.

"The same could be said from emerging out of the tunnels in broad daylight too," Felisha said. "That's all we need is some gang claiming this place while we are out hiding."

"Can we hide in the tunnels until dark?" Elektra asked Colt.

Alister cleared his throat. "It will be hard for a group this large to move quietly and safely through the dark ruins to find safe shelter."

"I can scout it out and then come back to guide everyone there," Rustin said, loud and enthusiastically. "I know that place really well and I have a couple ideas of where we can find shelter. I can go ahead of the group, scout it out, and then guide everyone there two at a time."

His smile was so big and genuine that Elektra wanted to hug him right there. The rest of the group may not trust her, but at least Rustin's optimism kept her motivated to stay with the group.

Lina and Lainie, Alister, Von, and Zuri seemed indifferent to her. They didn't try to connect or make eye-contact, but at least they didn't appear to outwardly hate her, like Felisha did. Elektra would stay and try to whip this group into soldiers worthy of standing up to the dictator, whether they liked her or not. But at least Colt and Rustin made it all worth it. They were the type of people she wanted to save the planet for.

She wanted to emphatically agree with Rustin's plan, but she was afraid the rest of the group would immediately dismiss anything she was in favor of; so, she bit her tongue instead.

Alister and Von verbally agreed while Lina and Lainie nodded their heads. Felisha shrugged.

"Alright then, it's settled," Colt said. "Let's head to the main tunnel."

It was surreal, re-entering the dark, damp tunnel. This was how she'd come to join the group, and she hoped that it wasn't a bad sign to be leaving the same way she'd entered.

No one spoke, and the sounds of their boots echoed off the walls. When the heavy door was closed behind them, it felt like all the life had been sucked out of her. She wondered if she was the only one who sensed the ominous weight around them.

The tunnel seemed longer than she remembered. When they reached the end, it was still daylight, so they sat down in the dirt and ate from their rations in silence.

When it was finally dark, Rustin climbed out of the tunnel alone in search of shelter. Elektra knew that he was familiar with the landscape, but she desired to go with him. She wanted to show her value to the rest of them but knew better than to offer. They would only assume she was planning some treachery.

Rustin would have to walk beyond the diamond district ruins and into a few outlying buildings to see if there were any unoccupied ones that would provide a roof and walls. The higher they could get, the better, so they could see their own hideout and watch for intruders there as well as in their temporary shelter.

The first time Rustin came back, Elektra was awash with relief. He'd found an empty building. It wasn't more than a few stories high, but he said that it would still give them a good view of the surrounding area come daylight.

Since they had agreed it would be too dangerous to all go at once, Colt took command of doling out the teams.

"Alister, you'll go first to confirm the location. Take Lainie with you," Colt ordered.

Elektra was starting to feel cold in the damp tunnel, and the space got darker every time a team left, taking their lanterns with them. Nobody spoke as they all strained to hear Rustin coming back.

Rustin returned and took Von and Lina the second time.

When he came back the third time, his eyes were larger, and his smile was gone.

"What is it?" Colt asked, grasping his forearm, and helping him down into the tunnel.

"I'm not sure," he said. "I thought I heard something on my way back, but now that I'm down here, I'm not sure if I heard anything."

A tingle crawled up her spine. She had the same feeling she'd gotten when KaLeah had disappeared.

"Zuri, you and I will go with Rustin this time and make sure the way is clear," Colt said. He looked back at Elektra and then Felisha. "If everything is clear, then we'll send Rustin back for you two. If not, then you're to stay here tonight. Don't go out until we come for you."

Neither one of them said a thing, but Elektra knew without looking at Felisha that she was not happy about the arrangement. The girl started clicking her fingernails together. Elektra watched Colt, Rustin, and Zuri climb back out of the tunnel with a sinking feeling in her stomach.

"This is not good," Elektra mumbled under her breath.

"Dragon's blood," Felisha exclaimed. "Of all the people to be stuck in a tunnel with…"

Elektra couldn't stand the girl's attitude any longer. "What's your problem with me?"

In one hot breath, Felisha was up and in her face in the dimly lit tunnel.

"You and your friend have messed everything up!" she yelled. "There was no danger before you came along. We didn't have a dictator to deal with. We had food, access to underground water, and shelter. We were safe and we were surviving. Now we are out running for our lives again. This is all your fault!"

Elektra felt like the wind had been knocked out of her. "You're right," she said, agreeing completely.

Felisha took a step back, her nose crinkled up in confusion, looking a little deflated.

"But I don't want to just survive," Elektra said. "I don't want to spend the rest of my days hiding out while some man destroys this world. I don't want to sit in a diamond district, being spoon-fed lies while ignoring the plight of the people right outside my door. While I am alive and while I can fight, I want to make this world better. I want to stop Keldon. I'm willing to risk anything."

"Well, I'm not," Felisha said, slamming a fist into the muddy wall. "I've already lost so much. We have already fought and our friends, our family, died. I'm done. I don't want to lose anyone else. You don't know how much we've fought and lost already. You have no idea who we used to be. This is all I have left and you're taking it from me."

"I'm trying to save us!" Elektra yelled.

"You're trying to kill us!" Felisha screamed back.

The manhole to the tunnel suddenly slid to the side with a thud. Elektra knew instantly that it wasn't Rustin above ground. Rustin had opened the trap door to the tunnel quietly and cautiously.

This was aggressive.

"Come out of there!" The voice was rough, but young.

Elektra put her hand against Felisha's mouth and pushed her up against the wall. The woman struggled out of sheer annoyance, but Elektra held firm.

"I know you're down there, now come up before I lower my weapon and start shooting." The man's voice yelled again.

"Alright, I'm coming out," Elektra said back, widening her eyes at Felisha to stay quiet when she released her hold over the girl's mouth.

She handed her guns over quickly to Felisha, who took them without a word. She quickly shrugged out of her wings too, not wanting them to be stolen.

"I'm not armed. Don't shoot me," Elektra said again, trying to buy time before edging over to the ladder. Felisha slowly backed away down the tunnel.

"We'd never shoot a lady," the man said with a chuckle.

"They are such rare finds nowadays," another man said.

Elektra wondered at her hands as she climbed up. Would she be able to claw an eye out? Throw a punch? She was better at shooting weapons and had neglected her hand-to-hand combat training.

Above ground, she saw that there were only two of them. They could be members of a gang, or just two guys trying to get by. They were both thin and taller than her, but they had muscles and guns.

"What are you doing out here? Where are your friends?" It was too dark to make out their features, but the one who had called down to her was also the one asking the questions.

"I don't have any friends. I was looking for a place to hide and found this hole in the ground, but the tunnel was all caved in." Elektra tried to make herself sound tired, her voice raw and scratchy.

"Looking pretty loudly for someone alone." The man started to peer down the hole, and she hoped that Felisha was halfway back to the hideout by now.

"I get mad and yell at myself," Elektra said, trying to bring a bit of crazy into her voice now. "I was yelling because I thought I had found a dry place to stay for a while, but it's obvious this hole leads to nothing and is nearly flooded with sewage. You ever been so mad and so alone you start talking to yourself?" she asked, staring the closest man dead into his dark eyes.

She spoke fast and with overly exaggerated wide eyes in an effort to appear a little unstable. She needed them to stay out of the tunnel and feel a little uneasy in her presence. It had the effect she'd intended, and the men both took steps backward from her and the tunnel entrance.

"Well, that's too bad about the tunnel. On the bright side, you won't be alone with us. Come along, girl. We'll help you find a nice, warm hole in the ground."

"She's not going anywhere."

Elektra turned to see Felisha leap out of the hole and point a gun at each man. Elektra moved quickly to Felisha's side, and grabbed an extra gun holstered at her hip. She drew and pointed it, moving from man to man.

"Now you've gone and hurt our feelings," one of them said. His eyes seemed to grow darker in the moonlight. They were white men, but their skin was covered in dirt to camouflage themselves in the night.

"It's time to go," Rustin said from behind them, more sternly than she'd ever heard him. Elektra was relieved now that there were three of them against two.

"You win this time, kids," one of them said. "Let's head out before this gets messy."

"You got it," said the other man.

The three of them kept their guns locked onto the men until they disappeared into the darkness.

"Are you ladies alright?" Rustin asked, coming over. Elektra kept her eyes on the darkness.

"Yes, but we need to close this hatch, maybe cover it up with some dirt and stones, and get out of here fast," Elektra said.

"Colt may want to permanently seal it up. For now, let's go meet up with the others," Rustin said.

"I think I turned them off of investigating it," Elektra

said. "I told them that it's caved in and flooded."

"Let's hope that's enough," Rustin said, his usual smile missing from his face.

Elektra dropped into the tunnel to retrieve her wings, and then quickly scrambled back up the ladder. They covered up all evidence of the entrance with mud and foliage and then followed Rustin through the darkness.

"Thank you for saving me back there, Felisha," Elektra whispered as they walked. The young woman didn't respond, but it was a start.

8 GHOSTS

Nikolat watched night fall across the barren land from another dirt hole in the ground. They had eaten large, leggy insects and drank dirty water from old, discarded cans the night before, and he was beginning to crave the disgusting things. Nikolat watched the young child with awe and pity as she stretched herself awake.

I wonder how long she has lived this way.

He hadn't paid much attention to the people of Naldash who had existed outside of his castle. He had always been so focused on his goal of taking the throne from his elder brother, that he assumed the kingdom itself and the people in it were fine.

He knew there were some on Naldash who lived in poor conditions, but he had no idea if their situations compared to Ash's. When he made it to the spaceship, would he be able to leave the girl to return to this way of living? He wondered what Ash had lived through so far in her short life and suddenly his mind was awash with memories.

He remembered his mother smiling at him while he and Bylex practiced swordplay. The night his mother died during childbirth came back in an unexpected flash, and he recalled hating the tiny, blonde-haired baby the nurses had carried from her chambers.

He had been alone in his grief, watching his father go on worshiping Bylex as if his wife were still there and everything was fine.

Nikolat had closed himself off from them all. It wasn't until KaLeah came to the castle that he began to feel emotions other than anger and misery. She had somehow even managed to soften his thoughts toward his young sister.

He didn't want to admit it, but he had started to feel different. Looking at the waif that reminded him of his own, innocent sister, he was slightly remorseful for the way he had treated Amirra and KaLeah.

But then he started to remember them both on that balcony, plotting to take the throne that was rightfully his and hot anger began to fire up again.

He rubbed his temples with his dirty hands, squashing the memories. He needed another annoying, selfish, conniving little girl in his life like he needed a pebble in his shoe.

"Come," said Ash, pulling him from his thoughts.

Nikolat's stomach grumbled as he emerged into the night. They started gathering small insects and dried foliage, Nik checked each new item with Ash before eating anything unfamiliar.

Once they had enough energy, they began walking. Even in the moonless night, he was beginning to relax each time he saw a figure appear. Even though a lot of the planet seemed to be dirt and mud, it must have rained enough to keep some plants and bushes alive.

At first, he'd been nervous about dark shapes in the night, but as they got closer, he noticed they always turned out to be short, prickly bushes that Ash would comb through for berries and leaves. They rarely saw people or animals.

Though sparse, if they heard any noises, they could hide behind the bushes for cover. Ash, being so much smaller, had a much easier time ducking behind bushes. Nikolat did the best he could.

They would pause periodically to listen for sounds in the night. Or, more specifically, Ash would listen. He heard things from all directions that made no sense to him, but each sound seemed to tell her a story and a course to take.

As they walked, Nikolat started noticing dirt mounds dotting the landscape. The mounds looked like they had entrances, and he realized they were similar to the dugouts they had been sleeping in, except three times as large. There were also small structures that seemed to be constructed of discarded scraps of metal. Pretty soon, he noticed people sitting around tiny fires who watched as they walked past.

Nikolat tried not to stare back at them, following Ash's lead who simply kept walking. She didn't seem concerned about the proximity of these folks, nor did she appear to want to steal food from them. He was glad about that, not looking forward to another run through the night.

"Friends," she finally told him, heading onward. He felt constantly out of place following her, letting a child take the lead, but she did seem to know how to get around, and he was still completely lost.

Ash veered toward a fire that was surrounded by mounds of dirt he assumed were more living burrows and dugouts. Although Ash seemed at ease, he still followed her cautiously. How would this group be any different than the group that took his shoes that first night? Or the group they stole and ran from? It looked like another group of poor, starving bandits to him.

They approached and a large man stood and spread out his arms. His ragged brown cloak spread out around him and was adorned in tiny, shimmery trinkets. It was too dark to make out any features, but Nikolat could see the man had a long beard and lightly colored eyes that reflected the firelight.

"Welcome," the man said in a calm, clear voice that seemed full of authority. "If yee seek to commit no harm here, then no harm will come to thee."

"We seek to harm no one ever, father," Ash said.

"Then please, come sit by the fire young one," the man said.

At first, Nikolat thought that perhaps this was Ash's father, but then realized he must be a religious person. There were those who prayed to the dragon spirits on Naldash, but Nikolat had never taken to religion, believing it all to be silly superstitions.

As he thought this, the memory of the dragon phantom on the balcony that had appeared above his sister and then sent him to Denlerack entered his mind. He shuddered.

Nikolat followed Ash's lead and sat by the small fire beside her. They were given hard bread and water, slightly cleaner than what he'd had so far on the planet, and he wondered how they were cleaning it. After a while, he noticed the spiritual 'father' staring at him from across the flames.

"The spirits have a message for you, young space traveler," said the bearded man.

Nikolat nearly choked on the bread, which wasn't terribly hard to do. He took a quick drink to swallow the lump down.

"What?" Nik asked.

"No matter your beliefs," the man said. He handed a small cup of liquid to the person to his left and the cup passed hands until it reached Nikolat. "Drink and you'll receive your message."

Nikolat took the cup that appeared to be made of hardened clay. He looked over at Ash, who nodded reassuringly.

He sighed and figured if it was liquid, his body probably needed it anyway. He lifted the cup and smelled sulfur. Then he swallowed it down quickly, tasting hints of fruit and dirt. He set the empty cup down at his feet.

Nikolat took a minute to observe the others sitting there. Some were dressed in robes similar to their host's robe, but without trinkets. Others looked much more desolate, barely clothed in rags, with tattered blankets wrapped over knees and shoulders.

No one was in a good place. Everyone appeared thin and malnourished. Everyone was covered in dirt. He looked down at his own arms, hands, legs, and shoes. He too was beginning to look as ragged as they did.

I'm a prince, and look at me, he thought, shaking his head. He figured that whatever he'd just had to drink must not be very nourishing, after all. Everyone looked near death, dazed, and staring into the flames of the small fire as if it would save their lives.

He started to feel woozy and the only thing that made him feel better was looking into the flames. His mind started to feel disconnected from his body, as if he were moments from falling asleep, but he was still sitting straight up on the dirt, watching the fire. The flames danced and grew before him, changing shapes, and pulling him into the pictures they were creating.

The people sitting around him, including Ash, began to fade as if they had only been a dream. They floated away into a fog creeping around the edges of his vision. There were dancing figures in the flames that started to solidify into one, moving shape.

He stared more intently, trying to identify a familiar frame. The fire shifted from red to a black shadow that had legs, a torso, and arms. A human stepped out from the shadow, and he thought he recognized the silhouette before him.

"Mother?" he asked, knowing this couldn't be real. He knew his mother was dead, and he was only dreaming.

What had the spiritual man said about a message?

"My son," said the deceased Queen Sorara of Belarone Kingdom.

She stood before him in a red-flamed dress, her brown hair looking gold in the firelight. Her features were just as he remembered them, especially since he had seen them more and more every day in Amirra's face; a sharp, petite nose, pointed lips, and thin eyebrows. Her skin was also golden-hued in the firelight, but shadows kept casting her in darkness over and over while the fire tried to maintain the image.

He knew she wasn't really there, but he was curious. What would this ghost of his mother, this spiritual messenger, have to tell him?

"You look well," Nik said, raising an eyebrow and trying to keep back any emotional response.

"Your life is in danger," Queen Sorara said.

"This isn't exactly new information. I'm stuck on a desolate planet—the wrong planet—and I'm being led by a strange little child to a ship I don't know how to fly. Can you help me?"

"I can warn you." Her voice was soft and lyrical. "If you don't make changes, if you don't embrace the man that you are meant to be, then your sister will be all that is left of my living children. You will lose everything. Your hubris will destroy you."

He looked away into the fog that hid all the people he assumed were still there on the outskirts of his vision.

"Again, this doesn't exactly help," he said, flippantly. Then he turned back to her. "I am trying to get back to Naldash and to my kingdom. I'll try to work things out with my sister. Maybe I'll help her find a nice man to marry so she doesn't have to leave Belarone. But it is my right to rule that kingdom. I will make it to the ship, and I will get back there. Ash is helping me."

"Help will only take you so far," she said, shaking her head. "You must figure out who you are and who you can be. You *can* be a good man. You *can* be a great king. You *can* earn KaLeah's love. You *can* earn your sister's respect."

"Earn KaLeah's love? My sister's respect? Are you crazy? They stole my kingdom from me. They are the reason I am here! They will be lucky if I let them live."

His mother's image gasped, and the fire shimmered

violently all around them. Nikolat bit back his angry outburst, thinking it unwise to upset a magical fire ghost.

"I don't mean that," he said, regaining control of his tone. "I am just angry at them, and we will have to come to an agreement when I get back, that's all. I just hope they don't try to fight me again, because I'll make sure they lose this time."

"If you stop the fighting, and if you step back and listen to them, love, and respect them, then you can have all that you desire and more. You will truly have a wonderful and loving life. I promise you. If you give up your place in Belarone Kingdom, you could still rule and have more beyond your wildest dreams."

He thought on that for a moment. He didn't understand what she was trying to say. What could possibly be better than Belarone Kingdom? He had wanted it his entire life. She wanted him to give that up and be nice to KaLeah and his sister in the hopes of getting something better? It was ludicrous.

"Thanks for this special message, mother. You can go now." He waved her off with a dismissive flapping of his hand.

The image started to dissipate back into the flames.

"It was good to see you," he said quietly, just in case it really had been her.

There was a mix of nostalgia, pain, and a little bit of shame. He had not treated his siblings, her children, very well in pursuit of his goal.

As the fog drifted away and his head began to clear, he let that shame go with it. He had made decisions, he had taken actions, and he refused to regret anything he had done in the pursuit of his dream. He would keep moving forward at any cost.

"Ash, are we going to keep moving?" Nik asked the girl he assumed was still sitting beside him, but she wasn't there. Everyone was gone from their places around the fire and the fog still loomed.

"What's going on?" he wondered out loud.

He squinted to try to make out figures he thought he saw in the fog. He heard voices begin drifting toward him.

"You can change."

"How could you treat your sister that way?"

"They say that a warrior who can hear the dragons will end the war and unite the sister planets once again."

"Do you realize who she is?"

"You saw the phantom dragon with your own eyes."

"You saw Anissa La Alani."

"How could you do that to them?"

"You had her kidnapped."

"Why didn't you just kill me yourself?"

"Terrible."

"Evil."

"Shame."

"Shame."

"Oh, shut up!" Nik yelled out into the night fog. He knew those voices. His father. His brother. His mother. All dead. How dare they try to tell him anything about who he is or what he'd done.

The fog suddenly dissipated, and he found himself standing in front of the fire with the circle of poor folk still sitting around the edges, eating from clay bowls, mending clothing, and sleeping.

Ash was looking at him but said nothing. He wasn't sure if they had been able to hear him or the voices.

It doesn't matter, he told himself. *I know exactly who I am, and what I want. And I always get what I want.*

&KaLeah&

KaLeah awoke in a large canopy bed in a young child's bedroom. The service bot had tidied up the room, but there was still a layer of dust on the top of the furniture, and on the bedding.

Dolls were lined up and stared at her from the foot of

the bed, and she found the stark differences between this room and the one she'd grown up in, both sad and a bit unnerving.

The KaLeah of Naldash had owned no toys, no dolls, and slept under furs of animals Clegg had killed and skinned. That child had learned to fish, hunt, swim, and fight with every weapon available as soon as she was walking. That child had never worn a dress, had never been pampered or coddled, and had never been promised an easy life.

The child meant for this room, with toys, dolls with their own large house, a closet full of colorful dresses, and handmade blankets, was more like a princess. KaLeah realized she would have been a completely different person had she grown up in this space. She would have been more like Princess Amirra.

The room was as large as Amirra's bedroom back in Belarone Kingdom. The bed was soft and comfortable, and surrounded by billowy white curtains. She lied awake and looked up at the canopied bed, running back the events of the previous day in her mind.

First, she couldn't believe she'd actually met her father. He hadn't come across as the evil dictator that Elektra, Colt, and the rebels had made him out to be. He had missed her and had been searching for her when his men found the crashed ship outside of her village.

He said that his men had taken Clegg in order to find out where Huntra and his child were. Clegg had told them that both Huntra and the baby had died when the ship crashed. Keldon claimed he never would have given up hope of finding her alive, and she believed that he was truly happy to finally be reunited.

In the half a day and evening they had spent together, they had eaten fresh meat and fruits, had the best drinks she had experienced so far on the planet, and shared stories. They laughed together and she was connecting with this strange man, excited to build a relationship with him.

Thoughts of Clegg made her hesitate at times. She had grown up so loyal to the man she thought was her father, that she felt a sense of shame with growing close to her actual father.

What did she owe Clegg? she wondered. He hadn't really loved her as a daughter or missed her as her true father had. At times, during the conversation, an anger toward Clegg started to build for his role in stealing her away from this man and from this life.

The life she had lived on Naldash was one fraught with struggle and pain. She had hunted and dragged home great beasts, toiled in the garden, labored to create wares for them to sell to survive. Her life had been hard where it could have been spent lavishly in a grand mansion. She could have grown up the way Princess Amirra had.

She moved to the edge of the bed and pushed the soft white bed curtains aside. There was a slight glow to the room from the light coming through the far window. She heard a faint clicking sound, and then a jolt, and the draperies started to slide open all on their own revealing large glass-paned windows. Feeling propelled, she stood up and walked to look outside.

As she walked up to the window, KaLeah recalled the first time she stepped up to a window from within Belarone castle. The views could not be more different.

From Belarone, she could see snow-capped mountains in the distance, rich forests, and vibrant patches of fields and gardens stretched out across the land. There were crisp, clean streams and lakes, and bustling villages. Everything in the kingdom had been colorful.

The view that greeted her from her new home was gray and desolate. Instead of gardeners tending diverse assortments of colorful foliage, there were soldiers patrolling a barren wasteland, wearing masks to protect them from the smoky fog.

What is in the air? she wondered.

No animals seemed to be thriving, and she worried that

maybe the soldiers knew something that no one else knew. The air was thick, warm, and always hazy, carrying a strange smell of dirt and smoke, but was it actually harmful? She made a note to herself to ask Keldon, her father, later.

"I have met my father," she said to herself in awe.

She could see her reflection in the window and tried to see the resemblance there. He had been nice to her, welcoming, and supportive of the struggles she has experienced in her life without him.

KaLeah hadn't told him everything, but he listened to her stories, asked her questions, and gave her more attention in one day than Clegg had in years. This was clearly a man who wanted to be in her life and who was glad to be reunited.

The view from the room, the planet itself, and the food were definite drawbacks. But when she turned back in toward her room in the military compound and admired the simple and lovely décor that had been prepared for the child KaLeah of Denlerack, nostalgia crept in her heart that was near to creating a desire to stay.

She walked to a nearby dresser and picked up a tiny green stuffed dragon that would have been hers. KaLeah lifted it up and the cute face with its black eyes and black nose made her smile. The green scales reminded her of the phantom dragon, the one the people called Klackire who was truly named Anissa La Alani.

Anissa had transported KaLeah to Denlerack to stop her father from invading Naldash, and yet, KaLeah hadn't seen a hint of a dragon shadow since she'd arrived.

Anissa hadn't come along to help save her in the alley—Elektra had. Anissa hadn't tried to stop her from coming alone to her father's house. And she wasn't here in what should have been KaLeah's childhood room to help her deal with the conflicting emotions now creeping in.

"Where are you?" she asked, and then angrily threw the stuffed dragon across the room.

It hit a door, popping it slightly open. She walked over

to investigate. There were two large doors that opened to a walk-in closet. She assumed that it had been filled with baby and young child clothing at one time and maybe for many years, as her father had said. But when she opened the doors all the way, she saw that the clothing had been replaced with items more appropriate to her size and age.

She stepped in and a row of lights immediately illuminated the space. It brought back the memory of walking into Princess Amirra's closet room and being greeted by her nurses to dress for the ball. She kept finding so many parallels between her two experiences.

KaLeah reached out and fanned between the garments until she found a pair of brown pants and a loose green tunic. There were dresses and nicer clothes, but she felt most comfortable in simple clothing.

She dressed and strapped on heavy black boots that were at the very end of a long line of shoes. Her own boots and clothing had disappeared, but she assumed that a servant, or one of the service bots must have taken her items to be cleaned and that her sizes had been deduced from those items.

She scrunched up her forehead, realizing that she had not actually seen any human servants within the keep, or the center mansion of the compound. She had only seen machines. She wondered if machines were the only things cleaning her room and picking out her clothing.

She headed toward her bedroom door and the closet lights went off automatically, the doors closing behind her. Before she touched the handle, her bedroom door opened. She watched it curiously and then stepped into the hallway. As she walked, lights flickered to life and then switched back off again.

Although the home seemed to have all the same robots and mechanical conveniences as Professor Wheelwright's had, this home was lacking in character. There were no pictures, no tapestries, no iron sculptures, or trinkets. The space had no human touch at all. Her bedroom had been the only space she'd seen so far with any color besides black, gray, and white.

She headed toward the dining hall, not sure where the kitchen was since they had been served by robots throughout the previous day and evening. Her father was sitting in a chair at the table, reading from some sort of screen.

"Ah, there she is," he said to her, switching off the device and making the screen vanish. "You finally made it down to eat. I assume that means you are all caught up on your sleep now?"

"Yes, thank you," KaLeah said.

"Wonderful," Keldon said. He patted the table. "Let's get you some breakfast before we start the day."

Three service bots on wheels suddenly emerged from a door at the back of the room. They came at the table rapidly and then stopped beside her chair. They were as tall as the table. With a few clicks and whirs, the robot tops popped open, slid to the side, and they raised plates with mechanical arms. They then placed the plates on the table.

There was a steaming hot bowl of oats, toast, some sort of red jam, and a plate of a meat she had never seen before. The last service bot placed a glass of water and a cup of hot tea down.

"Thank you," she said, immediately feeling dumb for thanking the robots. Luckily, her father responded.

"You are very welcome, my dear. I am just so happy to have you here with me after all these years." He smiled at her warmly. "Now, go ahead and eat. I'm going to continue reading if you don't mind."

"Not at all," she said, grabbing utensils.

After breakfast, he suggested they go for a walk around the compound, and then he wanted to show her how to drive a rover.

Before they headed outside, he took two large face masks off a wall and showed her how to wear one. The contraption fit over her face and strapped to the back of her head. The shield covered her eyes, nose, and mouth completely, and two filtered canisters let clean air in from the sides.

"It is a good idea to always wear a mask outside," he said. "I don't think you have been here long enough for the air to do any damage, but it isn't good for long term exposure."

"What's in the air?" KaLeah asked, feeling concerned for the rebels.

"Oh, all manner of things. Nothing for you to worry about." Keldon patted her on the shoulder dismissively.

The guards opened doors for them that led to a long interior hallway. They walked through many twists before reaching doors that led to the outside.

"The air and water in the interior of the compound are fully filtered."

KaLeah assumed her silence had prompted the answer to an unasked question. "What about the soldiers?" she asked, noticing the many men stationed or walking around the yards.

"They have their masks, and yes, their nightly quarters are filtered as well."

"And the diamond districts?" she asked.

"Oh my, yes, they have excellent systems setup there."

"What about the other people that live between here and the districts? There must be more than just the people in the slums? What about people living in their own houses or in the buildings?

He squinted as he looked off toward the buildings where KaLeah knew the rebels were hiding out. "It isn't really any of my concern," he said, shrugging. "This planet is what it is and cannot be fixed at this point. Ah, here we are."

They walked down a dirt path on the outside of the main mansion until they reached a smaller building with a wide opened doorway. There was a boxy, rust-red machine on four large wheels waiting just inside of what Keldon called a garage for them. Two soldiers opened doors for both Keldon and KaLeah, and they climbed into the vehicle.

KaLeah tried to talk to him more about the planet and its people while they drove around the complex, but he evaded most of her questions and she grew more interested in what he was showing her.

The cylinder towers were attached to factories that produced metals, compounds, masks, and food. He showed her underground reservoirs for recycled water, a necessity since most surface water had all dried up.

After a few trips around the compound, they parked the rover and returned to the interior of Keldon's mansion home. KaLeah was relieved to remove her mask, which had started to rub painfully against her skin and restricted her ability to breathe deeply.

"Well, dear child, I am going to retire to my room for a brief nap. I hope you enjoyed the tour."

"I did, thank you," she said, honestly. KaLeah felt good about slowly getting to know her father, regardless of the state of the world.

"And you will return to your room as well?" It sounded more like a command than a request, so she nodded politely.

"Wonderful. I'll see you back in the dining hall in about an hour for tea."

They both began walking the same direction and he veered off toward his room while she kept walking to hers. It wasn't far, but there was enough distance that once she rounded a corner, he was out of sight. She paused at her door after it swung open for her.

She wanted to do some exploring in this strange new place, but she didn't want to go far in case her father came looking for her. She started by going to the room right next to hers. The door didn't open when she approached, so she unlatched a lever and then turned the knob. It didn't open easily, as if it hadn't been opened for a long time. She pushed her shoulder into it until she could get through.

A few small lights flickered to life. It was another bedroom, but this one was adorned with tapestries on the wall, and many colorful rugs along the stone floor. There was a canopied bed similar to hers, but the sheets and curtains were much more clearly feminine instead of the more neutral colors of her room.

She went to the dresser, drawn to an ornate jewelry box that sat on top. It was made from a piece of wood so old that it had turned gray. There were two dragons carved on the top of the box. The dragons were similar but different, staring at one another through a mirror sitting between them.

"Beautiful," she said as she ran her fingers along the dusty carvings.

She lifted the lid of the box. Inside the lid was a small mirror and stuck to that mirror was a small painting. She squinted her eyes. It seemed too realistic to be a painting and it was faded and cracked, but she looked closer and realized that it was an image of her mother.

Her heart raced and she dared not touch the picture for fear of it crumbling under her fingers.

"Is this my mother's room?" she asked the shadows.

Then, in her hunger to know more, she began to dig through the jewelry, and then through the clothing in the drawers and in the closet. She searched the nightstand drawers and desk drawers, and even under the window bench and under pillows.

She didn't know what she was searching for. It was like she wanted to soak up as much of her mother as possible.

Was this all of her mother's belongings? Was there more? Were there notes or letters or a journal that would tell her who her mother was?

She found more pictures in a book that nearly crumbled away at her touch. She knew none of the faces but saw her mother's a few more times in the pages. Tears came to her eyes as she ran her hands over bedding and clothing, as if she were touching her mother's hands.

"What are you doing in here?"

KaLeah's voice caught in her throat.

"Get out of here! You are not allowed to come into this

room. These are not your things! Get out now!"

KaLeah scrambled to run past her father, feeling sick to her stomach with fear and sadness at leaving her mother's things behind.

Why wasn't she allowed? What was happening?

She went into her room quickly, pushing open the doors before they could open for her, and then leaning heavily against them to shut them fast.

She stood there for a few moments with her eyes wide. *Did I just get into trouble*, she wondered?

For some reason, she thought again of being in Belarone Castle when King Erazus had yelled at her and Amirra in his study. She stood up for herself then, but she couldn't bring herself to yell back at Keldon, at her father, even though she didn't know what she had done wrong.

There was a knock at the door, but she took a few steps into her room without answering. The door's automatic mechanism kicked in and it started to slowly swing open. Her father was standing there in the hallway.

"KaLeah, I apologize for my outburst," he said. "I'm sure you realize that was your mother's room. I have not been able to go into that room since she left me all those years ago. I have so many memories, so many terrible memories of her taking everything from me. I admit that I'm already afraid of losing you again, dear one. By seeing you in that room, around her things, it was as if I was afraid her ghost, the memory of her in her possessions, will convince you to leave me too."

He stepped into her room then and grabbed her hands with his. It was a strange feeling, having a father show her any kind of emotion, let alone touch her. She had to stop herself from pulling her hands back. He looked down earnestly into her eyes.

"Promise me that you'll never leave me, KaLeah, my child, my blood," he said. "Tell me, now that we have found each other, you won't leave me alone here as your mother did. Promise me."

She didn't know if she could make that promise. Surrounded by lavishness, being waited on by robots and protected by soldiers, and being offered an entire planet to rule someday, seemed like more than she was prepared to handle.

The memory of Hilip came upon her suddenly, and she felt the blade that he had given her strapped to her thigh beneath her dress. In her heart, she'd intended on returning to Naldash, returning to Amirra, and to Hilip.

She shook the memory off. He was just a man, like any other, and her father was offering her the world.

She was more than a guest to this man. She was his daughter, and she was being given a new chance to have a real father.

"I promise," she said, hoping that it wouldn't be a lie.

He nodded, smiled thinly, then released her hands and backed out of her room. She stood there and watched the doors close.

9 RISKS

Elektra, Felisha, and Rustin walked the short distance to the new hideout without a word, although the air hung heavy with their thoughts.

Whether Elektra wanted to admit it to herself or not, Felisha had saved her life, even though it was Elektra's fault they were having to leave their headquarters in the first place.

To be fair, she knew that she'd be angry too in Felisha's place. Elektra had always been protective of her mother and didn't let anyone new into their lives, until they had moved within the safety of the Morbel diamond district.

Elektra was angry at herself for trusting KaLeah and wished that she would have just left the girl either at the top of that building the day she rescued her or at least left her with Professor Wheelwright. Elektra felt guilty knowing that she'd endangered all of their lives.

Rustin guided them effortlessly through the darkness on a path he'd clearly taken many times before.

Elektra looked up into the sky as they walked, wondering what the moon, or the other planet, Naldash, would look like in a clear sky. She thought that maybe if she could at least see the other planet, it would make part of KaLeah's story feel real enough to trust her.

But with no visible planet, and KaLeah gone, Elektra had no faith in either of them.

They crossed over the ruins of the first diamond district, the place where Rustin had first found her and KaLeah. Beyond the ruins, she finally started to make out a tall structure up ahead of them. It was only a few stories high but looked to be solid and intact.

Rustin gave the door a few soft knocks, then a scrape, then two long knocks. The door swung open, and Colt stuck out his head, smiling at Elektra. Her stomach did a little flip, and she smiled back.

"We were attacked," Felisha said. "They almost took off with Elektra here, but Rustin came along just in time."

Rustin smiled proudly.

"Felisha saved my life," Elektra said, wanting to give Felisha credit. She rolled her eyes and brushed past Colt. Elektra was at a loss but felt good knowing she had tried to thank the girl and give her credit.

Colt furrowed his brows and grabbed Elektra by the shoulders, pulling her into the building entrance.

"What happened?" he asked. "Are you alright?"

"Men heard us and yelled for us to come up," she started. "I gave Felisha my gun and climbed out, stating I was the only one. When they were distracted, Felisha came out and Rustin walked up just in time."

"I'm so sorry, Elektra," he said. "We shouldn't have left you two behind for that long. I should have stayed or checked the area better."

"Then you might have gotten killed, Colt," she said. "Everything worked out fine... except."

"What?" he asked.

"Well, now they know where the entrance to the hideout is. We tried to cover it up the best we could before we left."

Colt was quiet as he pondered that information.

She took a moment to look around the dark interior, just making out the others scattered against walls.

She didn't think it would be a good idea to just completely abandon the hideout. They had years of supplies, live surveillance systems, and a fairly secure location.

"Do you think they'll come back?" Colt asked.

"It was really dark, so maybe they only found the entrance by following our voices. I told them the tunnel was caved in and flooded with sewage, but I'm not sure if they believed me. There may be another option."

"What do you mean?" he asked.

They started walking toward the interior of the abandoned building. There were candles lit, and the rebels had unpacked and settled into corners around the room.

"What if we wait for them and try to recruit them?" Elektra asked, already anticipating the negative response.

"Are you crazy?" Felisha asked, having overheard. "They would have kidnapped you or worse."

"We don't know that," Elektra shot back, defending her line of thought. "What if they are just looking for something bigger than themselves to believe in? You all haven't recruited or joined forces with anyone in a long time. But if we are going to be stronger, if we are going to have any chance of defeating an army, then we need to start growing our numbers."

"And how in dragon's blood do you propose we do that?" Felisha asked from across the small room they were huddled in.

"We split up into teams and we fan out and try to connect to other gangs," Elektra said.

"They'll rob us," Felisha said.

"Not if we don't take anything of value with us," Elektra argued.

"Not take our guns? Then they'll kill us for sure." Felisha continued arguing while the others stayed quiet.

"We take guns, but we don't come up on people with guns drawn. If we go with intent, purpose, and passion, then the worst they will do is say no. But if they say no, then they are saying they accept this world as it is. I don't think anyone outside of the diamond districts accepts this world as it is."

"It's a risk, though," Rustin said, his voice low and calm.

Elektra turned to him. He was the youngest and always the most optimistic. His smile was gone, and he looked thoughtfully at her.

She could see the fear and years of loss in his eyes. He'd lost parents, friends, maybe siblings, and more. She walked over to him and took his hands in hers, seeing a slight smile return to his cheeks.

"We could keep living this way until we all die," Elektra said softly. "Or we could take little risks over and over, working our way up to taking the biggest risk of all, standing up to the dictator. I think it's worth the risk."

Rustin finally nodded and Elektra looked around to the others in the dimly lit room on the bottom level of the dilapidated building.

"We don't want to live like this," Lina said.

"We want to help others get out of living like this," Lainie added.

Everyone was quiet, even Felisha.

"We don't need to decide tonight," Colt said. "Let's schedule rotations for the night. Has anyone inspected the higher levels for vantage points?"

"Yes, the stairs toward the back are solid and lead up to a few more floors," Von said. "All is clear. One can do rotation in four directions."

While they discussed logistics and decided who would do first watch, Elektra thought back to the men out by the tunnel entrance. If she could recruit them, if there were more of them, more groups like theirs just hiding out and struggling to survive, then maybe she could build a small army.

It was risky, but great change took risks. If she was going to change the lives of this world, she would have to risk her own. She always knew it, but it was strange to think it so definitively.

Later that night, Colt gently shook Elektra awake for her shift on watch. She stretched out and then headed up the stairs. She went to peer out of the first window on the third floor, checking the near parameter as far as she could see off into the dark. By the time she'd reached the third window, Colt was coming up the stairs.

"What's the matter?" she asked him.

"Can't sleep," he said, joining her at the window. "Do you think your plan will work?"

She thought about his question, playing out different scenarios in her head.

"Maybe some will shoot at us and chase us off. Some may try to rob or kidnap us. But maybe, just maybe, some will join with us. It's worth a shot. Hopefully, not literally."

They both smiled and looked at each other for a few moments. Elektra cleared her throat and turned to the window, but Colt grabbed her hand.

"I'm glad you found us, Elektra," he said. Her stomach twisted and she tightened her abdomen, pulling her hand gently out of his and setting both her hands firmly on the windowsill, trying to appear dutiful to her post.

"I'm glad that I came too," she said. "I think we have a real chance here."

He was quiet for a few moments, and then he turned to look out of the window with her.

"When do you want to start?" he asked.

"Tomorrow."

❧KaLeah❦

KaLeah woke up the next day with an unsettling feeling in her stomach. As soon as she sat up, the curtains clicked to life, sliding aside automatically to let the dull light in.

She had no desire to go look outside. She missed the blue sky, the green landscapes, and feeling the sun on her skin.

She had barely slept, fretting over getting into trouble. She tried to remind herself that she had been in trouble before. She had been yelled at and punished by a king.

Why did it feel so much worse now, she wondered?

This was a man that half the world despised, and the rest feared. Why should she care so much about him getting angry with her?

Her mother's room was right next to hers. She wondered why her mother and father had separate rooms. She felt pulled to go explore her mother's room more, try to find hints about the person she had been, why she left Keldon, and why she left Denlerack.

She took a quick shower, which was a brand-new experience for her and should have been more enjoyable, like standing beneath a waterfall, but the recycled water smelled of dirt and sulfur.

She dressed, pausing when she grabbed the dagger that Hilip had given her. It was small, made of a cold silver, and was sharper than it was lovely. She remembered the kind of man he was and wondered about how he compared to the man she was discovering her father to be.

KaLeah strapped the knife to her thigh and headed down to the dining hall. Her father was already at the table.

"There she is!" he exclaimed, showing a strange level of excitement. "Come, have a quick breakfast and then I have a gift for you."

They ate in silence, and he had a small grin on his face the entire time, rather proud of himself for some reason. He told her to go get her sword after breakfast. She didn't wear it around the compound, seeing no need with all the armed soldiers. When she came back, he led her through a door and down long corridors, then into a large open room.

The room had high ceilings and the walls were gray, just like everything else in the compound. There were no windows but when he flipped a switch, the entire space lit up. A tall, cylinder robot wheeled out at them from the darkness.

"This is the shooting range and practice hall for me and my top soldiers," he said.

KaLeah looked around and saw guns mounted to the walls in all shapes and sizes.

The robot came closer and KaLeah took a step back. The machine was almost as tall as she was and as round as a grown man.

"Ah, this big fella," Keldon said, just seeming to notice it. "I programed the dueling bot to sword fight with you so you may practice. We haven't had much use for such archaic weapons, but I polished up one of my antiques and now this robot can spar with you."

KaLeah tilted her head, looking at it curiously. The machine had no arms or anything that looked like eyes. The rounded top that looked like a dome was encircled by a narrow glass window.

How would this robot be able to move and anticipate like a human? she wondered.

"I would also love to teach you how to shoot a gun and get some practice in myself. I think it's important for my heir to learn how to make a stand and shoot straight. Which would you like to do first?"

KaLeah looked around the room at all of the guns, and the memory of Prince Bylex being shot and bleeding out on the floor came rushing back. She could still hear the loud boom and wasn't sure she was prepared to hear it again. She looked at the robot then and wondered how fighting a robot would feel.

At least it wouldn't be loud, she thought.

"Let's start with the bot," she said.

He immediately went and plucked a sword from a wall. She hadn't even seen it there amongst all the guns.

Keldon brought it back and flipped a switch on the back of the robot. Doors slid open on both sides and two long, mechanical arms emerged, unfolding at multiple joints, fingers clamping open and shut. He pressed the hilt of the sword into a hand and the robot gripped it automatically.

KaLeah's mouth was suddenly very dry.

"This way," he said.

KaLeah watched the bot follow him as if it were alive, and then she followed close behind.

They went to the middle of an open space where the floor was squared off with red lines.

"Here we are. Just stay inside the lines for an extra challenge, of course. Are you ready?"

Ready? KaLeah was about to practice swordplay with a robot. She did not feel ready.

"Just tap it's shoulder with your blade and it'll kick into action."

She drew out her sword and did as her father instructed. It held the sword in one robotic arm, so she tapped its opposite shoulder.

The machine clicked and clanked to life immediately, dropping the robotic arm that held the sword and twisting fully toward where she had tapped with its sword extended.

KaLeah pulled back her sword just in time. The dueling bot then pulled its sword back and came directly at her as if it could see her clearly.

She realized that the eyes must be within the narrow glass window, meaning that it had much better peripheral vision than she did.

Sweat beaded on her forehead and she remembered how long it had been since she'd truly practiced. Her arm still ached slightly from the bullet wound and she was going up against an unnatural machine.

What if it has some advantage? What if I lose? "Not today," she said.

Maybe it was a machine and something she had never dealt with before, but she had seen a dragon, she had fought an army, and she was the strongest person she knew. She could handle this.

The robot moved straight toward her and swung its sword arm back and forth in what seemed a little haphazard at first, until she realized that it was just warming up.

"Dragon's blood," she muttered, jumping out of its path, and striking its metal head with her sword. The room was filled with the clanging sound from the hit, and she saw a few blue and green lights flash from within the glass window eye.

"Good hit, KaLeah," her father exclaimed.

She had almost forgotten he was there.

"You'll need to hit it six times in order to end the practice session."

"Is it a real sword or a practice sword?" she asked, wondering what would happen if it hit her.

"Oh, well, yes, it is a real sword, but it hasn't been sharpened in some time. I hadn't really counted on it actually landing a hit. I may need to work on it a little more before it is coordinated enough to do any real damage."

As the machine spun and swung toward her, she realized its aim was real enough. Even a dull sword could injure her. She was having doubts about this situation. It whirred toward her again holding its sword inside right.

She met its sword and hit from her right, but the robot arm was stronger than a man's and didn't bounce back with her hit. It came straight at her, so she bounced away and spun around to its left side while staying inside the red marked square on the ground.

It spun again, faster than a human could, and attacked, holding the sword close right, higher this time.

KaLeah realized she wouldn't be able to knock its sword away or spin out of its way fast enough. Instead, she went into full attack mode, trying to run and hit it with her sword, bouncing back and away after each hit, circling it as it kept spinning to meet her blows.

She wasn't counting the hits, but it finally stopped moving, and its arms retracted back into its cylinder body. It seemed to let out a breath as its engines shut down.

"Beautifully done, my child," the dictator said with a smile, slapping her proudly on the shoulder. "I have never seen a girl in all my life sword fight, so this was quite a treat.

I hope you enjoyed my handiwork." He patted the bot, inspecting the surface for dings and scratches.

"How did you learn to create machines to do human actions?" She realized that she was still holding her sword in a combative stance as if the robot could reset and reactivate the duel on its own. KaLeah slowly tried to make herself relax and sheathed her sword.

"My father, your grandfather, used to say you can't trust anyone in your home, so if you want servants, you have to build and repair them yourself. The rebellion was just beginning when I was young, but he'd lived by that rule for years already. He taught me how to build and repair our robotic servants, so there would always be something in the house to cook, clean, serve, and protect me in my sleep. That was before we had the army, of course. Tinkering with machines became a hobby on long, boring days."

KaLeah felt relieved when he returned the robot's weapon to the wall rack.

"We even had robots programmed to drive our vehicles, but I decided to learn and do that for myself. Would you like a lesson later?" He turned his eager eyes to hers.

"Driving the rover?" she asked, part excited and part scared.

"Yes, but let's practice shooting first, while we're here!" He plucked four guns of various shapes and sizes from the racks, then headed to another wall of shelves where he gathered a box.

"This way," he called, heading toward a walled-off space.

When she rounded the wall, she saw long lanes in neat rows, with tables set up at the start of each lane. At the end, she could see outlines of men painted on the far wall. Lights lit them up from head to feet. She had to look twice to make sure they were paintings and not actually living people.

"This is our shooting range," he said, unloading the guns onto one of the tables. He opened the box. "First, we need to load the guns with ammunition, or fire bullets, as we like to call them. They are hot to the touch but only burn you once they get inside the skin. These are dangerous the moment I load and then pull back this lever here, see?"

KaLeah didn't want to get too close, but didn't want to appear rude, either. Although she didn't really want to hold or shoot a gun, she realized that, in this world, her life might be in danger if she didn't learn. She nodded to her father that she could see the lever.

He held up the gun, now loaded, then pulled back the top of it, released the lever, and aimed down the lane. "Now, you just aim carefully, looking down this notch here on top, lining your target up, and shoot." His finger pulled back the switch, or trigger, as he called it, and the gun made a click and whoosh. She furrowed her brow.

"Where is the loud bang?" KaLeah asked.

"Oh, well, my guns don't make that noise. It is very loud in this space, and it is much more enjoyable to practice with silenced guns. We don't need to protect our ears. Isn't that wonderful?"

He rapidly fired at the image of the man at the end of the lane. She noticed how every shot hit the target. She swallowed hard, knowing that no one could run from him without ending up full of holes.

"Ah, that feels better. Now, it's your turn. Let's get a few loaded for you."

He loaded two guns and showed her again how each latch, lever, and trigger worked. She held one up and looked down the barrel, realizing that it lined up exactly like her bow had.

If I can aim a bow, I can aim this thing, she realized. She pulled the trigger and without a sound, without a kick, the bullet shot and hit the painting of the man at the end of the lane.

"Wonderful shot, child. Maybe you don't need practice, after all. You're a natural, just like your ol' father here."

She smiled, feeling proud and happy that she'd now impressed her new father twice.

"It's just like hunting with a bow and arrow," she said.

"Oh yes, of course. I forgot you said you hunted with bows and arrows. How silly of me. Yes, I assume the same method would apply. You are a killer, aren't you?"

He smiled at her, and she didn't know how to respond. Did he know that she'd killed men back on Naldash? She hadn't meant to; it had been in self-defense. She wondered if he was also a killer, and the thought made her squirm uncomfortably.

He went to a separate lane and they both practiced shooting for a while longer. Then he said, "Now, for even more fun, let's go teach you how to drive."

They strapped on their face masks and then headed outside. The rover was already waiting with the engine running. After she sat down in the driver's seat, he instructed her on steering, and how to apply the gas and brake pedals.

"This moves your gear into drive, then back into park once we are done. Just take it slow and gentle, like the first time you rode a draggot," he said.

The memory of riding the draggot came back along with the thrill. It was different, moving the rover into gear, then listening to the engine get louder when she applied the gas pedal. She took it slowly, turning the wheel to keep the tires on the gravel road that went off toward the back of the compound.

The wind from the open windows felt good blowing through her hair, although she was aware of how much better she was breathing from safely inside her filtered mask.

She followed the road as it turned and twisted, and the dictator waved to his soldiers along the path, smiling proudly. They hit a few bumps in the road, but she felt confident enough to start picking up speed.

"There is a smoother stretch up ahead," her father said. "You can really open her up along that road for some speed."

She followed his instruction, and once they left the gravel and onto a smoother surface, she sped things up.

For a moment, she was happy, exhilarated even. She forgot about Naldash, Queen Amirra, Captain Hilip, and even Prince Nikolat. She wasn't concerned about Elektra and the struggles of the rebels and so many others on Denlerack. She ignored the smoke billowing from the towers ahead of her and the protective shield over her face.

She was just a kid, flying through the air, and making her father proud.

But the towers got closer, and the smoke got thicker. She started to slow down, seeing that people were moving up ahead, crossing the road from building to building.

She brought the rover to a slow stop.

"What's that up ahead?" she asked.

"My factories."

"What are factories?"

"Inside those buildings, we create parts for the many machines and robots we use on this planet, dear."

"Is all of that smoke the reason we have to wear these masks?"

"Unfortunately, yes," he said. "We make these too, actually. Although the people in the diamond districts don't need the masks, so I'm not able to sell as many as I used to. Still, a worthwhile investment."

"So, you create the reason they need to buy the masks?" KaLeah was trying to understand or draw some relation to a practice on Naldash, but the entire concept seemed stupid.

"You have a lot to learn about business, child. My grandfather was ingenious about creating diamond districts. Although they are self-sustaining, there are still things they need to purchase from us, like replacement parts and materials. You can't have the kind of sustained advanced life they enjoy without some risk and sacrifice."

"But haven't you, hasn't our family, risked the health of all of Denlerack? The smoke has blocked out the sun and so nothing can grow here. People can't grow food on the surface."

"Yes, but that caused everyone to innovate! Now they

can grow food underground, using the space that was just wasted before. It's very muggy underground, and so the farmers have to buy our masks and filters. We opened up an entirely new revenue stream. I know you are too young and simple-minded right now to really understand how the benefits outweigh the risks, but some day when I am gone and you are ruling both planets, I hope you'll see how to keep innovating through change. It is not as bad here as you are making it out to be."

"Who are those people?" she asked, realizing that the people going into and out of the factory were not soldiers.

"They work in the factories in exchange for food and shelter," he said, smiling.

She stepped out of the rover and started walking slowly toward the people and then turned around. Her father got out of the rover too, assuming that she wanted to look around.

"They are slaves," she said, shocked at her realization.

Her father made a dismissive gesture with his hand.

"I am helping them, and they are helping me."

"Do you pay them? Do you pay the soldiers?"

"Now, you listen here," his eyes went dark and stern. He took a few quick and aggressive steps toward her on the road.

"Their families did not protect them by getting them into diamond districts. They would all be starving in the slums, or worse, if I didn't offer them something better to do. I have created a fine-tuned ecosystem on Denlerack that ensures those closest to me are taken care of. You are now in that circle, and you better appreciate it. Perhaps you need some time alone to consider the alternative."

He stormed back over to the driver's side, climbed inside, and moved the rover into gear. He turned the wheel and sped off past her, then turned around off road and passed her again to head back to the compound, leaving her covered in a coat of dust and dirt.

She was glad for the mask and used the back of her

sleeve to wipe the dirt off the mask so that she could see again.

On the long walk back, she thought about Clegg, the man who had raised her. He never offered any praise or affection, and he had often criticized her for various failings. She thought about Nik and how he'd mistreated her by playing with her emotions.

Maybe I'm just not meant to have good men in my life, she told herself.

Just then, another rover pulled up beside her. A soldier motioned to her from the driver's seat, and she got in. The man, also wearing a mask, didn't appear to be much older than her. He drove her back to the compound without a word.

Being quietly rescued by a sandy haired man brought back memories of Hilip again. She was used to being the rescuer, and yet, Hilip had always been there to support her, just in case.

Sitting in the rover with this stranger made her feel a desperate longing for that kind of dependable presence; someone to make her feel like everything would be alright at the end of the day.

She thanked the soldier, knowing he had probably taken a risk by shortening her father's punishment. She hoped that Keldon wouldn't find out.

The soldier reminded her of Captain Daven. She thought about Hilip's smile and kind eyes as she removed her mask and slinked through the hallways to her room.

Hilip is a good man, she reminded herself. *Colt is also a good man. There are plenty of good men and women in the world, in both worlds,* she thought as she changed out of her dirt-covered clothes.

Maybe there is good in my father too. I can't give up on him. He has only known this world. She wanted to try to get through to him, despite the risks.

The mansion was quiet, and she headed up the floors to her room. Words traveled down a hallway halfway up the stairs to her floor and she stopped, curious.

KaLeah followed the sound down a long hallway until she reached a metal door that had been left ajar. She peeked inside and saw two rows of screens and a robot attached to a table. It was moving but the sound was coming from the screens. On the screens, mouthing the words, was a person. But it wasn't a person. Its movements matched the robot as if it were no more than a puppet.

"Rebels have been spotted attacking the Freely diamond district. Soldiers are on the scene now. All diamond districts should stay in red alert. Keep the gates guarded at all times and your Lord will keep you safe. All hail to the great Keldon, our savior. We give him thanks and praise. We have a new report of criminal activity in the…"

KaLeah backed up slowly and then ran down the hallway.

Was her father spreading lies and fear throughout Denlerack this way? She wondered. She remembered seeing an image of the same person on a screen in the rebel hideout.

Back in her room, she closed the door and locked it, a feeling of uneasiness spread throughout her body, prickling her skin.

10 RECRUITS

"This is crazy," Felisha said, shaking her head. Her arms were crossed, and she was leaning up against one of the walls on the third floor, peeking out to check the grounds the next morning.

"It is risky, but not crazy," said Alister in response. He was stationed at another window.

"We are just supposed to walk out into the wide open, go hunt gangs of thieves and starving criminals, and politely ask them to join up with us?" Felisha asked. "That sounds pretty crazy to me."

"Are we thieves and criminals?" Von asked quietly. HE was sitting cross legged in a dark corner.

"Exactly the point," Alister said. "We can't assume that everyone out there is bad. There must be more people like us who want to take a stand but just don't know how."

"They are hungry and just trying to do their best to survive this world every day," Rustin said, looking out from another window. "Maybe some of them turn bad, but most of them just need the opportunity to do better."

Everyone nodded in agreement and Elektra smiled. She had kicked off the conversation as soon as everyone had woken up. Felisha seemed to be the only one still hesitant, although Lina and Lainie hadn't said anything.

"What do you girls think about going out and recruiting?" Elektra asked the twins.

They turned their blonde heads to each other, as if reading one another, and then turned back to Elektra.

"We need to do *something*," Lina said.

"And we are willing to take the risk," said Lainie, nodding, sending her blond waves bobbing.

"Great," Colt said, clapping his hands together. "Let's eat and head out today in pairs. Lina, go with Alister, Lainie, with Von, and Zuri, with Felisha. Rustin, you'll come with me. Elektra, I'll let you decide if you join one of their groups or head out on your own. It isn't my place to tell you which team to join."

Elektra smiled, knowing that he wanted her to join with him.

"Thanks Colt," she said. "I'd like to stick with you and Rustin, if that's alright."

He couldn't hide the smile that came to his lips.

"That's fine," Colt said. Then, to the rest of the group, "Let's head out in four separate directions and travel for five days, gathering as many supporters as we can. On the sixth morning, turn back for here, picking up the recruits on the way or have them meet you here. Do not tell anyone where you are from or where you are headed unless you know without a doubt that they are joining with us and not just trying to steal from us."

"How are we supposed to know that?" Felisha asked.

"Zuri will know," Colt nodded at Zuri, who nodded back. Felisha rolled her eyes.

"Let's eat and pack up," Colt said.

Everyone started moving, but Elektra stayed at the window to keep watch over the surrounding land.

The ruins of the original diamond district were larger than she had realized when she'd met Rustin there the other night. Scaffolding had collapsed into it, but she could make out the original design. It made her wonder, briefly, how her mother was doing back in Morbel.

She could imagine her mother sauntering through the lively marketplace or staying in to watch her baby grow in his little tank. A mix of jealousy and irritation filled her. She wanted people on the outside to experience the same quality of life that she had given her mother—a life with more food, more comfort, and less death.

Elektra felt good about their next move. She knew they were going to succeed in recruiting people to their cause. There may be a few roughnecks and bandits, but she hoped that the small teams could handle the dangers and bring an army back with them.

They all took turns hugging one another and saying farewell. Lina and Lainie had tears in their matching blue eyes. Elektra never had a sister, so she couldn't exactly empathize. An image of KaLeah came to mind and she quickly brushed it away with bitterness.

She held back in the shadows, not wanting to assume she meant enough to anyone there to get a hug or even a goodbye. Elektra tidied up the space around her after she finished packing up.

To her surprise, two pairs of arms came at her from two separate directions, wrapping her up into a hug. Blonde loose waves of hair billowed around her. Her first instinct was to freeze up, but then she smiled and settled into the twins' hugs.

"Be careful, Elektra," said one.

"And take care of our friends for us," said the other.

"I will. You two be careful too. I'll see you in a few short days."

She, Colt, and Rustin watched the pairs head off in different directions. And then they closed the door to the abandoned building and headed out also.

They walked northwest beyond the ruins and across dry, desert dirt. She could see rows of buildings to the southwest as they walked. She wondered if anyone was in those buildings, watching them cross what appeared to be wasteland. There were low-lying bushes scattered about the landscape, but no trees or cover, other than remnants of metal and concrete that had sunk into the mud and hardened over time.

"Can people live out here?' Elektra asked.

"People have found lots of ways to survive on this planet, yes," Colt responded.

Nobody spoke for a long time after that. She wasn't sure if it was from exhaustion, sadness, or nerves.

After walking for some time, they sat beside a cluster of bushes to eat a snack and rest.

"Can I try out your wings?" Rustin asked.

Elektra smiled, although her body immediately clamped up. Different scenarios, many of them involving Rustin getting hurt, flew through her mind. Then, she remembered that KaLeah had taken to the wings easily and quickly. Of course, KaLeah was older, had quick reflexes due to years of swordplay, and could hear dragon spirits.

"Yes," Elektra said after some hesitation and against her better judgment. "But you'll have to be careful and follow my instructions exactly. Initial flights shouldn't really be done outdoors."

She looked out over the deserted, dry land, and up into the condemned buildings lining the edge of the desert. The buildings seemed so far away, and there was nothing but dirt stretching out in all other directions.

"You have to stay low so that if something goes wrong, you don't have far to fall. It isn't as easy as it looks."

"How long did it take KaLeah to learn?" Rustin asked.

"Not long, but we were indoors and KaLeah's... different. She took a bullet and managed to still fly, land, then walk, and fly some more."

They walked over to an area further from the buildings, as if she was preventing him from flying into them even though they were hundreds of feet away. She took the pack and wings off. She helped him get into it and then loosened the harness a little. He was young and thin, but still wider than she was.

She walked him through controlling the engine, getting lift, adjusting direction, and lessening the speed to lower back to the ground.

"Maybe just start by floating here for a little bit," she said, turning on the fans and stepping back. She wasn't sure why she wanted to be so protective of him, being that he's the one that saved her twice now. She couldn't help but think of him as a little brother—a strong, sweet, and clever little brother.

"Woah," he said, lifting off from the ground. The brown wings opened slightly behind him.

"Looking good there, Rustin," Colt said. "I wonder if these would give us some sort of advantage going against Keldon's men."

"It's a good idea until you are being shot at and can't out-maneuver a well-aimed bullet," Elektra responded. "We could use them to get over a wall in order to open a locked gate. There may be an opportunity at some point. Maybe even on this recruiting mission of ours."

Rustin started to fly a little higher and move out further into the desert. A shiver flew up her spine watching him floating away. She looked out over the land and to every side of them, making sure no one was around.

He was out in the open. She had been out in the open hundreds of times before but watching him made her worry.

"Not too far, Rustin. We don't know who is out there. There's no cover."

"Woo-hoo!" Rustin called back in response as he cut loose across the land.

"He needs to come back." She turned her worried eyes to Colt.

"Rustin, come back!" Colt yelled out, using his hands to create a megaphone. His deep voice carried across the land, but it made Elektra even more nervous.

She started to chase after Rustin then, afraid that someone could have heard Colt. Elektra yelled at him to come back, come down lower, and that it wasn't safe. Rustin's laughter came back at her in response as he whirled himself across the open land.

"You stupid kid," she said, frustrated and afraid.

A shot rang out.

"Not again. Rustin, get down! Now!"

Hearing the shot too, Rustin finally started to descend just as she heard another shot. She ran to where he was descending and protectively pulled him as low as possible, back toward cluster of prickly bushes.

"Are you alright? Are you shot?" she asked, looking him over from head to toe for blood.

"I'm fine, I'm fine, I'm good," he said.

Colt stood beside them stunned, looking off into the distance. "We should get out of here," he said. "I couldn't tell where the shots came from, but I don't think they came from the buildings. Maybe we should head closer to them for cover."

But Elektra wasn't listening. As soon as she saw that Rustin was unharmed, she turned on her heel and marched right back out into the open.

She had noticed how the dirt sloped up into a long hill bordering the area where Rustin had been flying. Something told her that the shooters were on the other side of that hill.

"Elektra! Where are you going?" Colt yelled, but she kept walking.

She was angry. All of the anger toward her mother for choosing a comfortable life and a bubble baby, anger at KaLeah for abandoning her, and anger at the dictator who had destroyed this world, flowed throughout her like liquid fire in her veins.

"Where are you, cowards?" Elektra yelled out over the deserted landscape. There were some smaller buildings and trees back along the edge of the clearing, but she saw no one.

"Who shoots at kids who can't defend themselves? You

are what is wrong with this planet. You are the reason that we will never heal, we will never prosper." She kept walking, hearing Colt calling from behind her.

"Dragon spirits curse you in your cowardice," Elektra continued yelling. "You refuse to fight to protect and improve your own cities, your own lands, but here you are, willing to shoot at kids from behind cover. Were you threatened by a kid with wings?" She was nearing the dirt hill with no fear or hesitation. "Come out and face me. I bet I can take you without your guns. You all hide behind your guns but there's no skill there, no strength. I'm sick of all of you acting like guns prove how tough you are, but at the end of the day, you are nothing more than bullies. You are a waste of humanity."

She stopped walking then, breathing heavily as her anger started to abate. A few short bushes on the hill started to move, and she realized that people were walking out from behind them, and onto the dirt all around her.

She saw the men first, leading the way, in their brown and green pants, guns latched to their belts, a few gripped in their hands but lowered. Muscles seemed to be under every tan shirt, and then she saw some women and older children walking behind them. They were all covered in dirt with long, unkempt heads of hair.

There were dozens of them now. Elektra stood still and waited for the leaders to approach. Two men and one woman came out ahead of the rest of the pack to stand before her.

"They were warning shots to scare you off of our land," the man in front said. He looked impossibly strong and towered over her, with a long, black bushy beard.

"No one owns land except for the dictator and the diamond districts. Are you members of a diamond district?" she asked.

"We don't recognize the dictator as our leader," the man answered nonchalantly.

"I don't either, but it doesn't change the fact that he still controls everything!" Elektra clenched her fists.

"He doesn't control us." The man raised an eyebrow.

"He would if he showed up with his army," Elektra said.

"Spirits curse his army," the woman said from behind the man. Then she made a spat sound and motion toward the ground. She had red hair that was long and wavy all the way to her waist.

"What are you doing here?" the bearded man asked Elektra.

"My friends and I are looking for help. We want to overthrow the dictator and take back this world."

The three people in front of her started to laugh, then the others who were close enough to hear, also started laughing, repeating her comment back to others in the crowd.

Colt and Rustin who was still wearing the wings, slowly walked up to stand beside Elektra.

"Is this your army, child?" the man asked, laughing even louder at his own joke.

Elektra was so used to feeling angry, that she found herself surprised to be feeling something else while these strangers were laughing at her—hope.

She started to smile.

"No, we don't have an army," she said. "We have a handful of rebellious kids, orphaned by the dictator. We have lost parents, siblings, friends, and livelihoods. We have lost the chance to walk the streets safely, to build homes, and to even feed ourselves. We have hope that we can find other people who are as angry as we are about what Denlerack has become, but who are willing to stand up with us and fight to take our world back."

The bearded leader crossed his muscular arms across his chest. "We are doing fine here on our own. We take care of ourselves."

"But what about everyone else," Elektra said, taking a small step forward. "What about the orphans and children of this world who don't have safe places, or food to eat, or clean water to drink? What about the people who turn to gangs and violence to survive?"

The man looked off into the distance then, thinking, or maybe feeling, the truth of what she said. He was silent for an uncomfortably long time.

"What's your name?"

"I am Elektra Dean. I was born in the slums of Sarda. These are my friends, Colt and Rustin. Our other friends are out trying to get more people to join us."

"We do not reveal our names so that no one may tell others about us. We three are the leaders of our tribe. We live and farm mostly underground, although our numbers have spilled above ground, and it is getting harder to stay hidden. Come with us and we'll discuss your futile plans over tea."

The group began to disband then, moving toward the hill they appeared from. Colt leaned in to whisper in her ear. "Do you think this is safe?" Colt asked.

"We knew there would be risks," she responded. "Look at all of these people.   There may be many more underground. These are the people we came to find, Colt. These are the people that we need if we are ever going to stand a chance against Keldon."

The three of them walked behind the three tribe leaders up over the crest of the hill that she could now see stretched on for miles, the perfect cover blocking visibility from the buildings.

Colt gasped when he reached the top. She stepped up beside him and froze.

Below them was an intricately camouflaged village. Each detail, from the trap door entrances, to pipes meant to capture rainwater, perfectly matched the color of the desert floor. Shielded by the long hill, it would be impossible to spot the community there without being right on top of it.

People were dropping down into the holes, pulling the trap doors closed behind them.

"Wow," Rustin said from beside her. "Do we get to go

in those?"

Elektra saw that the leaders ahead of them were waving them forward, toward one of the entrances. She led the way down the other side of the hill and onto the elaborate layout, watching her step to avoid falling into open hatches.

"This is impressive," she told the bearded leader, who was holding open a trap door. The other two leaders had already climbed down.

"As we dig out new burrows, we use the dirt to make the hill higher," he explained. "You are the first in many years to have made it this far alive, young one."

Elektra swallowed down the nervous lump in her throat and hoped that he meant they were safe with him going forward.

Take a risk and extend trust, she reminded herself.

She, Colt, and Rustin climbed down into the burrow, with the bearded leader going last in order to close and lock the trap door behind him.

She knew their secret existence was fragile. The trap doors were made from metal building scraps and painted brown. It wouldn't be too hard to accidently stumble upon them if anyone actually ventured out beyond the crumbling cities and into the wide-open desert. Which, of course, she knew the likelihood of that was slim, unless if you were a band of rebels looking for recruits.

The tunnels were wide at the bottom of the ladder entrance and well-lit with electrical bulbs all strung together. The others joined her and then the bearded leader guided them through the tunnels.

They walked by open doorways to other tunnels and rooms, where she saw people constantly working. Some people were patching cracks and reinforcing the tunnels, others sat in small groups mending clothing.

She saw a room with people sitting still but moving their legs, which seemed to be moving giant wheels.

"What are they doing?" Elektra asked, stopping to peer into the room.

"Creating energy for the lights, air filtration system, and water pumps," he said. "It takes continual work to make this space livable."

"What about food and water?" she asked.

"We pump water up from deep underground, and we created domes to capture moisture and convert it to water. We direct what we need to garden areas deeper underground where we can take advantage of naturally occurring moisture."

There were people everywhere. It was as if all the people in one diamond district had been shoved down into a tiny hole in the ground. People sat and worked in tunnels, so that she had to step over or around them. They passed so closely she had to hold her breath to keep from smelling whatever they'd recently eaten.

The tight space made her uncomfortable. She was used to finding corners to hide in back at home in Sarda, but there was no free nook within this underground world. Every space was occupied by a person.

"We are here. Have a seat anywhere," the man said.

They walked into a cave of a room. There were others, including the other two leaders, sitting around the edges of the room on tufts made from the same fabric as their clothing. Elektra sat down low and uncomfortable on one.

"As you see, we are safe and living a consistent life here," the bearded leader said, motioning to the room.

Elektra thought for a moment. He would not have invited them in if he wasn't at least a little intrigued by their plan.

"I smell mildew, mold, cold dirt, and dinginess," Elektra commented. "There are other foul, unsanitary smells down here, and although you have food, the dark circles under everyone's eyes and sunken cheeks tell me that it is not enough." Elektra looked around, making eye-contact with everyone. "I empathize with your struggle, and I commend the success you have had in surviving and protecting these people. But I feel we all deserve something better. We are all hard workers, but we are also fighters. We can take this place back for ourselves. We can live together, in peace, above ground. We can take out the dictator's polluting factories and help this planet recover. I don't know all of the steps to making this a reality, but I do know that the first step is removing the dictator. And we can't do it without a lot more help."

The three leaders looked at one another for a few moments, and then back at Elektra.

"We do want a better life for our people, young one," the bearded leader said. "But Keldon's men have guns. They are trained, organized, and live only for themselves. I fear that you ask us to sacrifice more of our lives for a very slim chance of success."

"But what if we can succeed?" Elektra said, passion in her voice. "What if enough of us come together and we find enough weapons? Do you want to die someday regretful of not taking a chance that could have improved the lives of your people? Or do you want to die knowing you did everything you could?"

"It seems that in either scenario, I die," he answered. "But in one of those scenarios, my death comes quicker than in the other."

❞Nikolat❞

Nik and Ash were walking again. Every day felt longer and more pointless than the day before. He was starving, thirsty, and tired. His shoes had almost been worn through.

He kept trying to picture himself flying the ship home. The image of him soaring across the universe was the only thing that kept him moving forward most days. He tried not to think about the fact that he wouldn't know how to fly the ship, even if he managed to get past the soldiers guarding it.

When he wasn't trying to envision the future, his mind was replaying the image of his mother walking out of the campfire flames.

"Who were those people back there?" he asked.

"Friends," Ash responded.

"You know, you aren't much for sharing information. Where are we? Who are these people? Where are we going? Maybe I wouldn't feel so angry if I had a little bit more information about the situation I'm in." He kicked a rock off into the night.

"There are many scattered tribes of people across Denlerack struggling to survive," she said without a hint of attitude. The girl always just spoke plainly, without emotion or inflection, even when he tried to push her. "Some people are good, helping others when they can. Some are bad, stealing and hurting others to survive."

"Where are the people like me," Nikolat asked, tapping his chest. "Where are the rich, the military, the royalty? Can they help me get back home?"

"They could, but they won't," Ash said. "There are some wealthier families spread out and living in diamond districts."

"That sounds nice," Nik scanned the dark horizon for one of these districts. "Why don't we go to one of those for food?"

"They will not feed you. They will not let you in at all. We are unimportant to them." Ash shrugged in front of him as she walked.

"I get it," he said. "We didn't let common folk into the castle either."

"The common folk are ignored here," she said without emotion. "It is as if the people inside the diamond districts are different types of people completely. Anyone outside of the districts are either soldiers working for the dictator or considered animals. I am an animal."

"So, there are no sweet mothers there who would see you and want to take you in and care for you?" Nik considered his own mother and whether or not she would have fed a hungry child who stumbled upon the castle, or if the soldiers would have shooed the child away.

"Not at all. The mothers would fear me biting and scratching them, and then taking all they hold precious, like their food and clean water."

"What about this dictator? Who is he? How did he get put in charge?" Nik asked.

"He comes from the wealthiest family of all," Ash explained. "His parents died, and he stepped in to supply the diamond districts. They pay him for soldiers to protect them from the animals in the slums. If anything breaks down, he owns all the factories that produce parts for the sustainability systems that create the filtered air and water for the diamond districts."

"Does he care about how disgusting it is here?" Nik curled up his nose. "Somedays, it seems harder to breathe, you can't see the sky, the water is filthy, and nothing grows. How can anyone in charge accept these conditions?"

"There is no one to pay him enough to fix it. He will not use his own wealth to improve the planet while he is making money off of its demise. He also knows that there is a backup planet he can go to once this one is completely uninhabitable."

"Naldash?" Nik stopped in the dirt, but Ash kept walking.

"Yes."

"I see," he said, moving to catch back up with her. "Well, we wouldn't let him have Naldash. Our armies would band together."

"He has advanced weaponry. No one on your planet can stand against the weapons of this one."

"How do you know what weapons we have?" Nik asked, curious but also feeling a little defensive. Who was this girl and this dictator to think they could take his world so easily?

"I have heard," she said bluntly.

"Well, maybe I'll take back some weapons from here and we'll just replicate them ourselves. We will defend ourselves against this dictator."

"Stop, quiet." Ash suddenly came to a halt in front of him. He nearly ran into her.

"What? Why?" he asked, dropping into a whisper.

"Something up ahead," she said quietly.

Nikolat rolled his eyes, growing impatient with Ash. "If we keep stopping at every little sound or bonfire, we'll never get off this rock. Let's just go another way."

He strained to see anything through the darkness. He swore that Ash had some special ability to see where he couldn't. Finally, he thought he saw a path in the dirt landscape and headed down it.

"Stop. Wait!" she called to him a little too loudly. But he kept walking, taking one careful step at a time through the dark desert.

"Let me go!" Ash yelled.

Nikolat dropped down to the hard ground, trying to blend in with the landscape, hiding from whatever had grabbed the girl.

"What do we have here?" A man's voice carried over to him.

"A delicate little creature," said another man.

"Woah, not that delicate! How about you keep those fists to yourself, little girl."

"I'm not a little girl!" Ash yelled back, clearly struggling with them.

"Let's take her back to the compound and put her to work in the factories," said the first man's voice.

"Good idea," agreed the other.

"Leave me alone! Let me go!"

"Come on, kid. It's hard work, but you'll have food and a bed at night. It's better than running around out here."

Nikolat listened to the soldiers drag Ash away. He got up and quietly followed, curious and thinking.

They took her to some sort of wagon, but he saw no draggots. In fact, he hadn't seen many animals at all on this planet. There were lights on the wagon, and he saw the two men. They were wearing masks that covered their mouths, noses, and eyes, and were lightly armored.

The weapons he now knew were called guns were strapped to their sides like small sheaths. One of the men put a metal device around Ash's hands and then lifted her into the back of the wagon, clipping the contraption onto some part of the cart.

"There, you aren't going anywhere except back to the dictator's compound with us now."

The men started to climb into the wagon, and he heard a loud rumble as the machine came to life.

They are going straight to the compound, he realized. *That's where the ships are. That's where I'm trying to get.*

Without hesitation, he jumped into the wagon's path, having to close his eyes against the bright lights as it steered toward him. It halted.

"Are you crazy? Who are you?" the men shouted.

Nik's brain scrambled to try to come up with a story.

"I want to be a soldier," he said back to the men, his eyes still blinded by the wagon lights.

Before he knew it, both men were out and standing on either side of him, spinning him around.

"He's unarmed."

"Looks like slum trash to me."

"Do you think there are any others? Is this an ambush?"

"It's just me," Nik said. "I want to be a soldier for the dictator."

"We only take diamond district boys," said one man.

"Yeah, and only the ones who messed up in the district. No one volunteers to join us."

"That's what I'm doing," Nik said, trying to keep a disrespectful tone out of his voice. "I'm not from the district. I just want something better than this."

"How much trouble could we get into for this?" one man asked the other.

"Yeah, it's risky, but we always need recruits. Listen kid, we'll take you back with us, but you have to say that you are from the Morbel district if anyone asks. Don't give any other details. Say you got hit on the head or something. You got it?"

"Yes, thanks. I got it. I'm from Morbel." Nik nodded at them.

"Get into the back of the rover with the girl," one of the soldiers said.

Nik did as he was told. He walked around and climbed up into the back of the wagon they had called a rover. It was open to the air around them while the two soldiers sat in an enclosed front cabin.

He sat across from Ash, who was glaring at him with her hands locked together in front of her and tied with a cable to a metal loop on the rover.

He smiled and shrugged in response. Maybe things didn't end like he'd planned, but at least he'd be getting to a ship sooner than expected. That's all he really wanted.

He wasn't responsible for what happened to Ash now. Maybe the soldiers were right. Maybe it'll be better for her with food and a bed at the end of every day. It had to be better than sleeping in a hole in the ground and foraging for food and water.

Things would be better for both of them now, he told himself as they bounced along to the compound.

&❧Elektra❧

Many days later, Elektra, Colt, and Rustin were standing in the middle of the diamond district ruins. Their feet ached from walking, and they sat around an open fire hoping to help guide back their friends and any new recruits.

Elektra rang her hands together, massaging the backs of her fingers and her palms. She was nervous, not certain if the conversations she'd had with the three leaders in their underground village, if the hope she sold, and the desperation shared had been enough to convince the strangers they had met that this was a worthwhile cause.

She wondered if the other rebels had any luck, and she

was anxiously looking forward to seeing them all again.

This was their only chance. If Colt's friends came back alone, then there were very few options left for them. They could try to sneak into the compound after dark, they could try to dig their way in, they could try to assassinate the dictator and probably be killed in the process.

There was no scenario she could imagine that would result in anything other than their deaths if they proceeded alone.

What if the rebels didn't come back at all, she worried?

What if they had been captured or killed already, shot down by gangs, or robbed and beaten for the food they carried? Would Colt want to go after everyone that was missing? Would she go with him to rescue his friends, or would she try to track down and assassinate the dictator herself? Could she leave Colt on his own?

Questions she couldn't answer and scenarios she couldn't help but imagine kept playing out over and over in her mind.

"Are you alright?" Colt asked.

"Yes, just anxious," she answered.

"Me too." Colt reached out and touched her arm.

"Me too," added Rustin, lacking his carefree smile.

Just as the sun was beginning to set, she heard them. Sounds came from every direction. She stood and turned, turned, turned, just kept rotating to every angle to watch for the people she heard coming.

"Do you hear them?" Elektra whispered.

"Yes," Colt responded, sounding surprised.

"Sounds like..." she trailed off.

It sounded like people were walking toward them from all directions. It wasn't just the rebels. It wasn't just the rebels plus a few recruits.

There were hundreds of people coming across the land toward them. Hundreds of armed recruits all coming to support them. Elektra smiled and let out a small cry of happiness.

She had an army after all.

She waited with a smile on her lips as the large, bearded leader, flanked by the other two, walked up to her. He nodded.

"Hello again, young Elektra" he said.

"Hello," Elektra responded, breathlessly. "Thank you for joining with us."

"You gave me a lot to consider. If my time is finished, I will go out fighting for what my people deserve." He stood up straight and tall, his voice increasing in depth and volume. "And if I am to die, let the people of Denlerack know that I, Ludwig Clandenstine, died protecting the future of the Mud Shadows people."

Elektra's chest felt as if it might burst. The man had just told her his name and the name of his people. He trusted them. She smiled even wider, and he went to help his people get organized.

She turned and faced the direction of the compound with determination. "We're coming for you, Keldon," she said, feeling stronger than ever. "We're coming."

11 BATTLE GROUND

It was too dark to see the smoke in the air, but Nikolat could feel it getting thicker and thicker. Every once in a while, the rover's lights would give him a peek of where they were headed. He could see towering structures lit up in the foreground and assumed that the smoke came from there, but he didn't understand why.

"Is there a forest fire?" he asked Ash. "I haven't seen any trees here."

"The smoke comes from the factories," she said.

"What are factories?" The word was strange to him.

"The dictator uses machines to make other machines, parts, materials, and large amounts of heat are used. Smoke is cast off into the sky, killing the planet." She spoke without looking at him.

"It does seem harder to breathe," he admitted. "Is that why the soldiers are wearing those masks?"

"Yes. This planet is dying. The smoke is hard to breathe."

"Why doesn't the dictator do anything? Why doesn't he stop it?" The solution seemed so obvious to Nikolat. He couldn't see himself doing something on Naldash that would result in destroying the very world he wanted to rule.

"Money," Ash answered, looking back toward the lands they were leaving behind.

He looked back too and briefly wondered if there were family members she was leaving behind or friends she would miss. For a moment, he was puzzled by why the child had helped him at all, and he felt a little bad about her being captured.

"Money and power," he said, nodding. "Those things are important to us on Naldash, too. At least, they are to me."

The dictator of Denlerack had both. He had an army. He was the king of the entire planet; no pesky kings continually trying to take what was rightfully his. Goosebumps appeared on his arms just thinking about becoming the king of all of Naldash.

Yes, he understood that much of the dictator very well, indeed.

The rover slowed down, and he heard men yell across the night to each other. Then they were rolling again through two tall gates.

There were artificial lights everywhere. Nik had never seen so many lights at night. There were sentries at every tower, which surrounded the compound. Soldiers marched with their weapons, casting curious glances when they passed.

"Long guns, rifles, semi-automatic weapons that are capable of firing multiple rounds over and over," Ash said, nodding toward the soldiers.

"I've never seen such weapons. We only had swords on Naldash."

He was concerned about how well he could pretend to be a solider, since he had no experience using guns. He wasn't sure how long it would take him to find and learn how to use a spaceship well enough to escape the planet.

It was clear that he'd be separated from Ash, although she probably didn't know how to fly one either.

The rover came to a sudden stop.

"Recruit! This is you. New recruit reporting to Barracks number three."

A soldier approached the rover on foot, wearing a gray uniform and the same masked headgear.

"Come along then," he said to Nik.

Nikolat jumped out of the rover and glanced back for a moment to catch Ash's eyes as the rover took her off toward the factories. He gave her a nod of thanks, not sure if she was able to see it in the dark. Then he turned and followed the soldier into the barracks for food, rest, and to start planning his interstellar escape.

❞Elektra❝

Elektra still couldn't believe how many tribes had come to join the fight against the dictator. They had all been hiding out for years, some underground, some moving from place to place, some staying in dilapidated buildings, and everyone struggling to survive. The rebels were able to convince them that fighting to get their world back was better than continuing to hide in the shadows of a broken world.

The rebels and tribes set up camps on and around the ruins of the first diamond district. Every morning, Elektra stepped out of the building that she and the rebels had stayed in that first night out of the tunnels. Tribes had set up fabric tents around and within the ruins, while others had started to fill in other abandoned buildings in the area. The rebels had all returned, but the tribes still trickled in, coming in larger groups that slowed down their progress.

Elektra climbed up onto a piece of rubble wall. She looked out around her, admiring the camps set up in every direction. Most tribes had sent a little over half of their men and older boys, and some women. They were armed, and Elektra felt exhilarated and hopeful looking out among them.

Finally, people were lining up for the same reason she was. They were committed to making this world better.

"There aren't enough people, and there aren't enough guns." Felisha came up behind her with her arms crossed.

Elektra rolled her eyes and tried to keep herself from snapping back. "It'll be enough," Elektra said, reassuringly. "We need a strategy and a strong plan. We won't just storm the front gates."

"But that's exactly what's going to happen. We can't bring along an army this big without them seeing us coming." Felisha waved her hand out over the crowds of tribes who were just starting the day. "They will literally hear us before they even see us. We are putting our guns against their guns. A lot of us are going to die."

"No, all we needed was an army to go against Keldon's army," Elektra said, hanging onto her hope. "We will match them gun for gun. We will take them out."

"Underground farmers and tribesmen are not going to take out a well-trained army, Elektra," Felisha said, flipping her brown hair. "His army practices shooting, exercises, and basically trains to kill on a daily basis. We can't just walk this untrained horde up against them."

Felisha turned to her and put her hand on Elektra's shoulder. It was strange to receive that physical touch from the young woman, and she froze as if trapped by the hand somehow.

"We want to defeat the dictator, we do, but we're going to have to come up with a better strategy than this," Felisha said. "We can't match them gun for gun. We can't match their firepower, their accuracy, or their experience. These people we brought out from hiding will simply be a minor inconvenience to the soldiers, a nuisance, or a distraction from their workout routines. And at the end of it, we'll all be dead, and Keldon will be sitting pretty in his fortress doing whatever in dragon's blood he does, since he clearly can't manage a planet."

Something tapped at the back of Elektra's mind, and she

took a few steps back. *What did she say?* Elektra saw the dictator sitting in a window, high above the attack, and safely watching as his soldiers decimated Elektra's friends.

He would be there, like Felisha said, safe from any bullet. She wanted to push Felisha off the edge of the wall, but she knew in her heart the girl was right.

They would battle, shoot bullets across the land at each other for maybe an entire day and night and still, the dictator would be safe behind a wall.

Felisha had called it a mere distraction. Her little army of rebels would be nothing more than a distraction to an otherwise dull day in the life of a rich leader.

Unless…

"What if *we* were the distraction?" Elektra asked.

"What do you mean?" Felisha raised an eyebrow.

"What if we created the attack as a diversion to cover some of us sneaking inside the compound to track down and assassinate Keldon?"

"Assassinate is a nice way of saying kill," Felisha said, crossing her arms. "You talk big, but have you ever actually killed anyone? I think not."

Elektra looked away but didn't answer.

"Hey, I haven't either," Felisha said. "This is new for all of us. We've seen people killed. Some of our own family members were killed for this and we are trying to finish what they started. But none of us actually know how. We don't know how to pull the trigger at a man staring us in the face."

"Then we are going to have to learn, Felisha." Elektra turned to face the girl standing across from her on the foundation wall. If we don't do something, then we'll just keep living like this until we die, or until the planet dies. Look at this place. This is the most amount of living people I have seen outside of a diamond district, and they can't live together at numbers like this without draining all of the limited resources this dying planet can provide. Something has to change. There is no great dragon spirit that is going to drop down from the clouds and save us. We are the only saviors this planet and these people have. We either try to take control of the planet, or we die trying."

"We'll either die slowly and starving, or fast and flying," Felisha said, curling up the side of her lip, looking at Elektra. "Do you think we could make a few more of those sets of wings?"

Elektra cocked her head to the side. "We could try, yeah. We'd have to scavenge for some materials, maybe see what we have back in the hideout."

"Let's do it then," Felisha said. "Maybe we can get an advantage in the air."

"Maybe," Elektra agreed.

Elektra and Felisha set off toward the hideout. She felt strange, as if she and Felisha were suddenly friends in all of this. The girl had definitely changed her attitude toward Elektra, but she wasn't going to get her hopes up that they would be friends, especially after being abandoned by KaLeah.

Never again, she told herself.

Trust and relationships were not something she would be trying to establish anytime soon. Her goal was to save the world from collapsing and help people; but she didn't have to be friends with or trust those people.

Hours later, the small band of rebels she'd come to know were all working together, sewing fabric, and welding metal to create wings.

"These are just gliders if we don't build engines," Alister said, working on a pair of wings using upholstery ripped from one of the couches in their sitting room.

"That will be the next phase," Elektra promised. "Rustin is scouting buildings for more machine parts. Once the engines are built, everyone will need to collect waste for fuel." Elektra's cheeks flushed. So far, they had been reverse-engineering the wing engines, but she'd not yet explained the fuel source.

"What waste?" Alister asked.

"Biowaste," Elektra said, avoiding eye-contact.

Colt let out a big laugh and Elektra couldn't help but smile. "The wings run on poop?" Colt asked.

"That is part of the brilliance of the invention, yes," Elektra said, selling it. "You don't have to dig for coal or scour for other natural resources. You create your own fuel."

"I'm going to skip the wings," Felisha said, looking pale.

Alister just looked more thoughtfully at the engine he'd dismantled in order to create more. "I see it, now," he said, then he continued at his work.

"And if we can't find enough parts, we'll come up with something. At the least, we can soar down from the fortress walls if we need to climb them." Elektra tried to picture the schematics in her head.

"Are we climbing walls?" Colt asked, looking perplexed. "What exactly is our plan? We haven't discussed—"

"I know we haven't, but I'm thinking about plans right now," Elektra said, interrupting him. "I'm sure some of the other leaders are thinking about plans. We should pull them all into a meeting and come up with a few of the best approaches to pursue. Felisha is right that we can't match them gun for gun. We have to have a strategy of some sort, and I'm not a military mind."

Colt looked at her with a smile. "But you are clever, he said. And you've pushed us all further than we thought we'd ever go. I trust you."

Elektra's cheeks reddened more, and she accidently pricked her finger with a needle, getting blood onto the fabric she was sewing. She looked away to hide her embarrassment, out across the field where the tribes were practicing their aim without wasting ammunition, cleaning guns, and trying to create other makeshift weapons.

She didn't understand the emotional responses that kept flooding throughout her body. She was giddy, excited, frustrated, and fighting with a deep distrust of not just Colt, but everyone.

What does Colt really want with me, she wondered? All the

men that Elektra had ever known had only wanted things from her and her mother. Even her mother's new husband, seemingly a nice man, only wanted a lovely and submissive wife.

She realized she was scared that Colt would leave her just like KaLeah had. She tried to push the thoughts and feelings back down inside of her.

The fields around them were filled with people, but she worried that it might not be enough. If she was the only one truly driving them all into battle, then if they died, it would be her fault.

She swallowed back the bile creeping up her throat, trying to convince herself that this was the best decision. There was no other life if they were not living freely in a world where everyone could eat, drink, and do more than just survive.

She looked back to her sewing and tried to think about finishing the task at hand. They needed to focus on one step at a time. First, build the engines for the wings for as many people as possible. Then, teach the people how to fly. And then they needed to finalize their plans.

Elektra, Colt, and Alister met later that day with the leaders of all the tribes who had come to fight. They stood on top of the ruins, both symbolically, and because it was the only place not crowded with tents.

Scattered around them, the tribe folk were making wings, throwing knives and axes, and cleaning guns. A few people passed out water and food, ensuring that everyone stayed as strong as possible, while rationing supplies.

Ludwig and the other two leaders of the Mud Shadow people were there, along with six leaders of other tribes, and a few gang leaders and smaller groups who came to join, but who were not leading any people. They had just been on their own, foraging and surviving for years.

"Thank you, everyone, for gathering to fight with us," Elektra started, greeting the people standing on the ruins with them. "I'd like for us to discuss strategies. I'm concerned Keldon's army is going to hear us all coming. A group this large is going to be loud and slow. So, I'd like to propose that I, along with Colt, go ahead and sneak into the compound. We can try to get to the dictator while our rebels and village folks head in for the attack."

"Wait one moment, now," said Ludwig, his voice booming. "That isn't a solution for our size. What you are saying is that you want us to walk into the mouths of hungry doquers, while you and your friend tiptoe around on the off chance of not only getting into the compound, but finding, and killing, a well-guarded dictator."

Murmurs began to rise among the group.

"It's just one idea, Ludwig, in order to take advantage of the fact that our large group will be a distraction. If Colt and I can get in and assassinate the dictator, then we can end this thing before anyone gets hurt."

"But we still need a plan in case you fail, and we face the army, which is what we came here expecting to do," Ludwig said.

Another man stepped forward. He had blond hair and a light beard. "We need to take inventory of weapons and list the challenges we expect to encounter, before we even begin to discuss strategies," the blond man said.

"We have guns and ammunition only for the people in our tribe," the fiery haired Mud Shadows woman said. "We have created enough wings for a third of our tribe and half of those have engines completed."

"There are fifty people here who do not belong to tribes, and each of the six tribes that came have about forty to eighty people."

Elektra leaned forward to see who had spoken up. It was an older woman with long, white hair. She was glad the woman had counted, as Elektra hadn't thought of doing that.

"Do we know how many soldiers are at Keldon's compound?" she asked, looking around. Elektra sighed, realizing how unprepared she was to lead this group into a real battle. "Will anyone volunteer to go count them?"

A few men and one woman from different groups stepped forward.

"Thank you," she said. "Please take wings with engines and fly to the buildings on the outskirts of his compound. Report back with a count as soon as you can."

The four of them nodded and walked off together.

The rest of the groups confirmed whether or not they had enough weapons and ammunition, and how many had wings. Some leaders began to negotiate trades with others to try to ensure everyone had some kind of weapon.

"Here is my proposal," Elektra said loudly, trying to get everyone's attention while also trying to sound confident. She took a stick and drew the compound fence in the dirt.

"We gather in the alleys between buildings in this area. Those with wings climb to the rooftops. We have a lot of open dirt to cross, and so, we'll be very visible."

"Why don't we go at night to avoid being seen," someone dressed in black from another tribe asked.

"Yes, we will gather before dark and attack," Elektra confirmed. "But even in the dark, we are crossing a wide-open space. We have to assume they will be able to throw lights on us. Hopefully, they will also have lights on themselves, and we can aim clearly at them. I have seen lights at the compound at night, so I know it's highly visible."

"I'll send a man to confirm," Ludwig volunteered.

"Great, thank you. I suggest that people with guns go in the first wave, to protect the people who only have knives and axes. Winged fighters with guns and engines fly in above them to draw attention away from the ground troops. And then the wings without engines follow behind. Ludwig, I was hoping that you and a few other leaders from a few other tribes, would lead the groups into battle. And while that is happening, Colt and I will already be inside the mansion interior, seeking the dictator out."

The leaders were silent, except for a few who quietly

discussed among themselves.

"I am open to other ideas," Elektra offered, wanting to clarify that she wasn't trying to be in charge of the entire attack. "But I think we should come to an agreement today, so that we can start preparations to march south."

She had never led a large, coordinated effort. Elektra had grown up without friends, a community, or even siblings, to protect. She realized the other leaders standing with her were way more experienced, and potentially, had better ideas.

The longer they were silent or discussed amongst themselves, the more fearful she was of them all changing their minds. Going up against an army was a daunting endeavor, and she worried that their convictions were waning.

Finally, Ludwig stepped forward. "I agree to this plan," he said.

Other leaders started speaking up. Everyone agreed and wanted to return to their tribes to lay out the details.

Elektra was relieved and she smiled at Colt.

"Who will co-lead each wave of the tribes with me?" Ludwig asked even more loudly.

Elektra stepped back, letting Ludwig coordinate ground and air advances with the other tribe leaders. She was proud knowing that she had not only pulled everyone together, but also gotten them to agree to her plan. She was coming into her own as a rebel and a rebellion leader. *Professor Wheelwright would be so proud of me*, she thought, smiling to herself.

Word spread quickly through the camp that Elektra and Colt would go ahead of the hoard to sneak into the dictator's mansion beyond the compound gates, flying over the wall with their mechanical wings. The rebel army would follow and engage with the enemy soldiers from land and air under the cover of darkness.

While the tribes attacked the soldiers, Elektra and Colt would try to find and assassinate the dictator. She knew it had to be done, but Felisha's words kept ringing in her ears. Elektra had never actually killed anyone. Would she be able to shoot the man in the back?

Deep down inside, she didn't expect to survive the assassination, but she refused to say the words out loud or discuss their chances with Colt. He'd been a rebel for so long, she hoped he was as committed to risking his life as she was. Although, the idea of losing him created a hollow, painful place inside her chest.

Word reached the building where their friends were staying before they'd returned from the meeting. Elektra walked in first, followed by Colt and then Alister.

Felisha stormed up to them, shoving Elektra out of the way. "You are not leaving us behind, Colt!" Felisha screamed from inside the doorway. "Absolutely not. I am going with you."

"We can take one of you with us," Colt said, trying to maintain a calm tone.

"Then you're taking me," Felisha said.

Colt turned to Elektra, who shrugged slightly. She didn't have a preference of who came with them. Three was better than two, but no more than three. More than three would draw too much attention. They had to fly in and then get past an unknown number of guards quietly.

"I want to come," Rustin said.

"No," Elektra and Colt both said simultaneously. Elektra smiled and tried to soften the response. "I'd feel more comfortable with you here, Rustin, watching out for Lina, Lainie, and the others."

"Oh, I see," he said, nodding, but turned his brown eyes down, disappointed.

"I'm afraid more than three would be too many people. We want to be stealthy out there. We'll have to sneak past soldiers to get into the compound." Colt looked around at everyone.

Lina and Lainie were agile and silent, but they didn't strike Elektra as killers. She needed someone who wasn't afraid to pull the trigger. She looked back at Felisha again.

"Felisha should come with us," Elektra said, trusting her instincts. The woman was wild and angry about something, clearly with the energy to aim and fire without question.

Felisha nodded curtly in response and got up to pack her things, grabbing a pair of wings that Alister had made and fueled for her. Felisha turned her nose up and placed them gingerly with her bag, as if the human fuel would somehow get on her.

Elektra stifled a laugh.

"Are you sure we shouldn't come along too? Maybe to at least follow you for a while?" Alister asked.

"No, thank you, Alister," Colt responded. "I think it's better if you all attack with the tribes, together, making sure that everything goes smoothly. You will speak for us in the camp. Just please be careful on the battlefield. Those soldiers have had a lot more target practice that we have."

The rebels began to prepare, and pack supplies and the wings they had built together, complete with the engines.

࿐

A few days later, the tribes were ready to start heading south to the compound. This time, Elektra didn't hesitate or hang back in saying goodbye. She wrapped the twins into an embrace, she shook Von, Alister, and Zuri's hands, and then she went to say goodbye to Rustin.

The young man smiled and hugged her so hard he lifted her up off the ground.

"You be careful out there, you hear me?" she asked, looking him directly in the eyes.

"I will," he said. "You be careful too. You have to come back alive, so you can help lead us to creating a better world."

Elektra smiled, but her heart was heavy. They were sneaking behind enemy lines, and she fully understood the risk involved. She wondered if he did too, or if he was still too young and innocent to realize that she may not be returning at all.

Elektra, Colt, and Felisha said goodbye to Ludwig and the other leaders who would be commanding the various waves. While everyone organized into groups to begin the journey, the three rebels took off ahead of them.

They left the open area around the ruins and headed into the building alleys. They found an old building with a sturdy interior staircase and climbed it to the roof.

Colt's and Felisha's wings were a patchwork mix of various green and brown fabrics, and scraps of black, gray, and gold metal pieces. Elektra stood on the ledge, spread her brown wings open, listened to the gold gears and rods move into place, and switched on the engines.

She felt at home in the air. "Are you both ready?"

"As I'll ever be," Colt said, climbing up on the ledge beside her. He and the others had only had a few days to practice.

"I guess," said Felisha, looking out at the landscape instead of at her.

Elektra took a deep breath and then leapt.

They flew for a day, stopping on rooftops to rest. They arrived on the outskirts of the dictator's compound as darkness was falling. They landed on a roof and ducked low, to stay out of sight, while they surveyed the land.

There was a tall fence that went all the way around the compound, and intermittent towers manned with armed soldiers. There were soldiers at the gates, soldiers guarding entrances of the interior buildings, soldiers by a handful of spaceships and rovers, walking from building to building, exercising out on the grounds, hand-to-hand fighting, and a few of them shooting at narrow targets in roped off sections.

Elektra let out a long breath she'd been holding.

"There are so many more than I thought. And why are they all wearing masks?" She had noticed that the air was slightly thicker and harder to breathe, but she had never considered making masks.

Maybe she should have made masks for everyone instead of wings, she thought.

Felisha backed away from the edge and started pacing. "We always knew they were trained soldiers, Elektra. We always knew there were more of them than there were of us. But we'll find a way in before our troops get here. I will find the dictator, and I will kill him, or die trying."

Elektra turned and saw that the young woman had her gun in her hand, and she was unloading, reloading, unloading, and reloading it over and over. She walked up and put a hand on Felisha's shoulder.

"Are you alright?" Elektra asked.

"It's just, it's just that I'm so close," Felisha said. "I never thought I'd be this close." Her eyes glistened with tears. She looked up and met Elektra's curious gaze.

"They killed my father. We were at a protest, protesting the dictator's pollution of the planet, and something went wrong. Shots rang out and I ran. I lost my father, and when the smoke cleared, when the soldiers had gone, I went back and found him dead in the street. He was all I had, and he was gone. Colt found me and brought me to the hideout. And I hid there. I've been hiding for years but now I'm finally here. I'm so close, and there are thousands of soldiers blocking him from me. It's not fair."

Tears started to stream down her face, but she didn't make a sound until she took a deep breath, sniffing the snot back and wiping away the tears.

"I can't fail at this. I can't fail my father."

Elektra understood, although she wasn't doing this for her own family specifically. She hadn't known her father, and her mother was safe with her new husband and new baby within a diamond district.

Elektra was doing this for future children who would be born in the slums, unable to breathe the air. Would they have to put masks onto babies someday? Would the poor be able to make the masks themselves?

No, she wasn't doing this for revenge. She was there, about to risk her life to save the dying planet of Denlerack and everyone on it. It wasn't just about the people who had died, or the people who were struggling to live.

It was about the children who would be born into a world, into a situation, that was not their fault. The children had no choice. Whether they were born naturally in the streets or bubble babies grown in protective tanks, the babies had no choice in the matter.

She hadn't had a choice.

She pictured her younger brother floating in the sack of goo in the diamond district living room. He was innocent in all of this, but he would continue carrying on the problem. He would be too comfortable to worry about everyone else on the other side of those walls.

The world would continue to get worse, and she wanted every baby to have the same chance at a beautiful life where they didn't have to worry about the next meal or if their lungs were strong enough to handle the polluted air.

Looking back out of the window, she was scared. But quitting now was not an option. There was no going back.

They made their move the following night, as soon as they saw their friends' signals on the horizon. They soared into the camp over a spot they'd discovered, which had no lights. They cut across the night sky unseen, then landed silently on the roof of the inner building. Based on everything they observed, the inner building made the most sense for Keldon's quarters.

It seemed like an unadorned mansion to her, and they needed to find a way inside, a roof access point. Without using any light, they crept along the roof until they found a door that led to a ladder down into the building.

"Are you ready?" Colt asked them, looking from one young woman to the other.

They nodded in unison, but Elektra felt that even though her mind was ready, her heart would never be ready. She froze for a moment, unable to leave the safety of the roof entrance. Her heart pounded harder in her chest.

Colt grabbed her hand and squeezed. She looked at him and he smiled. She couldn't explain why she felt better knowing he was there with her.

They climbed down the ladder, pulled out their guns, cocked them, then opened a door and walked into the dictator's home.

It was simple, dark, and bare. There were a few lights illuminating the hallway, but very few pictures on the walls. No decorations at all. The floors were hard, black stone and cool air hit their faces as they started to make their way down the hall.

They had absolutely no intelligence. There was no way of knowing which floor he could be on, the layout of the building, if there were guards, or where his bedroom was. All they could do was walk quietly and peek into rooms along the way. Most of the rooms were empty, with maybe one bed and one chair, but clearly unused.

It was as if he built a house for a family he never had, Elektra realized, almost feeling sorry for the man. It seemed like he was living a very lonely life.

She assumed the bedrooms would be along the floor they were on, while kitchens, dining halls, and gathering rooms laid below.

What else would this guy have, she wondered? *An armory, a library, a workshop?* She hoped they'd be able to find him before covering every inch of the cold mansion.

Finally, up ahead, they saw a door was slightly open with a triangle of light spilling into the hallway. They froze, standing next to the wall, and watched as a shadow passed across the light every few moments, as if someone were pacing inside the room.

"Is it him?" Elektra asked, although neither of them could know. Her mind started racing. "Do we just run in? Tell him to freeze and ask who he is first?"

"No," Felisha said. "If there is a man in that room, then that man is Keldon, and we need to put him down immediately before he can call in his soldiers."

"I think we should wait. Let's talk about this," Colt said.

"Dragon's blood," Felisha said, then she kicked herself off the wall, held her gun in front of her, and stalked down the hallway to the open door.

"Spirits," Elektra said.

She and Colt held their guns ready and followed fast, trying to step lightly.

Felisha stormed into the room, kicking the door open, pointed her gun and yelled.

"Keldon, you killed my father!"

Shots rang out and both Elektra and Colt immediately drew back into the shadows of the hallway.

A woman in a flowing, cream-colored dress came running out of another doorway in the hallway, going straight into the room where Felisha was.

"KaLeah?" Elektra asked, doubting what she'd just seen.

Elektra regained her composure and ran to the entrance of the room, peering from behind the open door, just out of sight.

She saw KaLeah on her knees, her cream skirt slowly soaking with blood while she looked over Felisha, lying dead on the floor.

Elektra started to go into the room, but Colt held her back, either out of fear or protection.

A shadow moved and she heard a man stomping across the floor and yelling.

Keldon wore a long, elegant red robe over a black tunic and pants. He grabbed KaLeah by the throat, lifted her off the ground, and stepped over Felisha's body, slamming KaLeah into the nearest wall.

"How do you know this woman?" he yelled.

KaLeah grabbed for his fingers at her throat, unable to respond. There was blood trickling down from Keldon's left arm, and Elektra realized that Felisha must have gotten one shot off before he gunned her down.

"I…met…on…road…here," KaLeah managed to

sputter out.

"Liar!" he screamed, spit flying and hitting her in the face. "You've been planning this all along, haven't you? You've been in a plot to destroy me. She has wings like the ones you were wearing when you showed up here. Do you think I'm an idiot?"

Elektra was so fixated on what was happening, surprised and shocked to see KaLeah in the mansion with the dictator, that she didn't hear the boots coming up from behind them.

Multiple sets of arms grabbed and disarmed her and Colt, then pushed them into the room.

"Are you alright, my Lord?" one soldier asked.

"We found these two in the hallway. They were armed." The other soldier reported.

"How did they get in here, you incompetent fools?" Keldon accused, his hand still holding KaLeah to the wall. "Lock them up and then scour the compound for other rats. This has ruined my evening. Get someone in here to clean up this mess."

He callously motioned to Felisha's body on the floor with one free hand, while the other one clasped KaLeah's neck.

Elektra stared at KaLeah, who seemed to be trying to say so much through her eyes.

Everything has gone wrong, Elektra realized.

Additional men came in and started to drag Felisha from the room. The soldiers holding Colt and Elektra pulled them back to the hallway.

She saw Keldon finally throw KaLeah to the floor.

"Lock this one in her room," was the last thing she heard Keldon yell as she was drug down the hallway. Three more soldiers ran past them, and Elektra heard voices on their communication devices.

"Rebels spotted outside the compound," said a man's voice.

Elektra took a deep breath and closed her eyes. The rebels were almost here, and she'd failed them all.

12 IMPRISONED

Soldiers ran in and out of the barracks gathering weapons. Nik had changed into a uniform with a new pair of black boots. He was lounging in his tiny bed, admiring the clean new boots on his feet.

"What's happening?" he asked, sitting up.

"We're under attack by locals," a soldier said before running back out again.

Nik was new, so he wasn't sure if he was expected to grab guns and join in the fray or not. Not wanting to draw any negative attention to himself, he went ahead and gathered up the gun and holster he had been provisioned, but he didn't try belting on the holster. He just clutched them both together in one hand.

He ran out into the night and was greeted by the sounds of gunshots. It wasn't a familiar sound and caused him to clench his teeth and jump unintentionally. He wanted to appear unfazed, but it was hard to do with the sound of explosions filling the air. He ducked instinctively, not knowing where the shots were coming from or headed toward.

While he crept across the grounds, more and more lights

popped on across the compound. The mansion in the middle was lit up more than he'd seen it so far. It reminded him of a castle keep.

This would be my best chance to go check out those spaceships, he realized.

Instead of following the other soldiers to the front lines, which seemed to be at the gates, he veered off toward the shipyard. It was dark but he could see the lights reflecting off the shiny metal ships. They were spherical in shape, like balls that had been somewhat flattened. They seemed to be about the size of four or five rovers. When he reached the first one, he held out his hand and trailed his fingers along the smooth exterior. It was cold to the touch but sparked to life, lights flickering across its surface.

"Spirits," he said, pulling his hand back. He looked around to make sure that no one had noticed the ship switch on.

"How do I get into it?" he wondered out loud.

A door started to drop down as if the ship had heard him. He walked up a ramp and into the ship, feeling more and more confident.

His confidence sunk when he sat down and looked at the control board. There were hundreds of lights, knobs, levers, and buttons. He could see out through the windows onto the shipyard and into the sky, but he didn't know which combination of steps would get the ship moving.

For a moment, he wondered if Ash would have some insight into how to fly one.

Don't be stupid, he told himself. That little girl knew how to get across the deserted wasteland and that was it.

I need to find instructions or talk someone into flying this thing for me, he realized.

It wasn't a draggot. He couldn't just kick it and steer in the right direction. He leaned back in the pilot's chair, feeling defeated.

"Hey, what are you doing in here?" a man yelled from behind him. Nikolat jumped up, startled, but then put his calm, charming expression back on. "I thought one of these would be useful against the intruders," he said.

"You are not to take any action unless explicitly ordered to do so. Is that understood?"

"Yes, sir," Nik said, standing at attention.

"Besides, these carry limited artillery we need to conserve for the Naldash invasion. We don't need something this powerful against meager rebels. We can take them out easily enough. You need to get back on the line. Now."

"Yes, sir," he said, trying to sound respectful.

He followed the soldier out and to the line of battle, his mind trying to figure out how to solve the puzzle of flying one of those machines off the planet and back home without being caught or shot out of the sky.

⅌KaLeah⅋

KaLeah watched helplessly from the window in her room as hundreds of people stormed the compound gates. Soldiers shot continuously from high towers and from behind the gates, and she cringed every time a rebel fell.

Elektra and Colt had somehow managed to find enough people to storm the dictator's compound, and yet, it would do them no good. KaLeah assumed their plan must have been to find and assassinate her father before the actual battle began.

It was a good plan and would have been better if she'd been aware of it. While she sat in her room, still wearing the blood-stained dress her father had given her, she wasn't sure if, or even how, she could have helped.

She felt torn.

Back in Belarone Kingdom, she would have grabbed her sword and headed to the battlefield to protect the royals, especially Queen Amirra. But here, she didn't know which side she would fight for if she ran out onto the battlefield now.

Keldon was her father, and yet, he had choked her, thrown her to the floor, and locked her in her room. He had yelled at her for trying to learn more about her mother, and he had made her walk back to the mansion from the factories for asking too many questions.

She came here thinking that she would discover a secret goodness within this man. KaLeah was the young woman who had rescued a princess in search of the man who had raised her. She fought in battles to protect the kingdom. She let a phantom dragon transport her across the stars in order to save an entire planet.

And she'd failed.

She was supposed to save Naldash, but instead, she'd tried to learn how to drive rovers and shoot guns with her biological father. She had tried to see if he could be changed, if he could take better care of this planet and not invade hers. But instead, she'd abandoned her friends to come up with their own failed attempt to assassinate the dictator.

"Keldon, my father, is not a good man," she said to the world beyond her window. "I made a mistake coming here. He doesn't care about me. He will never care about me. I am only his last chance at a legacy, a way to control the planets beyond his own death."

Saying the words out loud helped her feel more connected to them as truth. It was a hard reality to face. She touched Hilip's dagger at her thigh, seeking confidence in her decision, as if he were there with her. She could see his reassuring smile.

She knew that if she stayed beside the dictator, he would only continue to abuse and control her. There would be no bonding. She would grow cold, distant, and angry until she became exactly like him. He would eventually die, and she would become the new dictator of a dead planet.

Where are your friends?

KaLeah heard the words placed inside her mind.

"Anissa La Alani? Is that you?" KaLeah hadn't heard

the phantom dragon or seen her since she'd been sent to Denlerack. She'd assumed that she was completely alone on this quest.

Not alone. You have friends. Where are they?

She pictured Felisha lying in a pool of blood on the floor in her father's room, and she closed her eyes. She'd failed that girl.

"I should have been the one to assassinate Keldon while I had the chance. Even if the soldiers killed me for it, at least Denlerack would be free and Naldash would be safe."

Elektra and Colt had been dragged off, but she didn't know where they kept prisoners. If she rescued them, that meant she would never see her father again. She would never get him to change or have a relationship with him.

I could stay and slowly try to get him to change his ways, she tried to tell herself. But the memory of him leaving her to walk back from the factories, the memory of him slamming her against the wall and throwing her to the floor, came rushing back to her mind.

"He's beyond saving, isn't he?" she asked the phantom dragon.

Yes.

"Even if I can rescue Elektra and Colt, how would I get out of here? How do I get back home?"

Look beyond.

KaLeah was looking out of the window, so she looked past the soldiers battling with the invading rebels and out past the barracks buildings. There she saw black orbs shimmering in the night.

"Spaceships."

Everything clicked and she knew what she had to do.

She tore off the dress stained with Felisha's blood and grabbed black pants, a tunic, and boots.

Although cumbersome, she buckled on her sword and the holster belt that her father had given her with two guns. She looked at her black wings hanging in the closet. She strapped them on and fastened them across her chest. She stepped back and looked at herself in a mirror. This was who she really was.

"I'm a fighter, I'm a protector, and I am a fatherless-daughter. I determine who my family is and isn't from this point forward. It's time to rescue my friends."

The soldiers had locked her in her room, and she wasn't sure if anyone was standing guard. The windows didn't open since the outside air was contaminated. She would have to figure out how to break her window quietly.

KaLeah grabbed the blankets and pillows off her bed and laid the blankets on the floor under the window. She held a pillow against the glass with one hand. With the other, she pressed a gun into the fabric of the pillow. Luckily, her father had given her two of his special, silent guns they had practiced with in the armory.

She cocked it and pulled the trigger, the bullet shot out through the glass. She lowered the pillow and saw that the glass had a hole in it but had not shattered.

She holstered the gun and drew out her sword. She pulled back and then stabbed the hole with the tip of the sword, thrusting it through and splitting the glass into millions of pieces. Glass shards trickled down onto the blanket and the ground below. She hoped that everyone was busy with the battle and that no one noticed the falling glass.

With her weapons safely holstered to her, she launched herself out of the window, silently gliding across the hot air in her black wings. She landed, pulled in the wings, and ran across the yard.

She wasn't sure which soldiers knew about the assassination attempt or that she'd been locked in her room, but she had to take the chance. She stood up confidently and walked up to two soldiers heading from the gates to the armory.

"Tell me where the holding cells are!" she called to them, keeping her distance.

One looked her way and squinted in the darkness,

hesitating for a moment.

"Over there," he pointed. "Stay low, miss," he said. "Bullets are flying everywhere. You should be in the mansion with your father."

"I'll head back shortly," she said, trying to sound truthful.

The building looked like many of the others. In fact, she would have assumed it to be another barracks building, except for the two soldiers standing guard outside. She stormed up to them with her chin held high.

"They need you out there!" she screamed, making her voice sound panicky and childish. "What are you doing? My father called for men! Didn't they tell you?"

"No, I thought we were winning. It's just a few rebels," one soldier said, scowling down at her.

"Hundreds more have come up behind them. They have weapons I've never seen before. We need more men." KaLeah felt proud of her theatrics.

"Right," he said. Then to the other solider, "Come on, let's see what's going on. No one is getting out of here."

The men ran off toward the gates and KaLeah waited until they disappeared in the darkness before slipping inside.

The building had two rows of barred cages running the length of each side of a narrow hallway. It was exactly like barracks, except with bars separating the beds.

She ran through the aisle until she saw Colt and Elektra, standing across from one another in separate cells. They were holding the bars and talking, but stopped when she ran up, breathless.

"I'm sorry," she said, looking at Elektra whose eyes went wide. "I'm sorry, but I'm here now. I'm with you and I'm getting you both out."

❧Elektra❧

Elektra couldn't believe her eyes or her ears, but there in front of her was the KaLeah she had rescued from thieves in Sarda. She looked aged and defeated, but she had her sword, guns, and the wings that Professor Wheelwright had given her.

"Why were you in the mansion with Keldon?" Elektra asked, not able to believe this was somehow the same girl. "Why did you leave me with the rebels? Why did you abandon us?" She yelled the last question, feeling the anger bubble up.

"I'm sorry for not telling you, Elektra. Keldon is my biological father. I thought that maybe I could get through to him. I thought we would bond, and he would listen to me, but you were right all along. He isn't just a bad leader; he's a terrible person. But I couldn't kill him myself. He's my father."

Elektra couldn't speak. *Her father?*

It all made sense: why she seemed so mysterious, why it felt like she was hiding something.

It didn't quell the furious hatred in her heart.

"Get out of my face, traitor," Elektra said. "I don't care who he is or who you are. Felisha is dead, and your father killed her. You left us to fight him on our own. You sided with him and now our friends are out there dying."

"He is my father," KaLeah yelled back. "I had to find him. I had to see who he was for myself. It was the only way. I'm so sorry I wasn't able to save Felisha, but I didn't abandon you. I'm here now."

Elektra took in another breath in order to yell at KaLeah some more, but the girl's eyes went wide, as if she saw a dragon spirit. She clutched both sides of her head.

"They're coming back," KaLeah said.

Elektra looked to the doors but didn't hear anything. "How do you know?"

"The dragon spirits are warning me. I have to hide. Be quiet. Don't draw any more attention."

KaLeah ducked into a small shadowy corner of the barracks jail. Elektra turned to the door. It was three breaths before a soldier crashed through.

He said nothing, but glared at her and then at Colt, looked casually around the empty cells, and then left the room.

A few moments later, KaLeah was back in front of her cell with a smile on her face.

"I found your weapons and your wings while I was hiding back there. Can I let you out now so we can all leave together?" KaLeah didn't wait for an answer and started to unlock the cells.

Elektra narrowed her eyes but accepted her rescue. She didn't want to trust KaLeah, and she didn't want to like her, not after what she'd done. The girl handed her and Colt their weapons and wings. They armed themselves, strapped on the wings, and headed toward the only exit.

The same man who had stormed in to check on them was standing guard right outside.

"Don't kill him," KaLeah said. "He doesn't know any better. This world is all he's ever known. Can we just injure him?"

Elektra nodded curtly in response. She wasn't keen on killing either if she didn't have to. She shuddered, thinking about how many were out there fighting and dying right then and there, while the three of them planned their escape.

"We should make a stand and fight," Elektra said, not able to stand the thought of her friends dying while she ran away."

"Elektra, I've seen battles first-hand," KaLeah said. "You never go in behind enemy lines without a strong plan. Your plan to break in early and attack my father, the dictator, was good, except for Felisha. You didn't plan for her to get emotionally involved and fail to obey orders. I did the same thing once and it almost got me killed. We would be gunned down in an instant out there if they knew we had made it inside their front lines. We need to be cautious. There is a rover outside. We'll use my silent gun, take out the guard, and escape to the airfield in the rover. Agreed?"

Elektra hated taking orders from the girl who had betrayed her friendship—or at least, potential friendship. Her anger was mixing with the stirrings of logic and her brain felt muddy.

She gritted her teeth and nodded again.

"Let's go," KaLeah said. "On my lead."

KaLeah snuck out of the door first and shot the guard behind one of his knees. Elektra ran up behind him as he fell and shoved a handful of dirt into his mouth so that he couldn't call for help.

KaLeah smashed his communication device. Colt motioned that the coast was clear, and they ran to the rover, KaLeah jumping into the front seat.

"I've never actually been in one of these before," Colt said from the back seat. KaLeah hit the pedal to the floor, and they spun off into the night.

"Do you know where you're going? I can't see anything," Elektra said.

"I'm keeping the lights off, so no one notices us," she said. "I'm not sure if I could figure out how to turn them on anyway."

They pulled right up to a large, black sphere-shaped ship and came to a rough stop, jolting everyone forward in their seats.

"Sorry, I didn't get too many lessons at this," KaLeah said.

"Did you get any lessons on flying that?" Elektra asked, glancing up. "How do we get inside?"

They jumped out of the rover and approached the ship.

"Wow, a Shy Girl Mach 10," Colt said, running his fingers along the edge. Lights began twinkling to life across its surface. "We have to ask it to let us in," Colt added.

The ship must have recognized something in the comment because a door unlatched and started to drop down to provide a ramp into the interior.

Elektra and KaLeah both turned to him.

"You know what this is?" Elektra asked, impressed.

"Do you know how to fly it?" KaLeah added.

"I read about them back at the hideout," he said. "They had manuals on older versions that Keldon's father had designed. There were instructions on how to fly them in order to recruit men like me, but of course, nothing about the actual technology used to design them. I know which buttons to press. It's mostly voice-commanded."

He smirked and Elektra's stomach knotted. She smiled at him and then they all climbed the ramp into the ship.

It started to come to life around them. Lights and switches all began to light up and blink increasingly. It was overwhelming.

"Are we escaping in this? What are we doing here?" Elektra asked, stopping in the doorway.

"I want to fly you both to the other side, out of the compound, drop you off, and then head back to Naldash," KaLeah said.

"But I thought you were sent here to stop the dictator, your dear father, from invading your home planet?" Elektra said, raising one eyebrow.

"I failed." KaLeah shook her head back and forth. "How can I kill him? He's my flesh and my blood. But I can't stay with him either. I have to find a way to protect Naldash if and when he sends his army there. I know more than I did about this world, about the weapons, and about him. I'll figure something out, but I need to do it from there. I need to go home."

Elektra looked at the young woman and heard the sincerity in her words. It would be up to her and Colt to try and stop Keldon's army here on Denlerack, and if they failed, KaLeah would have to protect her own planet.

"Then let's get out of here," Elektra said, nodding. Colt?"

"I'm on it," he said. "KaLeah, come over here and I'll give you a lesson on takeoffs and landings. Luckily, all you have to do is chart your course verbally and the autopilot will guide you. It's really pretty simple. Press this here and this closes the hatch."

There was a slight clicking noise, and Elektra turned to see the trap door closing behind her.

Two hands slapped down onto the ramp, and one of Keldon's soldiers pulled himself in through the opening and rolled himself onto the floor. Elektra jumped back and pulled her gun on the man.

"Woah, woah, there. I'm just trying to get a ride out of here," he said.

His voice was smooth, and Elektra felt an instinctual nudge to shoot him, which she ignored to his benefit.

"Nikolat?" KaLeah asked from across the ship. "You're alive? You're... here?"

The man she'd called Nikolat took in a deep breath as if he'd just come back to life. His sharp blue eyes opened wide as he stared in disbelief. He started to move toward KaLeah, but Elektra blocked the path with her body, her gun aimed at his chest.

"Oh, huh-uh. You stay there," Elektra said.

"KaLeah... I can't believe you're here." Nikolat seemed to swallow deeply. "It's so good to see you. How did you get here?"

"How did I get here?" KaLeah asked. She took a few steps toward Elektra but stayed behind her. "The dragon transported me here through the blue flames, same as you. I thought she'd killed you at first, until she used the same method to send me here."

"Please tell me you're going back to Naldash in this? I have to come with you," the young man begged.

"I don't think so," Elektra said.

"Listen girl, I don't know who you are, but I am King Nikolat of Belarone Kingdom on Naldash, and I am going home," he said, staring her in the face.

There, she thought. *There is the killer I knew was behind those pretty eyes.*

"*Prince*," KaLeah said, correcting him. "Prince Nikolat. Your sister is queen now."

"We will see for how long," the prince mumbled.

KaLeah drew her sword and stalked up to the man, pressing the blade point to his throat. "Open the hatch," she commanded.

"No, no, no, no, no, wait, please. I'm sorry," he said. "You're right, she's the queen. I just want to get back home. I won't challenge my sister for the throne."

"He's lying," Elektra said. She didn't mean to get into the middle of whatever was going on between this stranger and KaLeah, but her protective instincts kicked in and she wasn't about to leave her friend alone with him.

Colt reached to open the latch when a large sound, a voice, filled the air around them.

"You in there, come out with your hands up."

"They found us," KaLeah said.

"Dragon's blood," said Elektra. "We need to go now, Colt!"

Colt ran back to the controls and gave the machine a few verbal commands. Gears released and the craft began to lift into the air.

That's when the bullets started flying. They heard them hit the spaceship from what seemed like every direction.

"Will those bullets penetrate?" Elektra asked Colt.

"I don't think so," he said, watching something on a screen by the controls. "KaLeah, you need to see how to fly this!"

KaLeah narrowed her eyes at Nikolat and then went to stand beside Colt. On her way, the ship tilted, sending all four of them flailing across the open space.

Nikolat tried to grab a hold of the sides of the ship while Elektra fell to the floor, losing her grip on the gun. It skidded over to Nikolat, who grabbed it, picked it up quickly, and pointed it at her.

Colt and KaLeah hadn't noticed. They were too busy trying to straighten the machine while flying it up and away from the soldier's guns.

"Up to that building on the other side of the fortress

wall, spaceship!" KaLeah yelled.

"Rerouting," responded a robotic voice.

"That worked? And straighten out!"

"Leveling the ship now," the voice said again.

"This is easy!" KaLeah laughed heartily and then turned around. "Are you alright, Elektra?"

"She is just fine. Elektra, is it?" Nikolat asked with a sugary tone, while pointing the gun at her.

Colt started to walk toward them, but KaLeah put her arm out to stop him.

"What do you want, Nik?" KaLeah asked him.

"I just want to go with you back to Naldash. I'm not going to hurt anybody, I promise."

KaLeah was quiet for a moment and Elektra wanted to tell her to ignore him, to just shoot him, but she didn't exactly trust KaLeah's aim or speed.

"Alright," KaLeah finally said. "But we are dropping these two off on that roof over there, and then you can come back with me to Naldash."

"Well," he made a show of a slow bow, "how gracious of you, Favor KaLeah."

"KaLeah, are you sure about this?" Elektra asked.

"We don't have a choice. Let's just get you both to safety."

13 SPACE TRAVEL

KaLeah was frustrated with Nikolat's last minute appearance, but she refused to let him ruin her plans or put her friends' lives in danger.

"We can't leave you alone with him," Elektra said.

Nik held a smirk on his seemingly fearless face, hanging onto the edge of the spaceship with one hand to keep his balance, while his other was extended and aiming the gun at Elektra.

Elektra's protective sentiment warmed KaLeah's heart. Maybe Elektra didn't hate her after all, she hoped.

But she had known Nikolat, and even if he wasn't a very nice guy, she wasn't afraid of him. He had tried to fight her and his sister in order to take back the throne, but he'd failed. He had been fighting for something he wanted so badly that it clouded everything else.

She wasn't angry at him. She was just surprised to see him after mourning his death and then moving on. She was surprised to feel a sense of relief at seeing him alive, but that relief was mixed with anxiety about being in his presence. She couldn't figure out if she still had feelings for him or not.

The ship had stopped and was floating a few feet above the roof of an abandoned building just outside of the fortress wall.

"It's not the first time I've had to deal with him," KaLeah told Elektra. "I'll be alright."

"I am right here," Nik said. "I can hear you, you know."

The girls ignored him and KaLeah grabbed Elektra's hand, looking into her brown eyes.

"Please forgive me?" she asked. "I should have told you everything about who I am and where I'm from. I should have listened to you. I never should have met my father, but now I know for sure. He is evil, and I can't change him. He will never love me as his daughter because he is incapable of loving anyone other than himself. I get that now. I'm so sorry we lost Felisha."

Elektra didn't say anything but looked as if she was considering KaLeah's words very carefully. Finally, Elektra shrugged.

"I'm not sure what I would have done if you'd told me the whole truth," Elektra said. "Maybe it was better you found out on your own. I'll always regret what happened to Felisha, but I'm not sure I could have done anything to stop her. She was so, so angry. She just ran in without warning."

"I haven't exactly told you the whole truth yet, actually," KaLeah said, feeling nervous.

She didn't want to damage the momentum that the rebels were making and what she had to say might shake their faith in their own movement.

"I am Huntra's daughter too," she admitted.

"What? But that would mean—" Elektra furrowed her brow tightly and looked over at Colt, who looked as equally confused.

"That would mean that Keldon and Huntra…"

"I am their daughter, but I don't know much about the relationship. I don't know the whole story. I know that they lived in separate rooms, and my bedroom was set up in between theirs. Maybe she infiltrated, or maybe she was captured. But whatever happened, a soldier named Clegg escorted her off of Denlerack in a spaceship like this one before I was born."

Elektra shook her head, as if trying to dismiss the idea. "But Huntra is our idol. She is the one who led our parents to rebellion. How could she make a baby with that man?"

"I don't know, but I'm here, and I can hear the dragon spirits just like she could. I will try to help save both our planets, but I don't know how."

KaLeah hugged her then, awkwardly, since both young women were still wearing their wings. KaLeah pulled back and looked into Elektra's brown eyes. "Be careful out there. Keldon may send his men looking for all of you now."

"I will." Elektra pulled back more from the embrace. "I'm not as angry with you as I should be for leaving me behind," she said. "I understand why you did it, and I might have done the same. I never knew my own father. I never even knew who he was. I would have taken the risk to find out too. I'm glad that I found you in that alley that day. You've changed my life."

"I'm glad I met you too. And you too, Colt." KaLeah looked toward the man who joined them in the center of the ship.

"You are both the strongest women I've ever known, and I'm honored to know you both. I still can't believe you're flying out of here in a spaceship. That's so cool."

The three of them laughed and embraced again.

"Destination reached," said the robotic ship voice.

"Open the hatch," KaLeah instructed.

They said a final farewell and stepped out of the ship and onto the rooftop. Then KaLeah closed the hatch and went to the controls.

"Touching scene," Nikolat said, sliding up beside her.

"If you could not talk to me until we get to Naldash, that would be wonderful."

"Why are you still mad at me?" his voice was dripping

with sarcasm.

"Spaceship, set coordinates for the planet Naldash, Belarone Kingdom courtyard," KaLeah instructed.

"Setting coordinates now," the ship's voice replied.

"I was only trying to secure my rightful place as heir to the throne," Nikolat continued.

"You tried to kill me and your sister."

"I am very sorry about that. Look at me. I'm a new man. I was sent here as punishment and barely survived out in the desert. I didn't eat or drink for days. I walked forever just to get a chance at redemption, and here we are."

"Why are you wearing a uniform?" KaLeah asked, not trusting anything he said.

"Just trying to blend in." He smiled even bigger and leaned in close. "The spirits have brought us back together again like this. We are meant to be together. Can't you see it?"

"You are meant to drive me crazy; I see that."

"Coordinates set," said the spaceship.

"Lift off and let's go to Naldash!" Nikolat yelled to the ship.

Its engines spun to life and KaLeah tried to catch a glimpse of Elektra and Colt one last time before they left the world forever. She was so grateful for Elektra's friendship and forgiveness. It felt good to be forgiven. KaLeah considered the three men in her life who had done her wrong and whether or not she should forgive them.

They had made mistakes, losing her faith and her love. They had angered and hurt her. But maybe they were incapable of love, incapable of comprehending the damage they had done, and incapable of true remorse.

Do you forgive men like that?

Do I forgive Clegg Trapper, the man who raised me, the man who was just trying to do the best he could, but who wasn't able to truly love me as his daughter?

Do I forgive Dayne Keldon, the father who was saddened by losing me, but treated me poorly out of his inability to love? An inability that was possibly created by losing his daughter in the first place?

Do I forgive Nikolat Belarone, the man standing beside me, declaring his love for me now as if the past, his actions, don't matter?

Maybe I'm the one who doesn't understand love.

Memories drifted into her mind as the spaceship lifted higher into the sky. She saw Amirra's smile and heard the girl's laughter as she rode her draggot across the castle lawns. She saw the young princess swirling around in a pink dress, silver blond curls bouncing. She remembered seeing Elektra for the first time, brown skin, brown hair, standing fiercely in her brown and gold wings.

I do know what love is, she told herself. *I can forgive the men who hurt me, but I will never love them.*

KaLeah stood in the ship as it sailed off into the stars and realized that she had only loved men who could not love her in return.

From now on, I will only love people who are capable of loving me back.

She was sad about leaving Elektra, but excited about finally going back home. The worst part of everything was feeling like she'd failed. The dragon, Anissa La Alani, had sent her to Denlerack to save Naldash, but instead, she'd tried to get to know her father. She was angry at herself and disappointed.

"You look like you are considering my apology," Nikolat said. "I have loved you since the moment I met you, KaLeah, and I can't stand you being angry with me. Will you talk to me, please?"

He was so close that KaLeah could smell the mix of dirt and smoke on him, maybe from a campfire.

"I'd rather not, Nik," she said.

"Oh, come on! You are making a big deal out of nothing. I was trying to get my kingdom back."

He stormed off to another area and KaLeah let out a long breath. He kept talking from somewhere behind her, but she ignored him. It was clear to her that they would never see eye-to-eye.

She also knew that the time would come where he'd want to try to take back his kingdom from his sister again.

If he just killed her now, he wouldn't have to worry about her standing in his way, but that wasn't his style. She realized he wanted to win her to his side. He wanted KaLeah to support his claim to the throne and validate it.

Well, she thought, *that will never happen.*

KaLeah stared in wonder as the clouds opened up into an endless universe of stars. Everything melted away. The anger, the fear, the confusion, and the feeling of failure. She would try, once again, to protect the queen and to protect Naldash, no matter what it took.

Nikolat came up from behind her and stood by her side, staring out of the window.

"So, this is what magic looks like," he said. "I know you don't want to talk to me, but I want you to know that I'm sorry. I missed you and I'll always love you."

KaLeah absently touched the dagger bound to her thigh, thinking of Hilip. It gave her a feeling of safety, comfort, and renewed hope knowing that when she did have to stand up against Nik, Hilip would be by her side.

She said nothing and kept her eyes straight ahead, looking for something better out among the stars.

☙Elektra❧

Elektra stepped onto the rooftop and quickly walked to the edge. She could see the wall around the dictator's compound, soldiers shooting and marching, and her people fleeing back to where they had come from.

"They are retreating," she said.

"That's good, right?" Colt asked.

"Yes, I think that's the best they can do for now."

She stared, watching as some ran, some limped, and others helped carry the injured. Some bodies were being left behind.

She closed her eyes tightly and pictured KaLeah back on

the ship.

KaLeah was the daughter of the dictator. Could she have used that information? Could they have put a better plan together if they'd known?

She shook her head. Probably not. And she'd meant what she'd told KaLeah. She did forgive her and probably would have done the same thing.

She let out a very long and heavy sigh.

"Are you alright?"

"No, I'm not alright, Colt. KaLeah is gone, Felisha is dead, and we didn't stop the dictator. We failed."

Tears streamed down her face. Colt gently turned her around to face him and wrapped his arms around her. She sobbed into his chest for a few moments before composing herself and pushing back from the hug.

"What are we going to do?" she asked, more asking herself than him.

"We try again," Colt said, holding her by the shoulders as if she might tip over. "We figure something out. We regroup. We don't give up."

"No, I'm not ready to give up, but I won't ask you or your friends to sacrifice their lives again."

She tried to push away from him, but he held her firm, looking into her eyes.

"I can't speak for the others, but I won't ever leave your side, Elektra. We're in this together. You give me hope in a better future."

"Hope? How am I supposed to have hope in anything anymore?"

Elektra pulled herself free from his hands on her shoulders and walked to the edge of the building, looking out at the rebels who were retreating, carrying their dead and injured.

Would they blame her, she wondered?

She didn't know how she'd be able to show her face to that group again. They all died for nothing.

Tears were welling up in her eyes and beginning to fall

again. She tried to sniff them back and lifted her head, casting her glance out toward the airfield across the fortress wall.

Something caught her eye.

"Wait," she said. "Colt, what is that?"

Colt was beside her in an instant with a small scope out. He peered through it.

"A child," he said.

"What?" she grabbed the scope from him and peered through.

Running over the ground, as if chasing KaLeah's spaceship, was a little brown-haired girl. She lowered the scope and watched the girl run.

As the girl ran, she started to transform. She grew larger and larger, greener, and greener, and sprouted two long, silvery wings that beat against the air around her.

The girl became a dragon right before their eyes, lifted up into the air, and chased the spaceship through the thick clouds and out into the atmosphere.

Elektra blinked a few times, then turned to Colt and grabbed his hand tightly. The transformation awakened something deep within her.

"Hope," she said, and then she kissed him knowing that he would never leave her side.

KINGDOM OF MONSTERS
SISTER WORLDS BOOK 3

She rules by title only. Can she become the champion her planet demands?

Queen Amirra worries her people will never accept a young woman as their leader. And her world's male traditions mean the inexperienced royal must show she has the grit to fend off violent invaders. So, when her treacherous brother unexpectedly returns to steal the throne, she finds herself clinging to power in a kingdom plagued by chaos.

Forced to act after her sibling divides the realm and pits her own army against her, the embattled queen makes a deadly decision. But her last hope for peace slips through her fingers when the neighboring country springs a vicious attack, compelling Amirra to lead her broken land into war...

Can the fledgling ruler win over her nation and claim victory?

Kingdom of Monsters is the dark third book in the captivating *Sister Worlds* YA fantasy trilogy. If you like determined heroines, feminist rebellions, and high-stakes action, then you'll love Tiffany Nicole Terry's girl-powered tale.

Buy *Kingdom of Monsters* to brave betrayal and battle today!

ABOUT THE AUTHOR

Tiffany Nicole Terry (TNT to her friends) is a corporate communications manager by day, a novelist by night, and a mother to daughters and dogs every moment in between. A bit of a bohemian nomad, she has lived in every time zone in the continental United States but prefers to live where she can see mountains on the horizon. She is passionate about equality, diversity, and inclusion and believes the world can be a kinder and more sustainable place. Her books are full of positive empowerment messaging for girls, especially those raised through trauma, neglect, and abuse.

FROM THE AUTHOR

I wasn't ready to tell my story at 15, at 22, at 26 or 35. It wasn't until I'd left an abusive marriage, was a single mom working full time, had lost my dream of having a fairytale life, and was journaling 100,000 words a year while I tried to make sense of it all at 38, that things clicked for me. I tried writing my story so many times but failed because I didn't understand why I needed to write it.

I now know I need to reach young girls and young women, so they don't repeat generational patterns of abuse. Instead of creating stories where the girls fall for bullies and abusers (like their fathers or through lack of good father figures), I'm determined to show young readers how to choose themselves and how to reject toxic people. We can be heroes in our own lives.

If you enjoyed this book, please leave a review, and spread the word. Help me reach more people who need this message. Thank you!

Love, TNT